MURDER
in the
COUNTRYSIDE

BOOKS BY HELENA DIXON

Miss Underhay Mystery series

Murder at the Dolphin Hotel

Murder at Enderley Hall

Murder at the Playhouse

Murder on the Dance Floor

Murder in the Belltower

Murder at Elm House

Murder at the Wedding

Murder in First Class

Murder at the Country Club

Murder on Board

Murder at the Charity Ball

Murder at the Beauty Pageant

Murder at the Village Fair

Murder at the Highland Castle

Murder at the Island Hotel

Murder on the French Riviera

HELENA DIXON

MURDER
in the
COUNTRYSIDE

bookouture

Published by Bookouture in 2024

An imprint of Storyfire Ltd.
Carmelite House
50 Victoria Embankment
London EC4Y 0DZ

www.bookouture.com

ISBN: 978-1-83790-058-9
eBook ISBN: 978-1-83790-057-2

To my middle daughter, Corinne, and her new husband, Joe, who got married while this book was being written. Wishing them many happy years together.

PROLOGUE

Blossomdown Farm apple butter, finest cloudy apple juice, honey, fresh eggs and cream sold from the farm gate. Call in or telephone Stoke Gabriel 271 to place your order. Top quality ciders also available.

Advertisement

First-class livery stables, boarding of horses long- or short-term. Riding lessons and ponies available for guided treks and hacks suitable for beginners or more experienced riders. Contact Mr and Mrs Pickering, Stoke Gabriel 224.

CHAPTER ONE

The September sun was still high in a clear blue sky as Kitty Bryant, née Underhay, pointed the nose of her little red Morris Tourer along the narrow Devon lanes. Bertie, her roan cocker spaniel, was happily sniffing the fresh country air on the back seat. The roof was down, and fat, lazy bees were buzzing in the hedgerows that spilled out onto the road.

The fields around them had all been harvested leaving behind a sea of yellow stubble. Ploughing for next season was well underway, exposing the rich, red loam beneath the last of the crops. Along the roadside trees were still groaning with the last of the fruit to be picked between brambles displaying plump, juicy blackberries.

Kitty had spent a pleasurable afternoon with her best friend, Alice. Formerly a chambermaid at the Dolphin Hotel, which was owned by Kitty and her grandmother, Alice now had her own business. Since her friend had started up as a seamstress a few months earlier she had been kept very busy. This had been a rare opportunity to meet up for a delicious lunch and gossip in a local tea room.

Torbay Private Investigative Services, Kitty and Matt's own

business, had also kept them on their toes with an influx of cases, so a day off was a thing to be treasured. Especially when the day was as beautiful as this one. She had left Matt to enjoy himself playing a round of golf at Churston Golf Club near to their house. Something he hadn't had much time to do just lately.

On the rear seat next to Bertie, she had the evening gown that Alice had shortened for her carefully wrapped in brown paper, and two empty stoneware cider jugs. She had promised Matt that she would take a detour to Stoke Gabriel, a small, local village not far away, to exchange the empty jugs for full ones. A refreshing drink of cider would go down very well with the pork chops she knew their housekeeper was preparing for their supper.

Matt had collected their last drinks from Wassail Farm, a place they had seen advertised in the local newspaper. Normally he called at a small stall run by Blossomdown Farm, which was along the same road on the route between Stoke Gabriel and Aish, but they had so enjoyed the cider from Wassail Farm that she was on her way there to restock.

Kitty drove carefully along the narrow lane looking out for the farm sign. Matt had warned her to leave Bertie in the car at Wassail Farm. Farms often let their dogs roam freely in the yards and Bertie was quite adept at escaping. Kitty didn't want to risk a skirmish, or her dog getting hurt.

She passed the well-kept, white-painted wooden gates for Blossomdown Farm so guessed she must not be too far away. She noticed that the stall by the gate was empty as she drove on to Wassail Farm. About half a mile further down the lane she saw a hand-painted sign on a rather battered black metal gate:

WASSAIL FARM
CIDER, APPLE JUICE, EGGS AND FRUIT FOR SALE IN THE
BARN.

Kitty pulled to a halt and peered through the windscreen for any sign of life in the farmyard. There was no one around that she could see and no sign of the farm dogs. She tucked her car in close to the hedgerow and collected the empty stoneware cider jugs from the back seat.

'Now, you stay here, Bertie, and be good. I shan't be long.' She patted her dog and checked that he was still secure and couldn't try to follow her.

Kitty opened the latch on the gate and squeezed through, closing it behind her. The farmhouse itself was directly facing the road. It was a traditional Devon longhouse painted white with a thatched roof, with small lead-pane windows and a black-painted, stable-style front door which was firmly closed. A few scrawny hens pecked about aimlessly in the dust at the front of the building.

Everything looked a little run-down and unkempt. The windows hadn't been cleaned for some time and the paint on the door was peeling. The barn was a brick building to the side of the farmyard. One side was open to the elements at the front revealing the freshly cut hay from the harvest of a few weeks ago. The other half of the barn had been bricked up and had a door with another hand-painted notice that said, 'Farm Sales'.

The door stood slightly ajar, so Kitty pushed it open and called out, 'Hello, is anyone here?'

The interior of the barn was gloomy. The only light coming from a dirty, cobweb-festooned side window and the door where she had entered. No one replied to her call. There was a shelf labelled 'Returns' which seemed to house a collection of empty stoneware jugs similar to the ones she had in her hand.

A wooden trestle table was loaded with what she could see were full jugs complete with stoppers. There were glass bottles of cloudy apple juice, jars of jam and honey and a few punnets of blackcurrants. Prices were written on cards in front of each item and there was a wooden box at the end with a slot in the top where she assumed you could leave the money.

The air in the barn smelt musty and of apples, dust motes whirled in the shaft of light from the window as Kitty's eyes adjusted to the gloom. She set her empty jugs down on the shelf and collected two full ones from the table, before finding her purse ready to drop the money into the box.

She pushed the money into the container and prepared to leave when something at the back of the barn, partially obscured by a rusting piece of farm machinery, caught her eye. Kitty blinked and took a step forward, not certain at first what she had seen.

Sticking out at a strange angle was what appeared to be a man's leg clad in dirty moleskin trousers with a mud-covered boot. Kitty's heart thumped as she walked forward towards what she assumed must be a man, or perhaps a scarecrow.

'Hello?' she called out again, her voice echoing against the bare brick walls and concrete floor of the barn.

Kitty rounded the corner and gasped in horror at the scene before her. A circular stone press, used for juicing apples, now held a human victim. Blood, dark red and sticky mixed with the apple juice on the floor, while wasps buzzed about the mess.

The poor man's head was crushed between the huge stone plates leaving his body to hang limply. It was clear there was no hope for him, and Kitty was only too glad she could not see his face. The contents of her stomach threatened to rise into her throat, and she turned and bolted for the door, desperate to get outside before she was sick.

Kitty bent forward, leaning her back against the outside brick wall of the barn for support as she sucked in air. Her heart raced and nausea continued to bubble at the back of her throat. In the distance she heard dogs barking and the faint rumble of cartwheels as a wagon of some kind made its approach.

She looked around to see if there was anyone about and to

try to discover where the sound was coming from. The farmhouse still appeared deserted, but just beyond the house she heard the cart and the dogs drawing closer. Kitty gathered her wits and hurried towards the side of the farmhouse hoping to find help.

Coming through the open gate to a field was a small horse-drawn cart loaded with wood and stones. The two black and tan collie dogs riding on the back of the cart started barking more loudly as Kitty approached.

''Ere, where's the fire, then? You all right there, miss?' The man driving the cart was dressed in working apparel, a flat cap on his head and a pipe clamped in the corner of his mouth. He seemed surprised by her sudden appearance at the side of the farm.

'I've just come from the barn. It looks like there's been a terrible accident,' Kitty gasped.

'Accident? What kind of accident?' The man clambered down from the cart and Kitty realised he was huge. Even next to her own five-foot two height this man had to be well over six foot tall and well built. He had a thick, black bushy beard making it difficult to determine his age.

'In the barn, the apple press. A man. His head is crushed.' Kitty couldn't think of another way of saying what she had seen.

The man stilled for a moment from where he had been hitching the horse's rein to the top of the gatepost clearly in readiness to go to the barn.

'Crushed in the press?' He looked at her in bewilderment. 'But that ain't possible.'

'Whoever it is in there is dead. We need to get the police.' Kitty started to shake. The shock of what she had just witnessed setting in as she attempted to tell her story to this huge man.

The man looked at her once more and called his dogs. The collies jumped from the cart and went to his heels as he strode off towards the barn.

'Bide there a while, miss.'

'No, don't...' Kitty called as she desperately tried to stop the man from entering, knowing how shocking the scene would be.

She scurried after him. 'Don't touch anything.'

She was too late to prevent him from going inside the barn. She petered to a halt outside the door and waited. A moment later the man lurched back out through the open door, dogs at his heels. His face was parchment white against the darkness of his beard, and he looked as nauseous as Kitty felt.

'Do you know who he was?' Kitty asked as the man started to recover.

The stranger nodded slowly. 'My father, Titus Blake.' He pulled a large red handkerchief from his jacket pocket and mopped his face as if trying to clear his thoughts.

'I am so very sorry for you.' Kitty paused, trying to collect her thoughts. 'We have to get help. Is there a telephone in the farmhouse?' she asked.

The man shook his head. 'No, Father wouldn't have none of that kind of trickery. No electric neither, he said as gas and candles were good enough.'

'I have my car. The farm along the lane, Blossomdown, is there a telephone there, do you know?' Kitty asked.

The man's mouth twisted into a peculiar sneer. 'I reckon so. There's nought as they don't have.'

'I'll go for help. Will you be all right here?' Kitty asked. On the one hand she was desperate to get help, but on the other hand she was worried about leaving the man alone.

The man nodded.

Kitty hurried to her car and dropped the jars she was still holding on the back seat. Bertie, who had been surveying her interaction with the man and his dogs with some suspicion, gave a small woof of surprise.

'Hold on, Bertie, we have to get the police.' Kitty swung her little car around and set off for Blossomdown, praying someone would be home and that they had a telephone.

The gate to Blossomdown Farm was already open when she arrived so she drove straight into the yard. She assumed that meant someone must be in. Unlike Wassail Farm, Blossomdown was a handsome, red-brick building with large windows and two stone planters full of flowers on either side of the front door.

Kitty pulled to a halt and hurried to knock loudly using the well-polished brass lion's head door knocker.

'Hello, can I help you?' A rosy-cheeked older woman clad in a floral-print summer cotton frock and a white pinafore had opened the door.

'I'm so sorry to disturb you, but I've just come from Wassail Farm. I need to use a telephone, there's been a terrible accident.' Kitty saw the woman's expression change to one of alarm, tinged with something else.

'Oh, come right in, my dear, yes we have a telephone.' She showed Kitty into the large, square-shaped hall. The telephone was on a small oak table with barley-twist legs near the foot of the stairs.

Kitty's hands shook as she picked up the receiver and dialled the number for Torquay Police Station.

'Chief Inspector Greville, please,' she said when the call was put through. 'Tell him it's Mrs Bryant. I need to speak to him urgently. There has been a murder.'

CHAPTER TWO

Kitty thought she heard the house owner gasp as she spoke, but her attention was focused on speaking to the chief inspector as her call was transferred.

'Mrs Bryant? Are you all right? Where are you?' The policeman's voice was calm and reassuring.

'I'm using the telephone at Blossomdown Farm near Stoke Gabriel. There has been an incident at Wassail Farm next door. The farm owner is dead, and I fear it is not an accident. His son is there now, I had to come away to call you as they don't have a telephone.' Kitty tried to keep her voice steady.

'Is someone in the room with you now?' the chief inspector asked.

'I'm with the lady at Blossomdown.' Kitty glanced across at her hostess to see the woman's previously pink cheeks were now as white as the walls of the hallway.

'Stay where you are, Mrs Bryant. I'll be right there. Ask the lady if there is anyone at Blossomdown who could go to Wassail Farm to be with the man's son,' Chief Inspector Greville said.

'The chief inspector is asking if anyone from here could be

sent to Wassail Farm to be with Mr Blake until the police arrive?' Kitty looked at the woman.

'I don't know as we would be welcome. Perhaps I can ask Jim, our cowman, to go. He knows Micah,' she said, pleating the hem of her pinafore between red, work-roughened fingers. 'Wasn't the housekeeper there at Wassail Farm, young Abigail? She never normally goes out much, unless it's to church or the market.'

'Everything appeared locked up,' Kitty told her before returning to answer the chief inspector. 'The lady says she will ask the cowman to go down.'

The woman bit her lip and disappeared. Presumably to find the elusive Jim to ask him to attend Wassail Farm.

'Thank you, Mrs Bryant. I'm on my way.' The chief inspector ended the call.

Kitty replaced the receiver on the black Bakelite telephone, before picking it back up once more. This time she dialled her own telephone number. She could only hope that by now Matt had finished his round of golf and was back at home.

* * *

Matt whistled a happy tune as he let himself in through the front door of the house he and Kitty shared. Rascal, their cat, twined lovingly around his legs, almost tripping him as he removed his golfing cap and hung it on the hall stand.

He bent to stroke his pet and was about to carry on into the sitting room when the telephone on the hall table rang.

'Hello, Kitty? What, slow down, darling. Where are you? Are you all right?' Kitty's voice filled his ear, her normal calm tones were jumbled and sounding slightly teary.

'Oh, Matt, I'm at Blossomdown Farm waiting for Chief Inspector Greville. There's been a murder at Wassail Farm. I was collecting the cider for our supper and... oh, it's so awful.' She paused for breath.

'It's all right, darling. Stay where you are. I'll be there in a trice.' He didn't wait for her to say any more before hanging up and collecting his motorcycling cap.

He hurried outside and was soon astride his Sunbeam motorcycle heading along the lanes towards Stoke Gabriel. He knew that whatever had happened must have been bad. He and Kitty had been involved in a number of murders and unpleasant deaths and it was unlike her to sound so rattled.

He arrived at Blossomdown Farm to find Kitty's little red Tourer parked in the farmyard. A glance at Kitty's car had revealed two stone jars of cider on the back seat and no sign of Bertie. He hopped off his motorcycle and knocked on the front door of the farm.

A second later, the door opened, and an older woman stood in the doorway. 'I presume that you must be Mrs Bryant's husband? She said as you lived not far away over at Churston.'

Matt introduced himself, shaking the woman's hand.

'Come inside, Captain Bryant. I'm Norma Blake, my husband Hedley is ploughing up on the top field, I've sent someone to find him. Mrs Bryant is in the front parlour with your dog.' Mrs Blake showed him into a pleasant sitting room just off the hall. Kitty was seated on the chenille sofa with a tray of tea in front of her, and Bertie at her feet.

'Oh, Matt, I'm so pleased to see you.' Kitty jumped up from her seat and hugged him. He could feel her trembling in his arms. Bertie greeted him enthusiastically with a wagging tail and a disapproving sniff at Matt's plus fours where he had not had time to change.

'Would you care for some tea, Captain Bryant? The police should be here very soon,' Mrs Blake said, picking up the teapot obviously ready to go and refill it with fresh tea.

'Thank you. That would be very kind.' Matt accepted her offer and took a seat next to Kitty.

Once the woman had left the room to go to the kitchen he asked his wife what had happened. Kitty quickly filled him in on her discovery. 'It has to be murder, Matt. I can't see how it could be anything else.' Kitty shuddered.

Matt rubbed his chin thoughtfully. He had seen the kind of press that Kitty was describing before. Basically, there was a stone base with a groove around the edge with a break to allow the juice to flow into a big bucket. Apples were placed on the base and another large and very heavy stone with a wooden plate was screwed down onto the base to compress the fruit. He dreaded to think what the result would have been like on a person's head.

It certainly wasn't likely to have been an accident. The stones were on a screw thread, someone would have had to stand and wind the top stone down. There was no possibility of it falling without destroying the machinery.

Mrs Blake returned bearing another delicate floral-painted china cup and saucer and a fresh pot of tea.

'Norma has sent her cowman down to stay with Mr Blake at Wassail Farm until the police arrive,' Kitty said.

'Are you related to the family at Wassail Farm, Mrs Blake?' Matt asked. He thought it curious that her surname was the same as that of the victim.

He noticed the woman appeared uncomfortable as she added more hot water to the teapot. 'My husband Hedley is Titus's brother. However, they don't get on and haven't for many years. That's why I sent Jim, our cowman, to Wassail Farm. I didn't think as Micah, that's Titus's son, would welcome any of us there. Not even after what Mrs Bryant has told me about what's happened to his father.' She shuddered delicately as she put the pot back on the tray.

There was a commotion at the back of the house. The

sound of dogs barking and a male voice. Mrs Blake rose from her armchair. 'That will be Hedley, my husband. I don't know if Saul is back. He's Titus's middle boy, Micah's younger brother. He works for us.' She scurried out of the room.

Kitty's brows rose as she stirred the tea in the pot and replaced the lid before pouring a cup for Matt.

'This all seems frightfully complicated. Norma's brother-in-law is the victim but there has been some kind of falling out between the families.'

Matt accepted his cup of tea. 'And yet she just said – Saul, was it? – her nephew works here at Blossomdown.'

He had barely finished speaking when the sitting-room door opened to reveal a large man of a similar age to Norma Blake dressed in farm clothes. He stood in his stockinged feet on the tiled floor of the hall just in the doorway.

'Captain Bryant, Mrs Bryant, forgive me for not coming in but I've just come right from the field. My wife has just told me what has happened to my brother.' He looked first at Kitty and then at Matt as if for confirmation.

'Yes, sir, the police have been sent for and should be here soon. I am so very sorry for your loss, sir. I think your wife said she had sent someone down to stay with Mr Micah Blake. He seemed very shocked and distressed,' Kitty said.

'Did he now?' Hedley Blake scratched the top of his head under his rather grubby checked-cloth cap.

'Did your wife say that your brother had two sons?' Matt asked. He was curious about why the nephew seemed to be working with Hedley rather than his father and brother at Wassail Farm.

'There are three boys. Micah is the oldest, he stayed with Titus running Wassail Farm. Saul is the middle one, he lives and works here, and Adam is the youngest, he got out of farming. He's in lodgings and works for a solicitor's office in Totnes,'

Hedley explained. He seemed almost unaware of what he was saying, and was clearly in shock.

Outside the front of the farmhouse they now heard the approaching sound of a police bell and the rumble of wheels as a car turned into the farmyard.

'I expect that will be the police.' Matt rose and set down his cup. 'Stay here, Kitty, and I'll see if the chief inspector needs you to return to Wassail Farm.' He could see that she had paled a little at the suggestion she might have to go back to the murder scene with the police.

Hedley Blake stood to one side as Matt accompanied Norma to the front door.

'Captain Bryant, I thought that was your motorcycle outside. I've sent my constables on ahead to Wassail Farm. I thought I should speak to Mrs Bryant first.' Chief Inspector Greville looked first at Matt and then at Norma.

'Of course, please come in,' Mrs Blake said.

'Kitty's in the sitting room,' Matt explained. 'She's rather shaken up.'

'I think we all are, Chief Inspector,' Norma said as they re-entered the sitting room.

Mrs Blake made introductions and explained the family's connections to the dead man. Chief Inspector Greville made notes in his book.

'I see, Mrs Blake, thank you. This other lad, your nephew, Saul, is he here on the farm today?' the chief inspector asked, after offering his condolences to the Blakes.

'Yes, he's working hereabouts, but he went off with the cart down to Galmpton Creek to get some supplies. He doesn't know what's happened yet.' Norma looked anxious.

'No, nor does Adam, that's Titus's youngest. He works in Totnes at a solicitor's office,' Hedley explained.

'I see. Thank you. I need to go to Wassail Farm as Doctor

Carter is meeting me there. May I ask if Mrs Bryant can trespass on your kindness a little longer, Mr and Mrs Blake? I may have more questions for all of you shortly,' the chief inspector said.

'Of course, we're only too glad to help, aren't we, Hedley?' Norma looked at her husband who was still in the doorway.

'That's right,' Hedley confirmed.

'Thank you.' Chief Inspector Greville looked at Kitty. 'May I borrow your husband for a few minutes, Mrs Bryant?'

Kitty nodded. 'Certainly, Chief Inspector.'

Matt followed the policeman past Hedley out into the farmyard.

'If you feel your wife will be all right for a minute or two, I should like to get your impressions of the crime scene,' the chief inspector said once they were out of earshot. 'It all seems a bit odd to me, with the family being at sixes and sevens with one another. I'm hoping Mrs Bryant may learn something more about the circumstances behind it if we are out of the picture for a while.'

Matt smiled. 'Oh yes, you can rely on Kitty to do some digging.'

He knew Kitty would certainly try to wheedle out more information about the family while they were gone. He also knew she would want him to try and find out more about what was happening at Wassail Farm.

He accompanied the chief inspector in the police car, leaving his motorcycle parked next to Kitty's car. Another black police vehicle was already parked outside the farmhouse at Wassail Farm when they pulled in. A uniformed constable stood on guard outside the entrance to the barn. There was no sign of Micah Blake, or the man who had been sent from Blossomdown Farm, although the door to the farmhouse now stood slightly ajar.

They had just left the car when another motor pulled in. This time it was a rather sportier dark-green, open-topped number that halted in a little cloud of dust just behind the police car.

'Chief Inspector, and Matthew! What have you got for me today then, eh?' Doctor Carter beamed happily at them from behind the steering wheel. A slightly chubby, cheerful man, nothing ever appeared to dismay him, no matter how grisly a scene he might be called to examine.

'I believe your services are required in the barn. I understand from Mrs Bryant this is not a pleasant scene,' Chief Inspector Greville said as the doctor pulled his brown-leather medical bag from the car.

'They rarely are,' Doctor Carter agreed in his usual affable fashion.

Matt followed the chief inspector and the doctor at a discreet distance as they walked towards the barn.

'Where is Mr Micah Blake?' Chief Inspector Greville asked the constable standing outside the entrance.

'Inside the farmhouse, sir, with the man from Blossomdown Farm. He was right shaken up. He said as their housekeeper, Miss West, is out and will probably be back anytime soon,' the constable said.

'Thank you, please keep a look out for her. I expect she will arrive by bus. We should keep her away from the barn. Inspector Lewis is also on his way here,' Chief Inspector Greville said.

Doctor Carter exchanged a look with Matt at this piece of information. Inspector Lewis was not very well regarded locally. Originally from Yorkshire, Matt and Kitty had first encountered him at a murder during Kitty's cousin Lucy's wedding. He had since transferred to join the Devon Constabulary hoping for rapid promotion.

Since their first meeting he had made it plain that he disliked private investigators, and, in Kitty's case, female investigators. Since then they had worked alongside him on several cases and although the relationship was marginally less frosty, it was far from being co-operative and cordial.

The constable pushed open the barn door. It took a moment for Matt's eyes to adjust from the bright autumn sunshine outside to the dim interior of the barn. As they made their way past the trestle table containing the goods for sale, they came to the grisly sight of Titus Blake lying exactly as Kitty had said.

Matt swallowed. He could see why Kitty had been so shaken. Chief Inspector Greville had also paled at the sight, before commencing to carefully examine the screw mechanism on the apple press. It was obvious to Matt that Kitty had been right, this was definitely murder.

Outside in the farmyard there was the sound of another vehicle pulling up and male voices at the door, before Inspector Lewis strode into the barn. He ignored Matt and continued past him only to halt at the sight of the grisly scene.

'Ah, Lewis, just in time. Give me a hand here, will you?' Chief Inspector Greville looked up at the approach of his junior officer.

Matt stepped outside the barn for a moment while the police wound up the mechanism to free Titus Blake from the press. He was not feeble but, even so, the scene was unpleasant. It also had brought a rush of terrible memories back to him of his time on the front during the Great War. This was something that still haunted him, leaving him with bouts of terrible nightmares and a fear of enclosed spaces.

He sucked in the fresh, country air before lighting up a cigarette, something he only tended to do when stressed.

'Well, Mrs Bryant was absolutely correct when she said it was murder. Poor devil didn't get in that press by himself,' Chief Inspector Greville said as he joined him. 'Lewis and Doctor Carter can carry on in there. Care to join me while I talk to Mr Micah Blake?' He clapped a friendly hand on Matt's shoulder.

Just as the two men were about to enter the farmhouse, a slender, young woman in a faded green-print dress carrying a laden wicker basket over her arm entered the farmyard. She halted in surprise at seeing so many motor cars.

'Miss West?' The chief inspector stepped towards the girl.

'Yes, sir.' She looked at him with wide brown eyes, reminding Matt of a frightened woodland animal about to take flight.

'Please, come into the farmhouse. I'm Chief Inspector Greville. I'm afraid there has been a terrible accident. Your employer, Mr Titus Blake, has been killed.'

The girl gaped open-mouthed at him for a moment, before unexpectedly falling to the ground in a dead faint.

CHAPTER THREE

Kitty finished her second cup of tea and set her cup back down on the tray. She was relieved to see that her hands had stopped shaking.

'Thank you so much, Mrs Blake, for the refreshments. You've been terribly kind. This must all have come as the most awful shock to you all,' Kitty said.

Mrs Blake glanced nervously at her husband who was still standing somewhat awkwardly in the doorway.

'Well, it has, and it hasn't,' the older woman said. 'You see, Titus was not, well, the easiest of men, and he had an unfortunate way of upsetting people.' She cast her gaze down to the hem of her pinafore, which she was continuing to twist on her lap. 'I suppose it was only a matter of time before someone set upon him.'

'My brother was one of the vilest men on this earth and sad to say his eldest son takes after him. They say the apple doesn't fall far from the tree and, in Micah's case, that's true.' Hedley frowned as he spoke. 'You can ask anyone hereabouts and they'll say the same.'

'Now then, Hedley,' Norma remonstrated. 'Titus wasn't

always that way and Micah might be hot-headed but he's not so bad as his father.'

Her husband snorted. 'Well, Titus has been that way the last thirty-odd years or so. I'm going to go and look out for Saul. This will be upsetting for him even though there was no love lost between him and his father.' The farmer stomped back towards the kitchen.

'How did Titus feel about Saul moving here and working for you and your husband if you didn't get on?' Kitty asked.

'Oh, it didn't go well at all, as you might have expected. Saul ran off from Wassail Farm three years ago and came here asking for a job and if he could stay. Titus followed him, threatened him and us with a shotgun if Saul didn't go home. Of course, the boy didn't want to leave. Working all hours of the day and night for his father and his brother for little or no pay and a beating every time something went wrong, or they had too much to drink. We told him he was more than welcome here for as long as he wanted. He's been here ever since.' Mrs Blake shook her head, her lips compressed together in a firm line of disapproval at her brother-in-law's actions.

'How awful,' Kitty murmured sympathetically. 'So, Saul didn't speak to his father, or brother, I presume, after that?'

Mrs Blake shook her head. 'No, not even at church. Wassail Farm kept to themselves, and we kept to ourselves unless we were forced to communicate.'

'That must have felt very awkward. What about the other boy? Adam? You said he worked in Totnes?' Kitty asked.

'Yes, he escaped as well. He's a clever boy, young Adam. His schoolmaster saw potential in him, encouraged him to find an apprenticeship. Titus and Micah were furious about that too. We got blamed for encouraging him to think he was better than he should be.' Norma pulled a lace-edged cotton handkerchief from the pocket of her pinafore and blew her nose.

'And Adam didn't see his father or older brother either?' Kitty asked. She was finding the story very interesting.

'No, only at church. He comes to us for his Sunday dinner. He lives in lodgings near his work, and he likes to spend a few hours with Saul. He and Saul have always been very close, right from when they were little boys.' Mrs Blake sniffed and dabbed her eyes. 'I suppose as I should telephone his office and let him know what's happened.' She looked at Kitty in alarm as if suddenly realising that no one had thought to inform him.

'I think it might be wise. It would be better coming from you instead of having the police telephone, or call at his place of employment,' Kitty said.

Bertie gave a soft thump of his tail as she spoke as if agreeing with her.

Norma tucked her handkerchief back inside her pocket and went out into the hallway. She pulled the door partially closed behind her, so her voice was muffled as she made her call to the youngest of Titus Blake's sons.

Kitty wondered how Matt was faring with the chief inspector. She also wondered where Inspector Lewis was since he would normally have been one of the first to arrive on the scene. She could only assume he must have been busy on another case, since Chief Inspector Greville had attended instead. It was a small mercy to think she'd be spared seeing his difficult behaviour today.

A shiver ran down her spine when she remembered the scene in the barn. She hoped Matt hadn't gone inside to see it. Since their marriage he had been much better at coping with his memories of the war. She hoped that seeing something so horrific wouldn't restart the violent nightmares that sent him sleepwalking and destroying the house.

There were more voices now coming from the direction of the kitchen. Kitty sat and waited and hoped Matt and the chief inspector wouldn't be long returning to Blossomdown. She really felt quite uncomfortable impinging on the hospitality of the Blakes while there was so much going on. Even if she was discovering some very interesting things.

The door to the sitting room crashed open, startling Bertie into a surprised flurry of barks. A young man of around her own age stood in the doorway, his eyes wild. 'Is it true, miss? What my uncle just said? My father is dead?'

Kitty nodded. 'Yes, I'm afraid so.'

'Saul, take off your boots. I won't have you trampling mud all about the place.' Mrs Blake tugged on his jacket sleeve as she scolded him.

The man shook his arm impatiently as if shrugging off a flea. His gaze was still fixed on Kitty. 'You are sure? He was dead? You saw him?' he asked.

'Saul! Where are your manners. Yes, Mrs Bryant saw him, that's why she's here. It was very upsetting for her. The police are at Wassail Farm now.' Norma's voice rose.

The man seemed to suddenly recollect where he was. 'Sorry, Aunt Norma, Mrs Bryant. It... it's just such a shock.' He bent and tugged off his work boots, before venturing into the sitting room and seating himself on a wooden rocking chair. A dazed expression was on his face.

Mrs Blake frowned as she picked up the discarded footwear and bore the boots away to the kitchen.

'Your aunt said that you and your father were not on good terms,' Kitty said in a gentle tone.

'No one was on good terms with my father. Even so, I can't believe it. My uncle said it was murder. Someone killed him. I mean how?'

Kitty thought it was perhaps understandable that Saul had not asked why Titus was killed but how. 'Saul, I'm so sorry to say this, but his head was crushed in the apple press in the barn.' Kitty could see no way to soften the truth to make it sound any better. Plus, everything would no doubt come out at the inquest anyway.

'And Abigail? Where is Abigail?' Saul asked. 'Did you see her? Does she know?'

'Your father's housekeeper?' Kitty was slightly surprised at his questions.

'Yes, she didn't find him, did she?' Saul asked.

'No, I found him when I went to buy cider. There was no one else at the farm when I arrived. Your older brother Micah got there on his cart just after I found your father.' Kitty was intrigued by Saul's obvious concern for the housekeeper. She wondered what this Abigail West was like and what she meant to Saul.

'Have the police gone to arrest Micah?' Saul asked.

'I don't think so. They have gone to look at the scene with the doctor. I presume they will interview everyone in due course. They asked me to stay here until they returned,' Kitty said. 'Why do you think they would arrest your older brother?'

The corners of Saul's mouth lifted in a mirthless smile. 'Well, he stands to inherit the farm and that's what he's wanted for years. It's why he always sucked up to the old man. Why he put up with having virtually no wages.' Saul shook his head as if trying to clear cobwebs from his brain. 'Father used to promise him that one day the farm would be all his since me and Adam had run off.'

'I see, but didn't they get on then? Living and working together?' Kitty asked.

'Micah is a regular chip off the old man's block. They used to fight all the time. Physically fight too, especially when they had both been drinking. That's why Aunt Norma won't have any alcohol in the house, even though we make it. She was always afraid that Uncle Hedley might be tempted the same way.'

Kitty thought that would explain why she had been offered

sweet, strong tea for shock rather than the usual medicinal tot of brandy. 'Is there anyone else who would want to harm your father?'

Saul's grim smile widened. 'A big, long queue of people. Uncle Hedley and Aunt Norma, me, Adam, Micah, Abigail, half the village. In fact, you can probably include most of the population of Stoke Gabriel in that list.'

Kitty could see the chief inspector's job was not going to be an easy one.

* * *

Micah Blake and Jim, the cowman from Blossomdown, were seated on wooden chairs at a scrubbed pine table when Matt and Inspector Lewis carried Abigail West into the room. Two brown bottles of beer stood open on the tabletop.

Matt assisted the inspector to lie the girl down on a small cot bed beside the range in the large farmhouse kitchen. It looked as if that was where she usually slept, judging by the simple wooden cross above her bed and a framed picture of the Virgin Mary.

Micah took no notice of the semi-conscious girl, not even turning his head to see what had happened to her. Jim had risen as soon as the party had entered the room.

'Is Miss Abigail all right?' he asked.

'She fainted in shock when she heard the news,' Chief Inspector Greville explained as he set down the woman's loaded shopping basket onto the table next to the beer bottles. He introduced himself and Inspector Lewis to the two men, while Matt took a seat beside Abigail and tried to revive her.

The girl's eyelids fluttered open as the chief inspector and Inspector Lewis took a seat at the table with Micah Blake. Now the police had arrived, Jim excused himself and set off back to Blossomdown Farm, clearly happy to be away.

Matt fetched the girl a cup of cold water and propped her up on the thin pallet mattress to get her to drink, while the police started to interview Micah.

'We appreciate this has been a terrible shock for you, Mr Blake, but we need to ask you when you last saw your father?' Chief Inspector Greville asked as Inspector Lewis took out his notebook.

Micah was hunched up over the table, his large hand around his beer bottle. 'We got up same time as usual just afore the dawn and had breakfast. Father said as he had work to do around the yard after we'd seen to the cows. I loaded the cart and headed out for the back field to do some repairs on the boundary wall. The stone had been damaged by a falling tree in the last gale. Plus, the horses from the livery stable have done some damage too.' He paused to take a swig from the bottle and wiped his mouth with the back of his hand before continuing. 'I reckon it must have been about half nine, ten o'clock when he were just sweeping out the byre.'

Abigail had fully roused now and was sipping her water obediently while Matt held the cup for her. Her sleeves had fallen back on the oversized, grubby pale-grey woollen cardigan she was wearing. Matt noticed her arms were covered in welts and what looked like burns.

'And did anyone see you while you were working on the wall?' the chief inspector asked.

Micah shook his head. 'Didn't see no one. It were just me and the dogs up there. I had to take some stone off before I could build it back up so it were a biggish job.'

'Were you and your father on good terms, Mr Blake?' Inspector Lewis asked.

Micah shrugged. 'We were all right, I suppose. We argued about the farm and stuff pretty regular. Father was old-fashioned. It took me all my time to have him put an indoor tap in the kitchen.' He nodded towards the large white Belfast sink. 'He said as the pump in the yard were good enough.'

Abigail's gaze met with Matt's, and he sensed that Micah was not being entirely truthful about his relationship with his father.

'Any recent arguments?' Inspector Lewis persisted.

Micah's cheeks turned red above his beard. 'No. No more'n usual.' He finished his beer and thumped the empty bottle back down on the table, glaring at the inspector.

'Is there anyone who you think may have had reason to harm your father?' Chief Inspector Greville took the lead once more in the questioning.

'You could try them at Blossomdown Farm,' Micah said.

'You mean your aunt and uncle, Hedley and Norma Blake?' Chief Inspector Greville asked.

'Maybe, and my brother, Saul. He had no love for Father.' Micah leaned back in his chair.

'Is there any particular reason why you are suggesting your brother and aunt and uncle may have wanted to kill your father?' Inspector Lewis scribbled more notes in his book as he posed the question.

'Uncle Hedley wanted our land. He'd been badgering Father for months. He got our Adam to send legal letters and such from those solicitors he works for. The big field is ours, see, and the water that's needed for the trees comes from the spring there. Well, he reckons as his copy of the land register shows the spring is on his ground when it rises on ours. He would have cut off our water.' Micah glared ferociously at Inspector Lewis as if he personally had been responsible for trying to take possession of the land.

The colour had returned to Abigail's thin cheeks now and she swung her legs off the edge of the cot bed and sat herself up. Matt set the empty water cup down on the large, pine Welsh dresser laden with crockery.

'I see. You mentioned your youngest brother, Adam. Did he too not get on with your father since he was acting for your aunt and uncle?' Chief Inspector Greville asked.

'He's a traitor, that's what he is. Thinks he's better than the rest of us working for that solicitor in Totnes.' Micah scowled as he spoke.

'And your other brother, Saul? I understand he lives with your aunt and uncle and works for them?' Inspector Lewis's tone was bland, but Matt noticed the inspector's foxy gaze was firmly fixed on Micah's face.

'He run off a few years ago. He were lured away by them with big promises of money and such. They don't have any children of their own, see. They were always fond of Saul. I reckon as Saul thought if he got in well there, then he might end up with Blossomdown one day.' Micah sniffed and rubbed the end of his nose with the sleeve of his jacket. 'Father was furious, went with his shotgun to get him back.'

Chief Inspector Greville's eyebrows rose at this revelation. 'What happened?'

Micah shrugged once more. 'Aunt Norma intervened. Father had a soft spot for her still, even though she threw him over for Uncle Hedley when they was young. That was what started all the bad feeling between Wassail and Blossomdown.'

'Oh?' Inspector Lewis said.

'Aunt Norma's parents owned Blossomdown, she was engaged to Father and threw him over for Uncle Hedley. Father inherited Wassail when grandfather died, after Uncle Hedley went and married her, so instead of combining farms they set up as rivals to us. They had money too, Aunt Norma's family did, where we just had the land. Father never forgave Uncle Hedley, even after he married Mother.' Micah blew out a sigh.

'Do you know if your father had a will? Who will inherit the farm now?' Chief Inspector Greville asked.

'He redid his will about three weeks ago at the place where

Adam works. He got it done at a good price, he said. Dealt with the senior partner, a Mr Frasier. He didn't want Adam knowing what was in it,' Micah explained.

'Did he tell you what he'd done?' Inspector Lewis asked.

Micah nodded and scratched his head. 'He left Wassail to me like he promised, for all my hard work.'

Abigail's eyes widened slightly at this statement.

'Nothing to your brothers or any other bequests?' Inspector Lewis asked.

Matt knew the police would be bound to contact the solicitors to check out Micah's claims.

'I think he might have left hundred pound or something to Abigail.'

For the first time since Matt and the inspector had carried the girl into the room, Micah glanced in her direction.

The woman startled at the mention of her name, almost flinching under Micah's gaze. Micah switched his attention back to the inspector, disregarding Abigail as if she were of no more interest to him than the ladybird that was scuttling along the edge of the windowsill.

'I need to go and start driving the cows in for milking.' Micah looked at the large grandfather clock that stood ticking quietly in the far corner of the kitchen.

'Of course, Mr Blake,' Chief Inspector Greville agreed as Micah rose from his seat, gave Abigail one last quick look, and whistled for his dogs as he left the room.

'Miss West, I trust you are feeling better?' Chief Inspector Greville turned to the girl.

'Yes, thank you, sir. It just took me by surprise.' She had a soft, low voice.

'Might we trouble you to make us all a cup of tea while we talk?' the chief inspector asked.

'Oh yes, of course, what was I thinking.' She slipped off the bed and picked up a white apron from a hook on the back of the door. After enveloping herself in the pinafore she filled the large kettle and set it on a hook over the fire while she prepared a tea tray.

'May I help you, Miss West?' Matt asked, getting up.

'Oh... I... well, thank you. I'll just get some milk.'

Matt carried the tray to the table and removed the empty beer bottles, standing them by the sink. Abigail disappeared inside a large pantry to re-emerge with a jug of milk which she added to the tray. Once the kettle was boiled, she poured the boiling water into a brown teapot and set it down beside the cups.

'I'm sorry as there's no biscuits or cake, only I wasn't here to do any baking today,' the girl apologised.

Matt bit back a smile when he saw the chief inspector's face fall slightly at this. Chief Inspector Greville was very partial to something to eat.

'Now, Miss West, you are the housekeeper for Titus and Micah Blake? How long have you worked here?' the chief inspector asked as Abigail set out the thick, white china cups.

'I've been here for six years. I was fifteen when I came from the orphanage when Mrs Blake were alive. When she was ill, she needed help, and I was sent. I've been here ever since,' she said.

'So, you must have witnessed a great deal of what happened in this house since Mrs Blake's death?' Inspector Lewis asked.

'I suppose so,' Abigail agreed as she carefully poured tea into the cups.

'Micah Blake told us what happened when Saul ran away to live at Blossomdown, but it sounded as if there has always been bad feeling between the two farms?' Chief Inspector Greville said.

'Yes, sir. They don't get on at all.' Abigail set the pot down and picked up the milk jug.

Matt noticed her hand was trembling slightly as she added milk to the cups.

The policemen added sugar from the glass sugar bowl to their tea.

'When did you last see Mr Titus Blake today?' Inspector Lewis asked.

'Just before I went to get the bus. He was in the yard. He had a cob on him about something. He was stomping about like usual with the broom and muttering about Micah. I called to him as I was going to town, but he didn't answer.' Abigail pulled her tatty cardigan closer around her thin shoulders.

'You didn't see Mr Micah Blake or anyone else near the farm as you left?' the inspector asked.

Abigail shook her head. 'No, sir. Micah had already gone off with the cart. I left and walked down the road to the stop to wait for the bus and I didn't see anyone else about at all.'

Inspector Lewis looked back at his notes, while Abigail took small sips of her tea. Her wide, brown eyes fixed on his face.

'Micah said that he and his father were on good terms. That the morning started as usual with no arguments? You said, however, that Titus was muttering about his son as you left?' The inspector met the girl's gaze.

'Mr Blake was always complaining about Micah, that weren't nothing new and they always squabbled over everything. Micah wanted to modernise the place, have electric lights instead of the gas and candles.' Abigail hesitated.

'Yes, Miss West?' Chief Inspector Greville prompted gently.

Abigail glanced quickly at the back door of the farm where Micah had gone. She ran her tongue nervously over her lips. 'It's just that the fighting had been worse lately between them. Especially after Mr Blake had been to Totnes about his will. And, well, a couple of nights ago, after they had been drinking, I heard Micah tell his father he wanted to kill him.'

CHAPTER FOUR

The momentary silence in the room was broken only by the sound of Inspector Lewis's pen scratching across the page as he made more notes.

'Do you know what may have caused Micah to say that? Any idea of what that particular fight could have been about?' the chief inspector asked.

Matt thought Abigail looked as if she was about to burst into tears.

'I try to lie low when they've been at the bottle. I swear I wasn't listening on purpose, but they was so loud I couldn't help but overhear them.' The girl looked around at the men as if seeking reassurance.

'No, of course not, Miss West,' Matt said.

'I heard glass breaking and I thought to myself, *well, that'll be a nice mess for me again in the morning.* Then they was cursing and I heard a chair go over. The words was hard to make out at first but I heard Micah say something about the will. Mr Blake started roaring really loud at him then and he says as it's up to him who gets what. There was more arguing and bad language and that was when I heard Micah say as he wanted to kill him.' Abigail bit her lower lip as she finished her story.

'Thank you, Miss West. Is there anyone else you can think of who may have wished to harm Mr Blake? Anyone who, perhaps lately, he has argued with or upset?' Inspector Lewis asked.

'Half of Stoke Gabriel.' The girl gave a weak smile for the first time. 'He would fall out with his own finger ends, would Mr Blake. He had a big argument last week with his brother Hedley Blake over the business with the land. He wanted to go after him with his shotgun, but Micah wrestled it off him.'

Inspector Lewis made more notes. 'Anyone else?'

Abigail shrugged her thin shoulders. 'I don't know, there was always somebody as he'd upset. He got barred the other week from the village pub for fighting. The landlord threw him out.'

'Which public house was this?' Inspector Lewis looked at her.

'The Church House Inn. It still has strong ties with the church, so they don't have no messing about. He was proper sore about it, blaming Saul for him being barred.' Abigail seemed to give the last piece of information reluctantly.

'Saul?' the chief inspector asked.

'That's who he was yelling at in the pub and then he tried starting a ruckus.' Abigail smoothed the palms of her hands down the length of her apron.

The interview concluded and they left Abigail to clear away the tea things as they walked back out into the farmyard. Doctor Carter's car had gone, and the sound of cows mooing emanated from a low brick building on the other side of the yard, which Matt assumed must be the milking parlour.

'Lewis, call down to the Church House Inn and see if you can discover more about the fight Mr Blake had with Saul. Afterwards try and see if you can catch the solicitor in Totnes before he finishes work for the day. We need to know what's in that will.' Chief Inspector Greville issued his instructions to his subordinate.

'Very good, sir.' The inspector walked off to get in his car.

'We need to go back to Blossomdown. It seems there are a few more questions for the other side of the Blake family. I'll interview Mrs Bryant too as I expect your good lady will be glad to go home after all of this.' Chief Inspector Greville opened the door to his motor.

Matt thought that if he knew Kitty she would only be glad to leave once she had finished digging. She would be very interested in hearing about everything that had gone on at Wassail Farm.

* * *

Kitty had just politely refused an offer of more tea from Norma when she heard the sound of the police car returning to the yard. Bertie sat up, wagging his tail joyfully, when Mrs Blake let Matt and Chief Inspector Greville back into the room.

Matt fussed the top of the dog's head and took his seat beside Kitty. Saul had left the room a few minutes earlier to go back out ready to help with the cows, now that Jim the cowman had returned from Wassail Farm.

Chief Inspector Greville dispatched Norma to make more tea while he took Kitty's statement, and she quickly told them what she had learned whilst she had been at Blossomdown Farm.

Norma returned with the tea tray, freshly laden with the addition of fairy cakes and home-made biscuits – something which caught both Bertie and the chief inspector's attention. After thanking their hostess, the chief inspector sent her out yet again, this time to find her husband.

'Now then, Mrs Bryant.' Chief Inspector Greville loaded

up one of the dainty china side plates with cake and allowed Matt to tell Kitty everything they had discovered at Wassail Farm.

He had just finished when Norma returned accompanied by Hedley, who seemed somewhat put out at having his work disrupted for the second time in a day.

'Thank you for coming back inside, Mr Blake. I wonder if I could just ask you a couple more questions about your relationship with your brother?' Chief Inspector Greville brushed a few cake crumbs from his tie.

Bertie happily pounced on them, deflecting the glare from Norma at having her immaculate sitting room marred by crumbs. Hedley perched himself warily on the edge of the wooden rocking chair Saul had occupied previously.

'I don't know as there's much more I can say, Chief Inspector. Me and Titus didn't get on, it's that simple.' He rubbed his face with his hand.

Norma Blake fidgeted anxiously in the doorway.

'I understand you and your brother fell out originally over your marriage to Mrs Blake,' the chief inspector said.

Colour mounted in Norma's cheeks. 'That was a long time ago,' she said.

'Titus had set his cap at Norma but it weren't her as he wanted, it was the farm. She found out in time and gave him his ring back. I love Norma for herself, and she felt the same way towards me. Titus didn't take it well and refused to attend our wedding. That were nigh on thirty-five years ago now,' Hedley explained, looking at his wife. 'It's gone on from there really. It settled a bit when he married Thora and had the boys. Me and Norma weren't blessed with children, so I suppose he thought as he'd got the upper hand over us with that one.'

Norma crossed the room to stand beside her husband and he took her hand. 'Of course, as the boys grew older and when Thora died, it all got worse again,' she said.

'Saul left home to live here,' Chief Inspector Greville said.

'Yes, about three years ago. Titus treated those lads terribly. The boy was half-starved when he came to us, and Titus would never pay him. Saul's a good lad and a hard worker, he deserved better.' Norma's chin rose as she spoke, and Kitty could see the woman clearly loved her nephew.

'You had another confrontation with your brother we understand last week about some disputed land.' Chief Inspector Greville set down his plate and gave the empty stand a regretful look.

Norma and Hedley exchanged glances.

'Aye, that's right. He saw me working on the boundary wall. I was marking it out ready for the land surveyor to visit. He started shouting about access to the spring and how I was out to ruin him by cutting off his water supply. He made all sorts of wild threats as usual. Apart from church, that was the last time I saw him, I think.' Hedley frowned as if trying to be sure of his facts.

'I see, thank you, sir. Do either of you know anything about an incident at Church House Inn a few days ago? Your brother was barred from the pub.' The chief inspector looked at them.

Kitty wondered how they would react to this given their stance on not allowing alcohol in their own house.

'We are not pub-goers, Chief Inspector. There was talk in the village, but then there is often talk about Titus. We don't allow alcohol in the house, nor do we consume it ourselves,' Mrs Blake said primly.

'Yet you make and sell cider?' Matt said with a puzzled frown.

'Cider has health-giving properties, but we in this house do not consume it beyond sampling a few mouthfuls to ensure it's good. We have seen too much of what overconsumption can do. Frankly, I wouldn't be surprised at all if Titus had been barred from the inn. Or Micah as well, for that matter.' Mrs Blake pursed her lips in disapproval.

Kitty looked at Matt and saw his eyebrows had risen in surprise at this reply. She guessed that the Blakes must not be aware of Saul's visit to Church House Inn.

'Thank you, Mr Blake, Mrs Blake. Do you know where Saul is? I could just do with a last quick word with him before I go,' Chief Inspector Greville asked.

'You'll find him out in the yard about now, Chief Inspector,' Hedley said.

'Thank you for your hospitality, Mr Blake, Mrs Blake. You really have been most kind to me. I appreciate this can't have been easy for you this afternoon,' Kitty said as she and Matt joined the chief inspector in taking their leave.

'Not at all, Mrs Bryant. It must have been a terrible thing coming across Titus like that.' Mrs Blake shuddered.

Bertie trotted on his leash at Kitty's heels as they accompanied the chief inspector out into the yard. Saul was sweeping up stray pieces of straw and mud near the entrance to the big wooden shed that Blossomdown appeared to use as their farm store.

'Just a few quick questions, Mr Blake, if you can spare me a minute?' the chief inspector said after introducing himself.

Saul paused in his activities and leaned on the broom, his stance wary. 'Certainly, Chief Inspector.'

Kitty and Matt loitered near Matt's motorcycle so they could hear the conversation.

'Can I ask when you last saw your father?' the policeman asked.

Saul shrugged. 'A few days ago, I suppose.'

'Was this when you had an altercation with him at Church House Inn?'

Saul froze momentarily, before casting a quick glance

around the yard as if making certain his aunt or uncle were not within earshot.

'Yes, sir. I don't usually go out to the pub. My aunt and uncle disapprove of drinking and I'm not a big lover of it myself, but I went especially to find him. I knew he'd be there.' Saul scowled at the memory.

'Why did you go there, Mr Blake?' Chief Inspector Greville asked.

'I wanted him to lay off hassling Uncle Hedley about the land. It was upsetting my aunt Norma. I knew he'd be in at that time, it was where he went most nights. That was one thing.' Saul stopped speaking and shook his head.

'And the other thing?' Chief Inspector Greville looked at him.

Kitty wondered what else the man was going to say. She could see he wasn't keen to discuss it with the police.

'It was about Abigail,' Saul admitted.

'Miss West? Your father's housekeeper?' Chief Inspector Greville asked.

'Housekeeper my eye. Slave more like. He treated her something terrible. The dogs was looked after better than she was. I'd found her that morning hiding under the hedge. She'd run off to hide, to get away from one of his beatings because she'd burned his porridge that morning. I've tried to get her to leave a thousand times but she's an orphan, no family and no money. And, of course, no reference if she goes.' Saul shook his head once more, a dark expression on his face.

'I see, and where were you today, Mr Blake?' Chief Inspector Greville asked.

'I was out collecting supplies for the farm. There was a delivery by boat down to the creek in Galmpton so I went to fetch it with the cart.' Saul moved the broom as if eager to return to his task. 'I've not long finished unloading.' He indicated towards the shed.

Kitty knew Galmpton well as it was the next village along the river from Stoke Gabriel. The creek was used more for loading and unloading local deliveries as it was quicker by river than by road.

'Can anyone vouch for you?' the policeman asked.

Saul scratched his head. 'I suppose so. The boatman who I took the load from and some of the others down there. They would have seen me.'

'Thank you.' The chief inspector turned away allowing Saul to continue sweeping.

Matt tugged his leather cap firmly onto his head, while Kitty stowed Bertie safely into the back of the car.

'Right, I'd best be off. I need to go and see Adam Blake to see if he can shed any light on all of this. I'm sorry you had to discover this murder, Mrs Bryant. Most unpleasant.' The chief inspector opened the door of his car.

'Yes, it was a dreadful shock.' Kitty shuddered at the recollection.

'Drive safely, and don't worry, I'm sure we'll find out who was responsible for this very soon,' the chief inspector said.

'I hope so. It seemed very, well, vindictive, what happened to Mr Blake. He didn't seem like a nice man, but even so.' She halted. To her the scene had looked as if whoever had killed Titus had hated him very much indeed.

The chief inspector nodded as if he understood what she meant. 'Yes. I'll be in touch if we learn anything new. Inspector Lewis may learn something useful in the village.'

Kitty watched him drive away, before following Matt's motorcycle back to Churston.

CHAPTER FIVE

Kitty was thoughtful on the short drive back to her house. Matt had already parked and was opening the front door when she pulled up beside his motorcycle on the driveway.

'Are you all right, Kitty?' he asked, turning around to help get Bertie from the back seat of her car.

'Yes, I think so, just rather shaken up by the whole thing. I was having such a lovely day until then.' She gave him a wan smile as she lifted the stone jugs of cider from the car. 'Not that we'll feel like these right now, but we had better put them away in the pantry.'

She suspected that it would be a long time before either of them wanted to partake of that particular drink. He took them from her, and she collected her parcel from Alice to take inside. Her lovely lunch with her friend felt as if it belonged in another world.

'I think you're right.' Matt placed his arm around her waist and gave her a hug before leading the way inside the house.

The tension seemed to drain from Kitty's shoulders once she was inside the comforting familiarity of her house. Their cat, Rascal, was curled up asleep in a pool of sunshine on the windowsill, the air smelt of lavender polish and the horror of the afternoon felt like a bad dream.

Matt stowed the cider jugs inside the pantry, below the marble slab where their housekeeper kept the butter, cheese and cold meats. He had hung up Bertie's leash on its hook in the hall and the little dog was busy slurping water noisily from his dish in the scullery.

Their housekeeper had left the vegetables prepared for supper in pots on the stove and the pork chops were ready on the cold shelf to be grilled or placed in the oven for later. A freshly made apple pie stood cooling on the side and a jug of cream to accompany it was placed with the other items.

Everything was clean, peaceful and orderly.

'Are you sure you're all right, darling?' Matt asked, looking at her curiously. 'That was quite an awful discovery this afternoon.'

'It was. It did affect me more than I thought given that you and I have seen quite a few horrific things since we've been working together,' Kitty admitted. 'It seemed such a vindictive thing to do, crushing his head like that.' She shuddered at the memory.

'Darling, I know you stumbled across Titus Blake by accident today, but if this line of work is too much for you then you know you can stop for a while. Take a break from it.' Matt gathered her to him, his face concerned.

Kitty shook her head. 'No, I enjoy our work. Even the murders.' She gave a wry smile. 'You know what I mean. It made me think about you, really.' She looked up at her husband.

'Me?' Now it was Matt's turn to regard her quizzically.

'Returning here with you now and everything is calm and safe and well, I just thought how awful it must have been for you during the war and losing Edith.' Kitty blinked back tears as she remembered all that Matt had lost during that awful time.

His first wife and child had been killed and he still lived with the memories of his lost comrades.

He held her close and kissed the top of her head. 'Now I know for certain that discovering Titus has upset you much more than you let on to Chief Inspector Greville. We can leave this up to the police. Inspector Lewis is on the case as well now.' His words seemed to have the desired effect as Kitty looked up at him with a slightly appalled expression.

'Really? Oh dear, let's hope he does better on this one than on the last few cases he's handled.' Kitty extricated herself from her husband's hold and picked up the parcel from Alice which she had carried in from the car.

'It's going to be an interesting case. It seems to me that any one of them has good reason to have murdered Titus.' Matt picked up an apple from the dish on the side and took a bite.

'Yes, and none of them appear to have very good alibis. In fact, most of them have no alibi at all. Then there are all these other people he is alleged to have upset,' Kitty agreed.

'I'd like to know what Titus's will actually says, and also what the youngest son, Adam, has to say about his father and his older brothers,' Matt said, before taking another bite of his apple.

'Micah Blake seemed to have a similar reputation to his father. What was your impression of him?' Kitty asked as she picked up Bertie's dish to refill it with fresh water.

'The same as yours, I suspect. He was obviously upset by his father's death, but he was quite indifferent to the housekeeper fainting. He showed no concern for her at all. He claims he was repairing a wall when his father was killed. He said he last saw him this morning when he set off,' Matt said.

'And no one witnessed him repairing the wall,' Kitty mused.

'I expect the police will check and take a look at the repairs.' Matt finished his apple and threw the core in the rubbish bin.

'I expect it's a drystone wall, so no mortar. It could have

been repaired at any time,' Kitty pointed out. 'I met him when he and the dogs were returning with the cart just after I'd found his father. He did seem quite shocked when he went inside the barn.'

The sight of Titus Blake trapped in the apple press was enough to shock anyone really, she supposed. Even if Micah had been the one who had killed his father it would probably still be horrifying to see the scene again.

'And Micah seemed to be expecting that he would inherit the farm. That's what his father had always told him,' Matt said.

'Yet Titus has made a new will recently and you said Abigail heard them arguing about it?' Kitty asked.

'That's what she told the chief inspector. She said she heard Micah say he wanted to kill his father. I noticed her arms while she was talking and she is covered in marks and bruises.' Matt looked troubled.

'That would seem to confirm what Saul said about how the girl is treated.' Kitty was concerned about this new information. It was too awful to think of what Abigail must have endured at Wassail Farm.

'I don't think she even has a bedroom of her own at the farmhouse.' Matt told Kitty about the pallet bed beside the fire in the kitchen.

'That's appalling.' Kitty was horrified.

'She fainted away when she was told Titus Blake was dead,' Matt said.

'She last saw him before she locked up and went off to buy groceries in the village?' Kitty confirmed.

'Yes, that was what she claimed. She had a basket with cold meat and bread with her when she returned. I helped pick the contents of the basket up when she dropped it in her faint. I suppose someone would have seen her doing her shopping and returning on the bus,' Matt agreed.

'She could have killed him before she left, I suppose,

though. I wonder if Doctor Carter will be able to say if he has any idea of when Titus was killed.' Kitty frowned as she spoke.

'It's possible. She's only a slight little thing but she must be stronger than she looks to have coped with all the work she does at the farm. She could have snapped if Titus had lost his temper and attacked her again,' Matt suggested.

'Hmm, then there are the occupants of Blossomdown Farm.' Kitty looked at her husband.

'Hedley Blake was fighting with Titus for the land rights over that field with the watercourse,' Matt said. 'It sounds as if they have been feuding for years, ever since Norma chose Hedley instead of Titus. This business over the water rights sounds bad though if Titus went to threaten him with a shotgun.'

'Without access to their main water supply for the crops and the animals, Wassail Farm would really struggle.' Kitty could see why Titus would have been so angry and concerned.

'I suppose if Hedley had won, he could have forced Titus into bankruptcy. He would have gained Wassail Farm's land and amalgamated it into Blossomdown. With Titus out of the way there would only be Micah to deal with. Perhaps he thought that Micah would be easier to win over than Titus,' Matt suggested. 'Micah also doesn't have an alibi.'

Kitty frowned. 'I headed straight to Wassail Farm since you got the cider from there last time, but when I was looking for the entrance, I passed Blossomdown and everything looked closed up. The little stall they usually have near the gate with eggs and honey wasn't there. I wonder if Norma was at home then?'

'You think Norma could have killed Titus?' Matt's brows lifted as he considered her suggestion.

'It's possible. She seems devoted to Hedley so she would know how much getting those land rights would mean to him. She is also very protective of Saul. I think she sees him more like a son than a nephew.' Kitty's shoulders rose in a slight shrug. 'It's not impossible that she could have killed Titus.'

Matt grinned, the dimple flashing in his cheek. 'Very well, it's possible I suppose. Although I can't picture Norma creeping across the fields in her carpet slippers to squash Titus's head in the apple press.'

'I said possible,' Kitty conceded. 'But, yes, it's slightly less likely. Then there is Saul. He had a fight with his father in the pub. He was very resentful of how Titus had treated him and how he treated Abigail.'

'He claims he had gone down to Galmpton Creek to obtain supplies for the farm.'

'I suppose people would have seen him there, but he still probably could have had time to come back, kill his father, and then arrive at the farm later on,' Kitty said.

'It's quite a conundrum,' Matt agreed. 'There is the other son too, this Adam, the youngest son. I suppose he was at work in the solicitor's office when his father was killed.'

'Norma telephoned the solicitors to tell him what had happened to his father. I was in the sitting room when she made the call. Unless he had a reason to be out of the office during the day, then I suppose he at least can be ruled out,' Kitty said with a sigh.

'True. I wonder if he knew what was in Titus's will? Even though the old man said he wasn't to find out.' Matt looked thoughtful as he moved towards the scullery door.

'Do you think that Titus lied to Micah about the farm and him inheriting it?' Kitty was intrigued.

She followed Matt as he unlocked the back door, allowing Bertie to go galloping out into the back garden.

'He was certainly a slippery fellow, anything is possible. There must be something in the new will that angered Micah.'

The late afternoon sun shone on a patch of white late-blooming roses and a pretty pair of butterflies danced around the trunk of the apple tree in the centre of the lawn. Kitty and Matt moved to sit down on the pair of rattan chairs that stood beside a small circular-topped table on the patio.

Rascal padded past them, tail in the air, ignoring Bertie who was busy playing with an old red rubber ball he had found in the border. The cat wandered along the stone-flagged path to vanish into the shrubbery at the far end of the garden.

'If Titus Blake had left the farm to Micah as he'd always promised, then why would they fight? You think he hinted that he had changed his mind?' Kitty tilted her face towards the sun, enjoying the last of the warmth on her face.

'I don't know. Perhaps Titus enjoyed keeping Micah on his toes,' Matt suggested as he stretched out his long legs to relax in the chair.

'I suppose that would fit with his personality, at least what we've found out about him so far,' Kitty agreed.

'It's all very interesting. I wonder what Inspector Lewis will find out in the village about any other likely suspects who may have wanted Titus Blake dead.' Matt glanced at her.

'Well, there must be others, I suppose. That's what everyone said. The one thing all the Blakes agreed on was that Titus had a lot of enemies,' Kitty said.

The following morning turned out to be another bright and sunny day. Matt left early to go to their office in Torquay to check the post and to meet with a potential client. Kitty decided to take Bertie and visit her grandmother at the Dolphin Hotel in Dartmouth.

Although her grandmother was now retired as a hotelier, she continued to reside in an apartment within the hotel and was also still involved with the local hoteliers' association. After everything that had happened the previous day, Kitty thought a few hours with her beloved grams would be good for her. No doubt news of the murder would have travelled along the river, and she didn't want her grandmother to worry.

The ferry from Kingswear to cross the Dart was busy and she had to queue for a while before she could board. The fine weather had obviously encouraged a spate of visitors to the pretty Devon town. But if she didn't take the two ferries to cross the river, it was a long drive round via Newton Abbot and Totnes to get to Dartmouth since all the villages were sited along the estuary.

She wondered what Alice would make of her adventures when she learned what Kitty had stumbled into after leaving her company. She resolved to telephone her later when Alice had finished work for the day. Once across the river, she drove the short distance to the Dolphin and parked near the embankment before taking Bertie out of the car.

The dog's tail wagged happily as she greeted a few people she knew.

'Your grandmother is in her apartment, I think, as Mrs Craven is with her,' Mary the receptionist informed her when she asked at the hotel desk if her grandmother was in.

Kitty's spirits fell a little at this news. Of all of her grandmother's friends, Mrs Craven was Kitty's least favourite. A former mayoress of Dartmouth, Mrs Craven had very decided opinions on everything and everybody. She was not overly enamoured of Kitty and was strongly inclined to disapprove of anything she might be doing. She also had a habit of trying to engage Kitty in various charitable works.

'Kitty, darling, and with Bertie too,' her grandmother greeted her happily as she opened the door into her grandmother's pleasant lounge. The sun was streaming in through the leaded glass panes of the large bay window that overlooked the embankment and the river below.

Kitty kissed her grandmother's cheek and took a seat on the sofa. Her grandmother occupied one of the fireside chairs and

Mrs Craven was installed in the one on the opposite side. Dressed in a smart navy suit, white blouse, pearls and a diamond brooch, Mrs Craven had greeted Kitty briefly when she had arrived. They were clearly just finishing their morning tea.

'This is a lovely surprise, my dear.' Her grandmother smiled at her and slipped a biscuit from the tea tray on the coffee table to Bertie.

'Yes, I would have thought you would be busy assisting Matthew with his typing or filing or something,' Mrs Craven said.

'Matt has gone to the office, so I thought I'd call and see you for a little while.' Kitty ignored the other woman's barbed comment to return her grandmother's smile.

'I was just telling your grandmother some shocking news I heard from my maid this morning. A dreadful murder not far from you, Kitty, at a farm near Stoke Gabriel yesterday,' Mrs Craven said.

'Oh dear, that's not far away at all.' Kitty's grandmother looked alarmed when her friend said where the crime had taken place.

'You must mean the murder at Wassail Farm,' Kitty said. She wondered what exactly Mrs Craven had heard about it all. The older woman knew everyone who was anyone in the area and often heard news before anyone else.

'That's the one. Titus Blake, the farmer, a dreadful man.' Mrs Craven's lips pursed in disapproval.

'Did you know him?' Kitty asked in some surprise. She wouldn't have thought that Titus and Mrs Craven would have mixed in the same levels of society at all.

'Only through my charitable work, my dear. The house-keeper, Abigail West, was placed there a few years ago from the orphanage. Of course, his wife, Thora, was alive then, poor soul. I wasn't happy about the placement at the time as he was most objectionable. However, Mrs Blake was quite ill, and the family required assistance, so I was overruled by the vicar. I believe the girl is still there. She must be twenty or twenty-one now.' Mrs Craven's expression grew flinty at the memory of the vicar's temerity at challenging her decisions.

Kitty thought the vicar had been a brave man to argue with Mrs Craven. Even so, she had to admit that the woman had been right in her reservations about sending Abigail to Wassail Farm.

'I heard that he was a most unpleasant person too,' Kitty's grandmother said as she placed her empty cup and saucer back down on the tea tray. 'I know when any of the charities used to apply for donations, they never received one from Wassail Farm. Now, Blossomdown Farm were always most generous.'

'Yes, you would never have believed those two men were brothers.' Mrs Craven looked at her friend. 'They say, though, that Titus Blake never forgave his brother for running off with Norma.'

Kitty was intrigued that both her grandmother and Mrs Craven knew so much about the Blake family. 'How long have you known the Blakes?'

'I've known Norma for many years. Her parents used to rent out rooms at Blossomdown Farm when Norma was a girl, before she married Hedley. Most respectable people, they were quite old when they had Norma,' her grandmother said.

'You know she tried to adopt one of Titus's boys when they were babies?' Mrs Craven wagged her head sagely. 'Norma and Hedley weren't blessed with children of their own and Titus had three under five at the time. Of course, Titus said no and turned away all their offers to assist them. Wassail Farm has never done as well as Blossomdown and they were struggling to cope. Poor Thora Blake, I swear being married to Titus helped send her to an early grave.'

'Saul ran away from home a few years ago and lives at Blossomdown now. Apparently, there was a huge row over it,' Kitty said.

'Saul is the middle boy, I think he was the one Hedley and Norma wanted. Titus Blake was always a hot-head, unlike Hedley. I wonder who will inherit the farm now?' Mrs Craven said.

'I thought Micah would inherit it. He's the oldest and he still lived there with his father,' Kitty said.

Mrs Craven gave a slight shrug. 'I wonder. I always thought there was a trust in place. I seem to recall something in the paperwork when we were placing Abigail. We needed to be sure the placement would be secure for her when Thora Blake passed on. No, I rather think it is to go to all the sons.'

CHAPTER SIX

Kitty came away from the Dolphin with that titbit of information buzzing around in her brain. If Mrs Craven was right, then it would certainly provide a motive for the fight that Abigail had overheard between Titus and Micah.

Micah might have discovered that his father didn't have the power or the intention to will him sole ownership of the farm. If a trust was in place that insisted it was split between all the heirs, then Wassail's ownership could be much more complex than they had imagined. She was deep in thought as she walked Bertie back along the embankment towards her car.

'Mrs Bryant, good morning.'

She was jolted out of her thoughts by Robert Potter, the son of her grams's favourite taxi driver and the former beau of Alice. He was a good-looking young man close to her own age and he too had his own business.

Alice and Robert had been walking out together for quite some time, and Kitty had been convinced that an engagement must soon be on the cards. Shortly after Valentine's Day, however, they had parted and Alice had embarked on her business venture. Alice had since firmly dismissed all discussion of courtship and marriage and her friend remained reluctant to tell her what had gone wrong.

'Robert, how are you? Your excursions are going well, I hear?' Kitty knew that Robert's own business, a coach hire that ran day trips to Exeter, the Moors and into Cornwall, appeared to be thriving.

Matt still saw Robert occasionally at the Ship Inn in Dartmouth and would have a drink and a game of billiards with him. He had hinted that he knew something of why Alice and Robert had broken up, but it was clearly something Robert had confided in confidence, so Kitty hadn't pressed the matter. Even though she had longed to know exactly what had occurred.

'Yes, thank you, Mrs Bryant, 'tis going very well.' Robert stood somewhat awkwardly in front of her, and Kitty sensed that he was trying to work out what he really wished to ask her. She had a feeling that it was something to do with Alice and she was not about to be disloyal to her friend.

'This fine weather must be keeping you very busy?' she said, hoping he would move out of her way a little so she could get by.

'Yes, indeed. I hope as Miss Miller's business is doing well?' Robert asked, his blue eyes anxious.

'I believe so,' Kitty assured him. 'She was very busy when I saw her yesterday.'

Robert seemed to relax a little when he heard this. 'That's good. If'n you see her again soon please tell her I asked after her and give her my regards.'

'Of course,' Kitty assured him. She hoped he had no further message that he wanted her to pass on. Alice had been dreadfully upset after ending her relationship and Kitty had no wish to bring that distress back to her friend.

'Thank you.'

To her relief Robert added no further message beyond the

seemingly heartfelt thank you as he touched his cap and stood aside to allow her to continue to her car.

Kitty fastened Bertie into the back seat and drove off towards the ferry. It was plain to her that Robert still cared deeply for her friend. She also suspected that Alice was still in love with Robert from the little things she had let drop during their lunch yesterday. It was all most frustrating that they were not together.

* * *

Matt had spent a productive morning dealing with correspondence at their office in Torquay, followed by a meeting with a local gentleman who suspected his chauffeur was stealing from him.

He was about to lock the office to return home to Churston when the telephone rang.

'Is that Torbay Private Investigative Services? Captain Bryant?' The female voice on the other end of the line sounded vaguely familiar, but Matt couldn't place who it might be.

'Yes, speaking.'

'We met yesterday, Captain Bryant, after the terrible events at Wassail Farm. It's Mrs Norma Blake.'

Matt sat down on his leather office chair. 'Mrs Blake, what can I do for you?' He wondered how she had discovered that he and Kitty were private investigators and what she wanted.

'I didn't realise yesterday that you and your wife were investigators until my nephew, Adam, telephoned me after he'd been speaking to the chief inspector,' she explained.

'I see, and was there something you wanted us to help you with?' Matt asked. Adam would no doubt have recognised their names from his work at the solicitor's office. His curiosity was piqued now about what the woman could want.

'This appalling business with my brother-in-law's murder.

Well, we had a visit today from an Inspector Lewis. Captain Bryant, I'm most anxious that my family are not connected to this murder at all. Blossomdown Farm has an excellent reputation, as do we, and I would like to keep it that way.' Norma sounded quite flustered as if she wasn't certain about what she was asking.

'Are you asking Kitty and I to investigate your brother-in-law's murder, alongside the police?' Matt cut directly to the chase.

'Yes, yes, I want to ensure that all of our names are cleared. People will say there is no smoke without fire you know and already I feel people are rehashing the past.' She sounded close to tears.

'Do you mean from when you married your husband?' Matt guessed she meant the stories about how she had chosen Hedley over Titus, and this was being recirculated by the local rumour mill.

A long sigh sounded gustily in his ear. 'Yes. I refuse to allow Titus to destroy everything Hedley and I have worked so hard for over the years from beyond the grave. We are respectable people, Captain Bryant, with a business. A good reputation goes a long way in farming circles.'

Matt frowned, he could tell that Norma was distressed. 'Mrs Blake, Kitty and I would be happy to take on an investigation into Titus's death, but you must understand that we may uncover some issues about people you are close to. It is possible that someone you know well might even be responsible for his death.'

There was a momentary silence before Norma spoke again. 'That is a risk I am prepared to take, Captain Bryant. I am confident that you will discover nothing untoward about any member of *my* household.'

'Very well. Kitty and I shall also be bound to pass anything that may be relevant to Titus Blake's death to the police.' Matt wanted to make sure that even if they were in the Blakes' employ he and Kitty would not be party to any kind of cover-up should they find something damaging about Norma's family.

'Thank you, I understand,' Norma agreed.

'Very well. I'll get a contract drawn up for you with our rates and conditions and send it out today.' Matt confirmed the arrangements and replaced the black Bakelite handset in its cradle.

Kitty would be very interested to learn of this latest turn of events. He drummed his fingers on the desktop, before picking up the receiver once more and dialling the number for Torquay Police Station.

Once connected, he asked for Chief Inspector Greville.

'Captain Bryant, good morning.' The policeman didn't sound surprised to hear from him. Matt thought his colleague had probably guessed that either he or Kitty would be in touch.

'I thought I should call and let you know that Mrs Norma Blake has just telephoned me and asked us to investigate Titus Blake's murder. She is concerned about any potential scandal or gossip attaching itself to her branch of the family.' Matt waited for the response.

'Did she now? Hmm, I presume you and Mrs Bryant will be taking the case?'

Matt thought he detected a hint of amusement in the chief inspector's voice. The policeman knew as well as Matt that Kitty would definitely want to investigate the murder.

'Yes, sir. I told her that we would, of course, be sharing anything relevant that we discovered with you,' Matt said.

Chief Inspector Greville chuckled. 'I'm sure you will. I presume that is also a small hint that we might reciprocate in some way with sharing information?'

'It would be helpful and appreciated, sir. You know that we can be trusted to keep your confidentiality.' Matt always appreciated Chief Inspector Greville's willingness to work somewhat cooperatively with them. Unfortunately, he knew from past experience that Inspector Lewis was less keen to do so.

'As you are aware I called on Adam Blake at his lodgings in Totnes yesterday. He claims he was at work all day, however he was out and about completing tasks for his employer, so there is a possibility that he may have had time to get to Wassail Farm and back without being missed. He has his own transport.'

'So he too doesn't have an alibi?' Matt said. 'Did you learn anything about the will?'

'Inspector Lewis spoke to a Mr Frasier, Adam's employer. As per Titus Blake's instructions Adam did not assist with the drawing up or witnessing of the latest will, which is kept in the safe at the solicitor's office. It seems that Wassail Farm was not Titus Blake's property to dispose of as he wished. A trust was formed before Titus and his brother Hedley were born, leaving the farm to be shared between all male heirs equally. This may mean that Hedley too would have a stake in the farm. It sounded as if the wording of the trust was unusual, and Mr Frasier needed to study it further to confirm all the details.'

Matt let out a low whistle at this unexpected piece of information. 'Then what was in the will, sir?'

Chief Inspector Greville cleared his throat and Matt heard paper rustle on the other end of the line. He assumed the policeman was checking his notebook before answering.

'Titus Blake, contrary to popular belief, was in possession of a sizable sum of money. He has over five thousand pounds in the bank and a collection of gold sovereigns which are worth a considerable amount,' Chief Inspector Greville said.

'That is unexpected. The farm is quite run-down and he didn't appear to have invested in it at all for quite some time.' Matt's mind raced to digest this news.

'Quite so. He didn't pay Micah much of a wage or the housekeeper, Miss West. He had a reputation for miserliness.'

'How has he left this money?' Matt was intrigued.

'A sum of fifty pounds to Miss West if she was still in his employment at the time of his death. Five hundred pounds to Micah Blake and the rest is left to Mrs Norma Blake for her own personal use. The solicitor said there were conditions that she was not allowed to gift the money to Hedley.' Chief Inspector Greville coughed. 'So, that makes your commission from Mrs Blake all the more intriguing.'

'I agree.' Matt was stunned. He hadn't expected that Titus would have so much money to leave, or that he would have left the majority of it to Norma. 'I take it there was nothing for Saul or Adam Blake?'

'No, just those people I have mentioned. He told the solicitor that they could fend for themselves since they had abandoned him. Oh, and Inspector Lewis called at the Church House Inn. It seems that Saul was telling us the truth about the fight with his father. The landlord confirmed that Saul and Adam rarely drank in the village pubs. Only Micah tended to drink there, although even he has not been seen in there as much lately.'

'I see, thank you, Chief Inspector.' Matt was about to hang up when the policeman added.

'By the by, Inspector Lewis will be heading this investigation. He is keen to create a good impression on our chief constable. I believe a move to Exeter Police Station with a possible promotion might be in the offing should he be successful.'

'I understand, sir, thank you.' Matt smiled to himself as he replaced the handset. It had sounded as if Chief Inspector Greville would be fully supporting his junior officer's move to Exeter.

He collected the paperwork from the cabinet that he needed for Norma Blake's contract and locked up the office. Kitty would be very keen to hear all of this.

* * *

Kitty had arrived home bearing freshly baked pasties from the bakery in Kingswear for lunch. Bertie, ever the optimist, followed on her heels as she prepared a tray with plates and linen napkins for herself and Matt.

When she heard his key in the front door she hurried into the hall, eager to tell him what she had learned from her grandmother and Mrs Craven.

'Just in time for lunch, I have so much to tell you,' Kitty said as Matt removed his motorcycle cap and hung it on the hall stand.

'And I you.' Matt grinned at her before following her out through the dining room onto the patio, where their lunch was waiting on the outdoor table covered by a clean linen teacloth.

'You first,' Kitty said as they sat down to eat, with Bertie sneaking under the table to wait hopefully for something to fall his way.

She listened attentively as Matt told her of their commission from Norma Blake to investigate Titus's death and his subsequent conversation with Chief Inspector Greville. Her eyes widened when Matt told her about the will and the bequests.

'That is a considerable sum of money, and to go to Norma Blake in her own right? Good heavens, if this becomes public knowledge then tongues will be wagging harder than ever.' Kitty was a little put out that Matt had already heard of the trust from the chief inspector, but it did confirm that Mrs Craven had been correct. 'Do you suppose that Norma had any inkling that Titus might have had such a sum of money and was intending to leave it to her?'

'I don't see how she would know. Everyone appeared to think that Titus had no money. The farm is run-down, he was a heavy drinker by all accounts and was stingy with his spending. Plus, there is so much ill feeling between Titus and Hedley I wouldn't have thought Norma would have had anything to do with her brother-in-law.' Matt had uncovered the pasties releasing a delicious aroma of steak and vegetables into the midday air.

'Hmm.' Kitty considered this as she cut her own pasty in half with a knife to allow the contents to cool a little before eating it. 'I wonder. Maybe she didn't know, but I suppose Adam could have found out, or perhaps Hedley?'

Matt chewed and swallowed a bite of his lunch before answering her. 'Chief Inspector Greville said that Adam's employer had taken great pains to follow Titus's instructions that Adam was not to know the contents of the will. It's locked in a safe at the solicitor's office.'

'It sounds so typical of Titus from what we've learned about him so far. He could have chosen to go to any solicitor in the area, but he went to the one where his son is employed. It could only be to make sure that all the family knew he had changed his will and to torment them by not revealing the contents.' Kitty shook her head. She was beginning to understand the mental games the dead man seemed to have enjoyed playing on his family.

'I think you're right. Being cruel seemed to be second nature to him. I can see now why so many of them said he had a list of enemies longer than his arm,' Matt agreed.

'Well, we have accepted Mrs Blake's commission, and it seems we shall be forced into working alongside our friend Inspector Lewis too.' Kitty gave her husband a wry smile. Perhaps *working alongside* was a little optimistic. Knowing Inspector Lewis he would take great pains not to tell them anything he discovered, while expecting them to share everything they found.

CHAPTER SEVEN

After lunch, Kitty completed the contract details ready for Mrs Blake to sign. They decided that a drive out to Blossomdown Farm was in order to deliver the paperwork. It would also provide the opportunity to probe a little further into the relationship between the two farms.

They left Bertie behind in the care of Mrs Smith, their housekeeper, who had just returned from the village, and set off along the country lanes. The roof was down, and the breeze was pleasant as they drove along beneath a clear, bright blue sky.

As Kitty turned the nose of her car into the white-painted open farm gate of Blossomdown, her heart sank when she spotted a black police vehicle already parked near the front door.

'It seems Inspector Lewis is already here,' Kitty remarked as she turned off the engine.

Matt smiled at her as she collected her handbag and climbed out from behind the steering wheel.

'Play nicely, darling, we might find out something useful,' he cautioned as they approached the front door of the farmhouse together.

Kitty obediently pinned a smile on her face and rapped the brass lion-head door knocker to announce their arrival. A few seconds later a slightly flustered looking Norma Blake opened the door to them.

'Captain Bryant, Mrs Bryant, please come inside. Inspector Lewis has just arrived.'

They followed her into the comfortable sitting room where they had been the previous day. Inspector Lewis was seated on one of the fireside chairs, a cup of tea in his hand. His sharp eyes narrowed when he saw them enter the room.

'Good afternoon, Inspector,' Kitty greeted him cheerfully and perched herself on the sofa, with Matt taking a seat beside her.

'Mrs Bryant, Captain Bryant. I might have guessed you would be along.' The inspector looked somewhat sourly at them as he set down his cup.

Norma seated herself on the chair opposite the inspector, her pleasant face flushed and anxious.

'I'm glad you're both here. The inspector said he had some news to tell me.' Mrs Blake looked at Inspector Lewis.

The inspector immediately took on a pompous air as he pulled his notebook from the breast pocket of his jacket. He cleared his throat as he flicked through the pages until he came to the one he wanted.

Kitty guessed what he was about to say and waited to see what Norma's reaction would be.

'I have spoken to Mr Frasier of Frasier and Dainton in Totnes regarding the last will and testament of your late brother-in-law, Titus Blake.' Inspector Lewis paused to shoot a sharp glance at Norma. 'From my conversation with him it seems that Wassail Farm is held in a trust to be shared between all three of Mr Blake's children. This has to be confirmed, however, as the trust documents are quite complex. It may even be the case that your husband is entitled to a share.'

Norma stared at him. 'Hedley always said he thought there was a trust. He said he had an idea as he might have had a half share himself in Wassail Farm at one time. He said it should have been split between him and Titus when their father died. He never bothered though after we were married as he was running Blossomdown. It seemed best to leave Titus to it. We figured it as perhaps we were wrong, and it was just left to Titus after all,' Norma said. 'Hedley was asking about it when we were looking at the land boundaries for the watercourse and the field.'

Inspector Lewis's eyebrows rose slightly at this information before he continued. 'Mr Blake did, however, leave several financial bequests. The largest of which was left to you personally, Mrs Blake, with proviso that your husband, Hedley, should not benefit from the money.'

Norma snorted. 'Titus had nothing to leave. He didn't have two pennies to rub together. What has he left me, a box of brass buttons?'

'Mr Blake has left you over five thousand pounds and a very valuable collection of gold sovereigns.' Inspector Lewis looked at her.

Norma gaped at him; her mouth open for a long few seconds. 'Nonsense. Titus had no money and any money he did have would have gone to Micah. Much as I dislike my eldest nephew, his father owed him years of wages.'

'You had no knowledge of this bequest, Mrs Blake?' Inspector Lewis asked.

Norma shook her head. 'No, how could I have? As far as I knew, so far as anyone knew, Titus had no money to leave anyone. He never paid Micah or Abigail what they should have had, he haggled over every mortal thing as he ever did buy, and he never invested in the farm.'

Kitty thought the woman was telling the truth, she appeared genuinely shocked by the unexpected news.

'Why do you think Mr Blake left his money to you rather than his children?' Inspector Lewis's eyes narrowed as he continued to survey the bewildered woman.

'I have no idea. I haven't said a word to Titus in over twenty-five years beyond a civil good morning if I met him at church or out and about. Not even when the boys were little. I used to talk to Thora then, but not Titus.' Norma plucked her handkerchief from the pocket of her apron and dabbed at her eyes and nose. 'I know as he had no care for Saul and Adam, but surely he would have left the money to Micah if it exists at all.' Norma was clearly having difficulty accepting the money she had been left was real.

'Inspector, when you spoke to Mr Blake's solicitor, did he know why Titus had decided to leave Mrs Blake the bulk of his money? Was this a change from his previous will?' Kitty asked.

She had been wondering why Titus had decided on remaking his will recently. His death coming so soon after the reordering of his affairs set alarm bells ringing in her mind.

'His previous will was several years old and hadn't been updated since Thora, his late wife, had passed away. Mr Frasier thought that Mr Blake had not been feeling well recently and had decided to put his affairs in order.' Inspector Lewis sounded reluctant to share the information.

'So, this was a departure from his previous will?' Kitty persisted. She wanted to know what had changed.

'Yes. His former will had left an annuity to his wife and the right to remain at Wassail Farm unless she remarried. His money had been left also to Thora and the sovereigns split equally between his sons,' Inspector Lewis confirmed.

'But he didn't say why he had decided to leave the money to me?' Norma asked, the puzzled frown on her brow deepening.

Inspector Lewis shook his head. 'No, Mrs Blake, he didn't. I had hoped that you might have some insight into that.'

'Well, I'm afraid I haven't. The only reason I can think of is that he wanted to stir up trouble. That was Titus all over.' Norma wiped her nose once more and returned her handkerchief to her pinafore pocket.

'He liked to pit people against one another?' Matt asked.

'He'd always make the bullets for somebody else to fire, would Titus. Then he would stand by laughing at the fallout.' Norma's expression was grim. 'He did it even with his own sons. He'd make more of one than another and think it was funny when they started fighting between themselves.' She gave a small shiver as if someone had stepped on her grave. 'He always had a cruel streak.'

'Does Micah know the contents of the will yet, about the farm and the money?' Matt asked, looking at the inspector.

'I am going to Wassail Farm next. I also need to inform Miss West of her bequest,' the inspector said.

'He remembered Abigail?' Norma looked surprised.

'He left fifty pounds to Miss West,' Inspector Lewis confirmed.

'Fifty pounds, it should have been five hundred with what that girl has put up with,' Norma declared.

'How do you think Micah will take the news about the farm and the money?' Kitty asked, looking at Norma. From what she had seen of Micah yesterday she suspected the news would not go down well.

'I don't know. He'll not be pleased though, I do know that. Especially about the farm. As I said, Hedley always thought there was something about a trust. He remembered hearing a whisper of it when his grandfather was alive, but he wasn't sure. It's only been lately with the row over the spring and all of that as we'd started to wonder.' Norma looked troubled.

Kitty hoped Micah wouldn't take a leaf from his father's book and show up at Blossomdown brandishing a shotgun to demand the money. He had a reputation for being hot-headed.

'What do you think Adam and Saul will say when they

learn they potentially own a third of Wassail Farm?' Inspector Lewis asked.

Norma shrugged. 'I don't know. Adam won't take much notice I don't suppose. He has no interest in farming, he's always preferred book learning. Saul, well, we intend to leave Blossomdown to Saul, he's like a son to us. I don't suppose he will be minded to quarrel with Micah about running Wassail with him. They never did get on. Saul is like his mother, may God rest her soul. Micah is all his father.' Norma shook her head sadly.

Inspector Lewis tucked his notebook back inside his jacket pocket. 'I had better get to Wassail Farm. I shall be in touch, Mrs Blake, if there is anything else I need to ask.' He rose from his seat and nodded to Kitty and Matt. 'Captain Bryant, Mrs Bryant.'

'I'll see you out, Inspector.' Norma too rose from her seat and took the policeman out into the hall. Matt exchanged a speaking glance with Kitty. They were certainly learning a lot about their new client and her family.

They heard the front door of the farmhouse close, then Norma popped her head into the room. 'I'm just going to make a fresh pot of tea, if that's all right. All that stuff the inspector was saying about Titus and the will. It's left me feeling a bit wobbly.'

'Oh yes, of course. Do you want any help?' Kitty offered.

'No, thank you, Mrs Bryant. It was just a shock, that's all. I'll be back in a minute or two.' She vanished down the hallway towards the kitchen.

'It was quite a lot, wasn't it?' Kitty murmured once the woman was out of earshot.

'Micah is not going to take the inspector's news about the farm well,' Matt said.

'No, I thought that too. I did wonder if perhaps he should have had a constable with him. Micah didn't seem a very reasonable sort of man from what you said yesterday.' Kitty looked at her husband.

'Perhaps he had an idea he wasn't going to inherit the farm. That could have been the argument Abigail heard,' Matt said.

'The one where Micah threatened to kill him.' Kitty didn't envy the inspector's task of breaking the news to Micah if indeed that had been the cause of the fight the housekeeper had overheard.

There was little chance to say much more before Norma returned bearing a wooden tray laden with tea things. She set it down on the coffee table and retook her seat on the armchair beside the fireplace.

'Tea?' Norma asked, setting out delicate china cups on the matching saucers.

'Thank you,' Kitty and Matt both accepted her invitation.

The act of making and then pouring tea for her guests seemed to restore Norma's equilibrium. Her cheeks were back to their usual pink colour, and she looked less shaken than when they had arrived.

'We came to bring you a copy of our contract and terms of agreement,' Matt said as he accepted his drink from her.

'Oh yes, of course. Do you need me to sign anything?' Norma asked as she offered Kitty a plate containing slices of fruit cake.

'Only once you've read it through,' Matt confirmed, 'but there is no hurry, you can read them later and let us have them back once you are certain you would like us to proceed.'

Kitty took the brown envelope with the papers from her handbag and passed them across to Norma.

'You see, this will of Titus's makes everything seem even worse,' Norma said with a sigh as she accepted the papers from Kitty. 'First he goes and gets himself murdered and now this. Even those that weren't raking over the past will start if they find out as he left me his money.' She gave Kitty and Matt a troubled look. 'As I mentioned on the telephone, Captain Bryant, they'll say as there's no smoke without fire and then Hedley will be all upset. Goodness knows what it will do to the farm's reputation.' She put the envelope on her lap.

'Even if people did gossip, I'm sure it would only be a seven-day wonder. They would soon move on to something else,' Kitty tried to reassure the woman.

'We are pillars of this community, Mrs Bryant. We are good, honest, hard-working God-fearing people. That bequest of Titus's was just to make mischief. That clause, or whatever the inspector called it, about Hedley not benefitting from the money.' Norma scowled as she helped herself to a slice of cake. 'He never forgave me for breaking off our engagement.'

'I didn't realise that you were engaged to Titus. I thought you had just been walking out,' Kitty remarked in a sympathetic tone. She had heard that Norma had been engaged but she wanted to see what Norma's version of the story was now that Hedley wasn't in the room.

'Oh yes, he was very courteous to me back then and he was a good-looking man.' Norma shook her head sadly. 'You'd not believe it seeing how he looked now. But he was considered a bit of a catch. He came calling on me after church and offering to take me dancing at the village hall.'

'What happened?' Kitty's curiosity was roused.

'Hedley was much quieter than his brother. He was studious, always had his head in a book. He still likes to read.' Norma waved her hand towards the fireplace and Kitty suddenly realised there was a low oak bookcase stuffed with books just behind the other fireside chair.

'Titus was quick tempered and liked to poke fun at his brother. I had been dazzled at first by his looks and how he courted me. He proposed after eight weeks and I was a giddy young thing then. I got caught up in the romance of it all. We started to talk of the wedding, but I realised I was talking about the wedding, and he was talking about the farm and what he was going to buy for it.' Norma's voice slowed as she became caught up in her memories.

'With your money?' Kitty asked.

'My parents' money. I realised he had his eyes more on Blossomdown than on me. There were other things too. He would be cruel for no reason. He had a dog, a collie, for working the sheep and she ran in front of him the one day in the yard. He stumbled and he kicked out at her. That was when I knew I couldn't marry him. I took off my ring and gave it back. I couldn't be with anyone who would hurt an animal. There were other things too.' Norma's eyes were bright now with unshed tears.

'And Hedley?' Kitty asked.

'He was quiet and kind. He waited a while to let the dust settle then he offered to walk me home from church. He took time to listen to me and he always treated me right. We fell in love and were married by the following Christmas. Titus never forgave either of us,' Norma said. 'Not even after he got married himself to Thora. She was a nice girl from a farming family near Newton Abbot. Everything became a competition for him. When Hedley and I found we couldn't have children he was delighted.'

Kitty placed a comforting hand on the older woman's arm when a tear ran down Norma's cheek.

'We were better off than Titus and when he had a bad year, crops failing with the bad weather and a disease that took a lot of his lambs...' Norma paused and pulled out her handkerchief once more to blow her nose.

'Was that when you offered to take in one of the boys?' Kitty asked softly.

Norma looked surprised. 'Yes, I didn't think as many people knew about that. Yes, Adam, the youngest was only a baby and he was sick, the bills for the doctor were a lot. We were always close to Saul even then. Thora was struggling, Micah was a handful and Saul, being the middle one, never got any attention. Titus, of course, wouldn't accept any money to help them out.'

'What happened then?' Matt asked.

'I tried everything to help. I'd go round when I knew Titus was busy on the farm and leave a basket by the back door of baked goods and a bit of money and treats for the children that I thought as Titus wouldn't notice. I didn't want him to take it out on any of the boys or his wife.' Norma wrung her hands together, the retelling of the story clearly still causing her anguish. 'I loved those boys when they were little.'

Kitty swallowed hard; she couldn't help but be deeply affected by Norma's story. 'I presume he found out?'

Norma nodded. 'Yes, eventually, then there was hell to pay. He was furious. I took all the blame; said I had forced things on them.'

'You took the blame to protect the children?' Matt asked.

'And their mother. He used to beat her, especially when he'd been drinking.' Norma dried her eyes and sat up a little straighter in her chair. 'But, that's the past. Nothing we can do to change any of it now. Hedley and I don't drink, we've seen too much of what can happen. I know that seems strange as we make and sell cider, but that is good for the health if taken in reasonable amounts. Our main business from the apples is apple butter and juice,' Norma explained.

Kitty knew the farm's advertisements in the local papers did indeed promote more of the other products that the farm produced.

'Take your time to read the paperwork and be certain before you sign the contract,' Kitty advised as Norma turned her attention back to the envelope Kitty had given her.

Mrs Blake fumbled in the large front pocket of her pinafore

once more to produce a pair of wire-framed spectacles. She put them on and studied the documents.

'That all seems in order.' She took a fountain pen from a small oak bureau at the back of the room and leaned on it to sign the papers before returning to her seat.

She passed them back to Kitty. 'I just want whoever did this caught. Not for Titus's sake but for the boys and our sakes.'

Kitty placed the papers safely back inside her cream leather handbag. 'We shall do our best, Mrs Blake.'

CHAPTER EIGHT

Matt seemed thoughtful as they said goodbye to Norma and stepped back out into the autumn sunshine of the farmyard.

'Where shall we go next?' Kitty asked as she opened the driver's door of her car.

'Inspector Lewis will be at Wassail Farm, and I think it may be best to let the dust settle there before we ask any questions of Micah or Abigail West,' Matt said as he got into the passenger seat.

'I agree.' Kitty was in no hurry to return to Wassail Farm. The image of finding Titus in the apple press flashed into her memory and she shuddered. She suspected too that Inspector Lewis would be most annoyed if they followed him there.

'Everyone seems to feel that Titus had other enemies beyond those in his immediate family. It might be useful to discover if there is anyone else who might stand out as a possible suspect.' Matt looked at Kitty.

'Any specific names, you mean? Shall we take a drive into Stoke Gabriel? It's such a lovely afternoon there is bound to be someone about we can talk to,' she suggested, starting the car engine.

'I believe there is a nice tea room there, perhaps an ice cream might be in order?' Matt grinned at her as she put her car in gear and set off along the lane to the village.

Stoke Gabriel consisted of a small cluster of whitewashed cottages topped by a mix of thatched and slate roofs clustered along the edge of the estuary. There were two roads leading into the centre which met at one of the junctions. Since the village was at river level the lanes were steep in places and high walls built of local grey stone lined the route. Famous for its fresh crabs caught in the clear water and the local cider, it was also a popular spot of late for walkers and visitors exploring the area.

Kitty drove down through the narrow streets towards the water's edge where she knew there was parking available near the tea room. They passed the Church House Inn with its steep flight of narrow stone steps and drove to the quay. She and Matt knew that places like post offices, public houses and tea rooms were often good sources of local information.

They parked the car and strolled over to the tea room. It was housed in one of the cottages that faced out onto the wide stretch of water. A green lawn stretched from the open French doors and tables and chairs were set out on the grass beneath gaily striped umbrellas.

At the water's edge on a wooden jetty, there were various men and boys fishing for crabs. A pair of white swans bobbed about nearby. Some of the outdoor tables were already occupied by couples taking afternoon tea and enjoying the sunshine.

They found an empty table closer to the tea room itself, but which still afforded a pleasant view of the river. Once seated, a plump older woman, her dark hair caught up in a bun beneath her white starched cap, scurried out to greet them.

'Good afternoon, welcome to the Swan Tea Rooms. How may I help you?' she asked, taking her order pad from the pocket of her crisp white apron.

'Do you serve ices?' Matt asked.

'Oh yes, sir, made with local clotted cream. Strawberry or plain?' The woman had a strong local accent.

'That sounds delicious. Plain, please,' Kitty said. 'This is the most delightful spot.'

The woman blushed with pleasure at the compliment as she noted Kitty's order on her notepad. 'Thank you, miss.'

'I'll try strawberry, please,' Matt added to Kitty's request. They added iced lemonade too and settled back to enjoy the sunshine and await their order.

The woman returned within a few minutes bearing a loaded tray which she set down on the table.

'This is such a lovely, peaceful place,' Kitty praised their surroundings for a second time as the woman lifted the lemonade jug from the tray to set it on the table.

'It is, miss, although there was a terrible murder just up the road from here only the other day. Not as you'd ever think such an awful thing could happen in a place like this.' The woman tutted and shook her head as she placed a glass each in front of them.

'Oh, I think we saw that in the newspaper. A farmer, Titus somebody?' Matt said as the woman set a pressed-glass boat-shaped dish of strawberry ice cream in front of him.

'That's right, sir. A terrible man, not that you'm supposed to speak ill of the dead, but 'tis no surprise really as he came to a bad end.' The woman placed a dish of vanilla in front of Kitty.

'He had a lot of enemies then?' Kitty said, picking up her spoon ready to dig into hers.

'He would have fell out with his own shadow that one. His eldest boy, Micah, is the same way. There are a good many as think as he might have been the one as killed him,' the woman said, glancing about her as if not wishing to be heard.

'Oh dear,' Matt said in an encouraging tone.

'Mind I reckon as them on the other side of Wassail Farm will be glad as he's dead. They had arguments with him time enough.' The woman picked up her empty tray.

'You mean, Blossomdown Farm?' Kitty asked.

'Oh, Blossomdown is owned by his brother and there is no love lost there to be sure. No, I mean the other side. 'Tis more of a smallholding really rather than a farm. Tillycombe Stables, the Pickerings' place. They hire horses for people wanting to take a ride out down along the lanes and such. They was at sixes and sevens over Titus Blake accusing them of trespassing on his land. There was a big argument last week at the market.'

'Gosh, it seems the police will have a long list of suspects,' Kitty said. This was the first they had heard of a dispute with Titus Blake's neighbours on the other side of his farmland.

'I dare say so. Nice people, the Pickerings; he's a war veteran. Still, I know where I'd place my money on who killed the old skinflint if I were a betting woman,' the proprietor said darkly and returned inside.

Matt looked at Kitty as he picked up his spoon to tackle his already melting ice cream. 'Well, it seems Norma Blake was correct when she said no one liked Titus.'

'That was a new name though, Pickering,' Kitty said. 'Land and its ownership seems to have been a big thing for Titus.'

Matt dug into his ice cream, savouring the cold, creamy taste before replying. 'How good are your horse-riding skills?'

Kitty eyed him, unsure if he was serious. 'I can ride a horse. But I haven't done so for quite some time. What about you?' She guessed what he was about to suggest.

A dimple flashed in Matt's cheek as he grinned at her. 'Perhaps a refresher lesson might be in order?'

Kitty glared at her husband. 'You didn't answer my question. How are your riding skills? Maybe you should be the one taking a ride along the lanes.'

Matt's smile widened. 'I suspect my riding skills are as rusty as yours. Perhaps we should just call in on our way home and make some enquiries about lessons or going out on a supported hack,' he suggested.

'I don't mind making enquiries, but I really am not dressed for riding today,' she warned, waving her ice-cream spoon at him. She was wearing a very nice pale-blue cotton print summer dress that Alice had recently shortened for her.

'And most charming you look too, darling. Very well, we'll just call in and see what we can find out,' he agreed.

Mollified by his assurance that he didn't expect her to go cantering off around the lanes within the next hour, Kitty returned to her bowl.

'Now we have one name for our suspect list, is there anywhere else we can try for information?' she asked as she dropped her spoon down into her now empty dish.

'Inspector Lewis has already been to the pub,' Matt said.

'There is always the post office. It's only a short walk from here into the village centre,' Kitty suggested.

'Sounds as if it may be worth a try.' Matt removed the crocheted net, weighted down with tiny blue glass beads, from the top of the lemonade jug. The proprietor had placed it there to keep any wasps or flying insects from landing in their drink. He poured himself and Kitty a glass of lemonade before replacing the cover.

'Sitting here with you like this, it makes what's happened at Wassail Farm feel like an awfully bad dream,' Kitty remarked as she stared out at the peaceful scene in front of her.

'I know. Yet out of all the people who disliked Titus Blake, one of them hated him enough to place him in that press.' Matt's tone was sombre.

Kitty finished her lemonade. 'Yes, you're right and even if he was as awful as everyone says, he still deserves justice.'

Matt smiled at her. 'That's my girl. I'll go and settle the bill and then we'll walk to the post office.'

He downed the last of his drink and went inside the tea room. Kitty gathered her bag ready to leave and tried to ignore the sudden shadow that briefly covered the sun.

CHAPTER NINE

Matt settled their account at the tea room and added a generous tip, delighting the lady who had served them.

Kitty was ready and waiting for him when he rejoined her at their table, and they set off together to find the post office. Kitty rested her hand lightly on his arm as they climbed the gentle curving slope that led into the village centre.

The houses in the village mostly had thatched or slate roofs and seemed to huddle together over the narrow streets. The post office was housed in one of these buildings and doubled as a small shop selling various groceries. It also sold postcards and gaily painted children's tin pails along with hooks, lines and nets for crabbing.

The shop was tiny, with barely room for two customers at a time thanks to the plethora of goods that were on display. Kitty waited outside ostensibly looking at the postcards displayed on a metal wire stand. Matt went inside to obtain some stamps and to try for information.

He had expected Kitty to want to be the one who asked the questions, but for once she appeared content to let him lead. He suspected it was because the scene she had witnessed the previous day had distressed her far more than she was willing to admit. This worried him and he hoped she would soon recover her usual inquisitive nature.

The interior of the shop was dark and stuffy after the bright sunshine and fresh air outside. Two fat flies were circling lazily around in the ceiling just above his head as he approached the small dark-wooden counter.

At first he thought the shop unattended, but then a sharp female voice in the gloom asked, 'How can I help you?'

He realised that a very elderly lady was behind the counter, dressed in rusty-black clothing and of such short stature he hadn't noticed her when he had first entered the shop.

'I'd like half a dozen stamps, please,' he asked.

The woman huffed and pulled open a shallow wooden drawer in the counter to find the stamps.

'It's a lovely day out today,' he said, trying to initiate a conversation, hoping to draw her into a general chat so he could ask some questions about Titus and the other members of the Blake families.

''Tis for them as can afford to be out enjoying themselves,' the woman said as she selected the stamps and slid them towards him.

'I suppose so. Could I have two pennyworth of peppermints too, please,' Matt asked, knowing that Kitty always liked to keep some sweets in her handbag.

The woman sniffed and dragged out a small wooden step-stool so she could climb up to lift the glass sweet jar down from the shelf.

'I'm sorry, I can get that for you if you like.' Matt immediately felt guilty that he hadn't realised the woman would struggle to reach the jar.

'No, thank you, I can manage,' the woman retorted sharply

as she lifted the heavy jar down and poured a few sweets into the set of scales she had on the end of the counter.

'You have a very well-stocked shop,' Matt tried again as the woman added lead weights to the scales and adjusted the amount of sweets to make them balance.

''Tis my daughter's business. I'm just minding the place while she sees to a couple of her jobs in the house.' The woman tipped the sweets into a paper cone and twisted the end to seal it, before adding the bag to the stamps.

'Have your family had the shop long?' Matt made one last try for some kind of conversation as he reached for his wallet to pay for his purchases.

'Long enough. 'Bout hundred years or so. This was my father's shop before, then mine, now 'tis my daughter's,' the woman said as she placed the lid back on the sweet jar ready to set it back on the shelf.

'How remarkable, you must know everyone in the village I should think, being here for so many generations,' Matt said in an admiring tone as the shopkeeper climbed back on her steps to replace the jar.

'I reckon so,' she said as she got back down.

'Such terrible news about that man being murdered yesterday,' Matt said as he opened his wallet.

'Good riddance to bad rubbish, that's what I say.' The woman totted up what he owed on a scrap of paper and asked for the money.

'He wasn't popular then, that Mr Blake?' Matt said, handing over some coins.

'No, he weren't.' The woman took his money and rummaged in her drawer for change.

'Here you'm not one of those newspaper people, am you?' she asked suddenly, her beady black eyes sharpening with suspicion.

'No, not at all. I live in Churston, and I came out with my wife for afternoon tea.' Matt indicated Kitty who was still studying the postcards outside the shop.

The woman dropped his change into his outstretched hand. 'Can't be too careful. There's no one as'll miss Titus Blake, I don't suppose. Not unless his sister-in-law still has any kind thoughts towards him.' The woman gave a short mischievous chuckle.

'Oh?' Matt said as he collected up the stamps and the sweets from the counter.

The old woman tapped the side of her nose with her forefinger. 'Proper close they were at one time. I'm not one to gossip mind, but 'tis said they still were.'

'Ah, I see.' Matt smiled politely and said goodbye to the shopkeeper, before joining Kitty outside on the pavement.

He handed her the sweets. 'I got you some peppermints for your bag.'

'Thank you.' She dropped them inside her summer handbag and fell into step beside him as they walked back towards Kitty's car.

'Did you learn anything new?' she asked.

'It was like trying to get blood from a stone. The only thing she did say was that she believed Norma and Titus were still on friendlier terms than they wished anyone to believe.'

'Oh.' Kitty was quick to realise the implications of this remark. 'That's interesting.'

'She also confirmed everyone else's view that the world was a better place without Titus Blake.'

* * *

Kitty turned her car around and they set off back along the lane leading out of the village.

'Where is this riding school?' Kitty asked.

'I thought I noticed the Pickerings' place as we were coming in. If I'm right, then it's just along here.' Matt indicated a point just beyond the bend in the road. Sure enough as they rounded the bend Kitty spotted the neatly painted sign in the hedgerows.

TILLYCOMBE STABLES
STABLES AND GRAZING TO RENT. TREKKING, HACKING AND RIDING LESSONS.

Kitty turned in through the open white-painted wooden gates and they found themselves in a small yard. Tillycombe Stables was another Devon longhouse made of cob, with lime-washed walls and a thatched roof.

A row of stables stood to the side forming an L-shape as they looked up the yard. A wiry middle-aged woman dressed in riding breeches and a check shirt was trundling a laden wheelbarrow out of the stables as Kitty switched off the engine of her car.

The woman set down the barrow and pulled off her gloves, wiping her brow with the back of her hand when she noticed the car.

'How can I help you?' the woman asked as Matt and Kitty climbed out and approached her.

'We were just talking to the lady who runs the tea room in the village, and she said that you offered hacks for beginners and riding lessons,' Kitty said.

The woman eyed them both curiously. 'Have either of you ridden before?'

'We both have in the past, but we are rather rusty now. We thought it might be nice to take it up again.' Matt gave the woman a disarming smile.

'I see. Would you want lessons or to try out a hack first to see how you feel?' the woman asked.

Kitty looked at Matt. 'Um, probably a hack. Not today obviously,' she said as the woman looked her up and down appraisingly.

'Best follow me to my office and I can see what we have available.' The woman abandoned her wheelbarrow to lead the way over to a small timber building opposite the stables. She unlocked the door to reveal a tired-looking pine table piled up with notebooks and an old biscuit tin shaped like a thatched cottage. A battered chair with a grubby dark-green cushion was at the side and a calendar from last year showing a portrait of the King hung on the back wall.

'When were you thinking?' the woman asked, pulling a diary from the top of the pile of notebooks.

'Um, next week?' Kitty suggested, hoping the woman would say they had no availability. She hadn't admitted it to Matt but her last experience of riding a horse had not been good. Her horse had been difficult and on the way back from the ride had made a sudden bolt for his stable, hurling Kitty off into the biggest, muddiest puddle around.

'Splendid, you're in luck,' the woman said briskly. 'Would Monday afternoon suit you both?'

'That sounds super, doesn't it, darling?' Matt replied before Kitty could come up with an excuse not to go riding.

Kitty suppressed a sigh. Today was Friday, so she had all of the weekend to find a reason not to do this. 'Perfect,' she agreed.

He gave the woman their names and address and paid a small deposit.

'Thank you, Captain Bryant. We shall look forward to seeing you and Mrs Bryant on Monday at two o'clock,' Mrs Pickering said, closing the book.

'I don't suppose we could see any of the horses now, could we?' Kitty asked.

'Of course. We have six horses here at the moment. We did have ten but we've had some bother from the farm next door, so we lost some of our boarders,' Mrs Pickering explained as she came out of her office and closed the door behind her.

'Oh, I'm sorry to hear that,' Kitty said as they followed the woman across the yard to the stables.

'I don't like to speak ill of the dead, but Mr Blake at Wassail Farm caused us no end of trouble. I expect you'll have seen that piece in this morning's papers about the murder?' Mrs Pickering stopped by the first open stable door and a pretty bay pony popped her head out.

'I think I did see something, was that near here?' Matt feigned ignorance.

Kitty reached out a gloved hand to stroke the pony's nose.

'Yes, just next door, a right to do by all accounts.' Mrs Pickering smiled approvingly at her pony. 'This is Bramble, a lovely gentle ride, she is.'

'She is lovely,' Kitty agreed, feeling much better about Monday now she had seen one of the horses.

Mrs Pickering moved along to the next half-open door. A white horse, taller than Bramble looked out and started to snuffle as if expecting a treat.

'What kind of trouble did you get from Mr Blake?' Matt asked as Kitty patted the side of the white horse's head with a tentative touch.

'What didn't we get?' Mrs Pickering scowled. 'Blackening our name around the place, breaking down our fences and walls to let our horses onto his land, then claiming as they had damaged his crops. Trespassing.'

'Oh dear,' Kitty sympathised. 'That sounds dreadful.'

Mrs Pickering appeared to collect herself. 'It was, Mrs Bryant, I don't mind telling you. Now this horse is Shadow. He might be good for you to ride, Captain Bryant.'

Matt eyed the horse and Kitty thought she detected a faint trace of nervousness in her husband. She bit back a smile.

Perhaps he too was not as terribly confident about riding as he'd made out.

Mrs Pickering showed them a couple of the other horses who all appeared gentle and well kept.

They said their goodbyes after Mrs Pickering had emphasised they should dress appropriately for their ride with good footwear on Monday.

'That has been an illuminating few hours,' Kitty said when they were back in the car once more and heading for home.

'Yes. I had thought originally that perhaps the Blakes were prejudiced when they said that Titus had a lot of enemies,' Matt said.

'They weren't exaggerating though, were they?' Kitty slowed down to turn into Yalberton Lane to cut across to Churston. 'Are we still going to turn up to ride on Monday?'

Matt looked surprised at her question. 'I think it would be a good idea. So many of the arguments Titus appears to have had seem to centre around land and land use. A ride out to see what the problems were could be very useful.'

Kitty could see he had a point. On horseback you were above the hedgerows and stone walls, and it would give them that view of the boundaries. It might also show the route through the fields between the farmhouses. That could show them how feasible it was for someone to get to Wassail Farm and not be seen.

It seemed she would have to hunt out some suitable riding attire for Monday and hope it still fitted her.

'Norma was also correct about the gossip starting up again about her and Titus,' Kitty said as she took the turn towards their house.

'Yes, the old lady looking after the post office was not very nice about it.' Matt sounded thoughtful.

Kitty pulled her car to a halt outside the house and switched off the engine. 'No smoke without fire?' she repeated Norma Blake's expression with a slight shrug.

'Perhaps. We shall have to see what else we can discover over the next few days,' Matt said as he climbed out of the car. 'I have a feeling there is a lot more to come.'

CHAPTER TEN

The following morning dawned just as bright and sunny as the previous days. There was a distinct nip in the air, however. Condensation had formed outside on the glass of the French doors and Kitty shivered as she finished her breakfast.

'We shall have to start lighting the fires more often again soon, I think,' she remarked looking at Matt.

'At least we have a good supply of firewood ready for the winter.' Matt folded his morning newspaper from where he had been studying the article on Titus Blake's murder. It had gone from a small paragraph the previous day, when the news had broken, to filling most of the front page.

'Alice is coming over later,' Kitty reminded him. 'We thought we could all have lunch together before she goes to her mother's house for tea.'

'That'll be nice. I haven't seen much of her since she's been so busy with her new business.' Matt smiled at Kitty.

'There will be a lot to tell her about our case.' Kitty nodded towards the lurid headline on the front page of the newspaper.

'I wonder if she knows the family. After all, your grandmother and Mrs Craven both knew the Blakes,' Matt said.

Alice's family had lived in Dartmouth for a long time and knew many of the local families.

'You should know by now that Mrs Craven knows everyone. And if by any chance Alice doesn't, then her cousin Betty does.' Kitty grinned back at him. Mrs Craven knew everyone who was anyone and Alice's cousin had usually worked for them at some point.

Alice's cousin Betty was a little older than Alice and was an only child, unlike Alice who had seven younger brothers and sisters. She was also what Alice's mother called a 'flighty piece'. She often changed her employers and dressed less modestly than was generally considered appropriate by the older ladies of the town.

Kitty liked her though, as Betty usually had a fund of interesting stories and was an easy-going girl with a good heart. She wondered if Betty would know anything about the Blakes.

'That is very true,' Matt agreed.

Kitty had just finished clearing away the breakfast things and had put the kettle on to boil for a fresh cup of tea when there was a knock at the door.

From the kitchen she could hear the murmur of voices and a few woofs from Bertie as he inspected the visitor. She glanced at the kitchen clock. If it was Alice, then she was unusually early as she had been expecting her friend to arrive on the later bus.

Kitty added an extra cup to the tea tray she was preparing and took the precaution of placing a plate of biscuits there too when she heard Matt showing the visitor into the drawing room.

Matt popped his head into the kitchen a few seconds later.

'Adam Blake has arrived to see us.' He glanced at the tray and saw she was already prepared.

'The kettle is just boiling, I'll be there in a minute,' Kitty assured him and finished her preparations, while Matt returned to their guest.

When she arrived in the drawing room bearing the tea tray a young man in a smart grey suit was seated on the modern black leather and chrome chair beside the fireplace. He stood when Kitty entered and set down her tray.

'Mrs Bryant?' He extended his hand to her. 'I'm Adam Blake, Titus Blake's youngest son. My aunt Norma suggested I should call on you. I hope this is not inconvenient?'

'No not at all, Mr Blake, do sit down. May I offer you some tea?' Kitty perched herself on the edge of the sofa and set about serving her guest a drink. Adam looked about two years or so younger than Saul and was a very different kind of person to both his older brothers in appearance.

Where Micah was unkempt with a big beard and straggly hair, Adam was well groomed and dressed smartly. He was tall, like his brothers, but built more leanly. Saul, the middle brother was very much a farm labourer, with a ruddy complexion from working outdoors and rough, working hands. Adam had silver cufflinks in his shirt and a pale-blue silk tie.

Once the niceties of hostessing were dispensed with and Adam Blake had a cup of tea and a biscuit, Kitty settled back on the black leather sofa.

'Now, how may we assist you, Mr Blake? You said your aunt suggested you call on us?' she asked.

Adam glanced first at Kitty and then at Matt before replying. 'My aunt Norma is a very sensitive soul. I think she has made you aware that she was expected to marry my father many years ago but married Hedley, my father's brother, instead?'

'Yes, she told us all about it. She is very concerned, I think, that the terrible nature of your father's death might stir up old gossip, which would be unpleasant for her and for your uncle,' Kitty said in a sympathetic tone.

'Exactly. Then there is the matter of the will and the financial bequest left to my aunt.' Adam paused and looked at them once more.

'Your aunt said Wassail Farm is subject to a trust? Although, the terms of the trust seemed to still be unclear,' Matt checked this with their visitor.

'That's right. It seems that the farm is to be split with ownership between all three of us. As you said though, my employer is looking into whether, in fact, Uncle Hedley has a prior claim. For myself, I don't care. I want none of it. I've no desire to be a farmer. Saul, well, I think Uncle Hedley and Aunt Norma will probably leave Blossomdown to him.'

'Micah, however, thought Wassail Farm was to be entirely his?' Kitty said.

'That's right. He hasn't taken the news too well. He went to the pub in Stoke Gabriel last night and got roaring drunk. Then he went round to Uncle Hedley and Aunt Norma's afterwards spoiling for a fight with Saul.' Adam shifted uncomfortably in his seat.

Bertie lifted his head hopefully from where he had been lying near the table, no doubt hoping for biscuit crumbs.

'Oh dear, what happened?' Kitty asked. She guessed this was why Norma may have asked Adam to call on them.

'Micah tried calling Saul outside wanting to fight but Uncle Hedley was having none of it. He made Saul stop in the farmhouse and ended up threatening Micah with his shotgun to stay away from the farm. No one was hurt and no shots were fired, but from what Aunt Norma told me it was very upsetting.' Adam stared gloomily into his teacup.

'I take it Micah hoped to push Saul into relinquishing his share of the farm?' Matt asked.

Adam shrugged. 'I think that was the gist of it. I'm expecting him to try something with me too. I don't mind giving up my share, and I don't think Saul would mind much now that he's settled in at Blossomdown. Micah does deserve the farm in many ways. He's put up with Father all these years and he's owed I don't know how much in back pay.' Adam paused again.

Kitty could tell the man had more to say. 'But?' she asked.

'Wassail Farm has been in our family for five generations to my knowledge and Micah, well, I can see that he'll run it into the ground left to himself. He drinks too much and there's a side to him...' Adam's voice tailed off for a moment and Kitty looked at Matt.

'Like your father?' Matt said.

Adam nodded miserably. 'Yes, and that's what's holding me and Saul back from just walking away from it.'

Bertie looked hopefully at Kitty and she gave him the last biscuit from the plate.

'Your aunt said none of you knew about the trust? The way the farm had been left? Is that correct?' Matt asked.

Adam looked uncomfortable. 'I knew there was a trust, and so did Saul because I told him. I found out by accident. Father's posturing with Uncle Hedley over the big field and the water rights meant my employer asked me to find the original deeds and documents for the farms. The deeds showing the boundaries were with the trust paperwork, but it was worded in a very complex way.'

'Your uncle Hedley said he thought the trust left the farm to the male heirs. He had never claimed his half when your grandfather passed away because he had married your aunt by then and was running Blossomdown,' Kitty said.

'That was what he told me when I let him know I'd been looking at the documents. I presumed that meant he had signed his portion over to Father at some point in the past.' Colour tinged Adam's cheeks.

Kitty could see this meant that all of the Blakes would have had some knowledge about the ownership of the farm not being straightforward. The only one in the dark appeared to be Micah.

'Why did your father choose to make his will at your place of work when he could have gone to any other firm of solicitors?' Kitty asked. She was curious about this as to her it had seemed a strange choice.

Titus had apparently made a huge fuss about Adam not being allowed to know the contents of the will and it being kept secret, so why go there at all? Why had he not chosen to go to another law firm?

Adam gave a wry smile. 'He had several reasons, I expect. One being that the company I work for has always dealt with any legal business for our family. All the documents and deeds are there going back over a hundred or more years. There is also the aspect that Father liked us to know what he was doing. Letting us know he was remaking his will gave him power over us. At least in his head anyway, and he loved to feel he had power over you.'

'You realise, obviously, that if the initial interpretation of the trust is correct and the farm is left to the three of you, this could be considered a possible motive by the police for you and Saul wishing your father dead. Obviously, Micah has the same motive since he thought your father had left the farm solely to him,' Kitty said, setting her cup down on the table.

Adam shrugged once more. 'It's not a motive for me. I don't want any part of the farm. I couldn't wait to get away. Micah and I have never seen eye to eye. I've always been closer to Saul, but I like books and he likes mud. I'm doing well for myself now where I am.'

'Has Inspector Lewis asked you where you were the day your father was killed?' Matt asked.

Kitty recalled that the chief inspector had told them that although Adam had been in the office he had been running errands for his employer.

'He did. I haven't much of an alibi. I was in the office all morning and then in the afternoon I had to take some papers to the court in Newton Abbot. I suppose people there would remember seeing me,' Adam said, before taking a sip of his tea.

'How did you travel there?' Kitty asked. She supposed he could have taken the train since the towns were linked on the rail network. She was sure though that Chief Inspector Greville had said that Adam had transport.

'I have a car.' Adam's expression lit up and she could see this was a source of great pride.

Matt glanced at her. If Adam had a car, then he could have driven to Stoke Gabriel, murdered his father and returned to Totnes. It seemed his alibi was as weak as that of his brothers.

'How lovely, driving gives one such freedom,' Kitty said.

'Why did your aunt ask you to call today? Was there something she thought we should do for her?' Matt asked.

'She's worried about Micah being so, well, unstable. That incident last night frightened her. She's afraid for Uncle Hedley, Saul and me. Plus, she thinks that gossip about her and Father is already taking hold in the village. Public opinion is very important to Aunt Norma, she sets great store by being respectable. She wanted me to call and offer any help to you that I might be able to give to catch whoever killed my father.' Adam finished his tea and placed his cup beside Kitty's.

'What do you know about the people who own the stables on the other side of Wassail Farm?' Kitty asked, changing the subject slightly.

'Mr and Mrs Pickering? Not very much. They bought the land about four or five years ago, around the time I left home. It used to belong to Mr Gilligan, he was quite elderly and let it get into a bad state. The Pickerings seem to be making a go of it now though.' Adam looked slightly surprised by Kitty's question.

'You aren't aware of any ill feeling between Wassail Farm and the Pickerings?' Matt looked at Adam.

'No, but then again, I didn't visit Wassail Farm very often, usually once a month and I stayed for as little time as possible. Saul doesn't visit at all if he can help it, unless he is hoping to see Abigail. He would see Father and Micah at church when they bothered to turn up. Unless Micah or Father complained or told us about something or someone they had quarrelled with, then I wouldn't know. You have to understand that living at Wassail Farm after my mother died was impossible.' A bleak expression settled on Adam's face.

'I'm sorry, that must have been hard for you all. Abigail West came to the farm just before you lost your mother, to help her when she was ill, is that right?' Kitty said.

Adam nodded. 'Abigail came from the orphanage. She took on all the heavy work and helped look after Mother. Then, when Mother passed away, Abigail ended up doing everything. She works hard and Father and Micah treat her terribly.'

'Why does she stay?' Kitty asked.

'She has nowhere else to go. Father never paid her very much and if she left, he wouldn't give her a reference, so she stopped.'

'Your brother Saul seems to have been kind to her.' Kitty was curious to hear what Adam had to say about that. She had her own ideas about Saul's possible affection for the young housekeeper.

Adam smiled. 'I reckon he's sweet on her. I think everyone knows that. Even Father seemed to guess there was something going on, but they were careful to keep it from him as much as possible. He would have made her life hell if he had thought it was anything serious.'

'Mr Blake, is there anyone specific who you may know of who might have wished to kill your father?' Matt asked.

Adam raised his hands in an open-handed gesture. 'Truthfully, Captain Bryant, I'm not sure. My father upset a good many people. It may be that he simply pushed one of them too far. He enjoyed upsetting them, causing trouble, stirring things up. He would bad-mouth tradespeople; delay paying bills till the last moment, or not pay in full. In short, he was a dreadful man.'

Kitty suppressed a sigh. It seemed the list of suspects wasn't getting any shorter. Yet, the manner of his death had been so awful, she thought it must have been someone who had truly hated him. She had been sure that by now at least a few more names would have come up.

'Thank you, you've been very helpful. We shall continue to investigate and will be in touch with your aunt in due course,' Matt said.

Adam rose, ready to leave. 'Thank you.'

'Please assure her that we are doing everything we can to get to the bottom of your father's death,' Kitty added as she and Matt went to see Adam out.

She had just opened the door so Adam could leave when she found Alice on the doorstep, her hand raised ready to knock.

'Oh, you took me by surprise. Good morning, Kitty, Captain Bryant. The bus has just dropped me off.' Alice looked curiously at Adam Blake as she spoke and a faint blush coloured her pale cheeks.

'Mr Adam Blake, Miss Alice Miller. Mr Blake is the nephew of a client.' Kitty performed a brief introduction as Adam and Alice passed each other on the doorstep.

'Nice to meet you, I'm sure,' Alice said.

'The pleasure is all mine, Miss Miller.' Adam smiled at her, causing Alice's blush to deepen further before he strode away to get into a slightly battered dark-blue car. He raised his hand briefly in a farewell wave and reversed out of the driveway.

'Come inside, Alice, and we'll catch you up with all the news,' Kitty said, ushering her friend into the hall.

She thought Alice looked very pretty this morning. Her lovely auburn hair was fastened in a neat bun at the nape of her neck under a straw hat trimmed with daisies and her corn-flower-blue dress emphasised her trim figure and bright eyes. It was no wonder Adam Blake had seemed to notice her.

Alice took off her hat and followed Kitty into the drawing room, where she bent to fuss Bertie who was wagging his tail enthusiastically at her arrival.

'Let me make a fresh tray of tea and I'll tell you everything that's happened since I saw you,' Kitty said.

'That sounds ominous.' Alice perched herself on the edge of the sofa. 'Don't tell me as you'm involved in investigating that murder that's on the front page of this morning's newspaper? I should have known you'd get involved when you telephoned to tell me you found the body.'

Kitty flashed an apologetic smile at her friend as Matt grinned cheerfully and picked up the tea tray.

'I'll put the kettle back on while you tell Alice about Titus Blake's murder.'

CHAPTER ELEVEN

Kitty told Alice everything that had happened after she had left her that day to go and get some cider on her way home. She had already spoken to her briefly on the telephone to say she had discovered Titus Blake's body. It had helped enormously to listen to Alice's soothing, common-sense talk.

'That's awful! I can't believe it. What a complicated family. I don't know them at all and even our Betty couldn't tell me anything when I asked her.' Alice stared at her, her eyes wide and her hands pressed to her cheeks in distress.

'I know. It is quite shocking. He really was not a well-liked man at all,' Kitty said. She was privately amused that Betty, for once, had failed to deliver any information.

'Are you all right now though? You were so upset when you called me. I don't even want to imagine how dreadful it must have been finding him like that, and now it sounds as if it will be quite a job to work out who killed him,' Alice said as Matt re-entered the room bearing a fresh tray of tea things.

'It seems there is quite a queue of people who disliked Titus Blake,' Matt agreed as he placed the tray down on the table.

Bertie sniffed around hopefully for a minute, before settling back at Kitty's feet when he realised there were no biscuits on the tray this time round.

'I read all about it in the newspaper this morning when I went to the workshop to check the post and see a customer. I had a lady coming from Stoke Gabriel to collect a dress I'd made for her little girl, and she was talking about it.' Alice settled back with her cup of tea.

'What did she say?' Kitty asked. She had declined another cup of tea and Matt had discreetly taken Bertie out for a walk to allow her to talk freely to her friend.

'She said much the same as you've found out already. That Titus Blake and his son Micah aren't liked much at all. Everyone were a bit afraid of Titus on account of him being handy with his fists. He would be always bullying people or being rude to them,' Alice said. 'Micah, the eldest son, he drinks a lot and is a bit hot-headed.'

Kitty frowned. 'Did she say anything else at all?'

'She said that Mrs Blake, the one married to the brother, well they had used to be sweethearts until she threw Titus over to marry Hedley. She said as she'd heard as Titus never got over it and that he's left all his money to her.'

Kitty hadn't told Alice yet about the money being left to Norma, so she was curious about how this had apparently become common knowledge so quickly. She couldn't see that Norma herself or her husband would be spreading that around. Especially as Norma had been very keen to eradicate any gossip, not fire it up.

'Where did she hear that?'

Alice looked at her over the brim of her cup. 'Is it true then? My customer said Micah got drunk at the Church House Inn and was telling anybody who'd listen how he'd been hard done by. She said as everyone was surprised as Titus had any money to leave.'

'It is true. Titus has left most of his money to Norma and it's a large sum. She says she doesn't know why he did it,' Kitty said.

Alice's brows shot upwards. 'Do you think it was because he still had feelings for her even after all this time?' she asked.

'That doesn't fit in with what we know of Titus. Norma, Mrs Blake, thinks he did it to cause trouble,' Kitty said with a wry smile.

Alice looked slightly disappointed by this less romantic view of Norma's unexpected legacy. 'Hmm, you're probably right. My customer said as it's the talk of the village right now.'

'Did she say who everyone thought might have killed Titus?' Kitty asked. She knew that if everyone was talking about the murder there was bound to be some speculation about who could have done it.

'She said as everyone thought it were probably Micah, the son. He wanted the farm and his father had always promised it to him. She reckoned as his father probably pushed him too far.' Alice finished the last of her tea and placed her cup down.

'I wonder though,' Kitty said. 'Micah seems hot-tempered. I could see him fighting his father, or even shooting him in the heat of the moment, but crushing his head in the juicing press seems more, well, cold-blooded.' She shivered as she spoke.

'True, but who knows what somebody is capable of if they'm proper riled up. I expect as well as whoever did put him in the press must have knocked him out first as he wouldn't have just lay there else while his head was squashed,' Alice said.

'I suppose so.' Kitty tidied up the tray ready to take it to the kitchen. Her housekeeper, Mrs Smith, had left her a nice large cottage pie for their lunch, so she needed to pop it in the oven to start warming it up for later.

'So, that gentleman this morning? You said he was the nephew of your client?' Alice asked as she followed Kitty into the kitchen.

'Yes, Norma Blake has engaged us to find out who killed

Titus. Adam is Titus Blake's youngest son. He has nothing to do with the farms, he works for a solicitor in Totnes,' Kitty explained as she took the prepared pie from the cold slab in the pantry ready to place it inside the oven.

'He must be the one as my customer said was doing well for himself,' Alice observed as she started to wash the teacups in the large stone sink.

'Yes, he has a car and was dressed nicely,' Kitty remarked primly as she slid the pie into the oven. She waited to see what Alice's response was to that.

'Humph.' Alice splashed the water noisily in the sink and scrubbed vigorously at the cups.

'Um, talking of young men with cars, a certain Mr Robert Potter asked me to give you his regards yesterday when I saw him in Dartmouth.' Kitty picked up an Irish linen tea cloth ready to dry the cups and braced herself for Alice's reaction.

'Did he now?' Alice let the water out of the sink and reached for a towel to dry her hands.

Kitty knew better than to say much else to her friend on that score, much as she longed to know how Alice felt about the matter. She knew her friend had taken the parting of the ways with her former beau very much to heart, even though Alice had been the one to initiate it.

'You don't think that perhaps you might...?' Kitty couldn't help herself however.

'I don't think on the matter at all,' Alice replied firmly. 'Kitty Bryant, I've said all I have to say on the subject of Robert Potter.'

'Sorry, Alice,' Kitty said repentantly as she placed the damp tea cloth over the Sheila Maid hanging rack in the scullery to dry out.

Alice fixed her with a firm gaze. 'Just leave that particular subject alone. If you see Robert again you may tell him you've passed on his message, but I have none to send back.'

. . .

After lunch, Kitty ran Alice down to Kingswear in her car so her friend could take the ferry across the river as a foot passenger. They parted amicably and Kitty promised to go to the pictures with her in Paignton on Wednesday evening.

Lunch had been a pleasant interlude amongst all the investigating they had been doing since Kitty had discovered Titus's body. Alice had been particularly amused about Kitty and Matt's intentions to go riding on Monday. Unlike Matt, she knew what had happened the last time Kitty had ridden a horse.

Matt was making another attempt at the daily crossword in the newspaper when Kitty returned.

'What are our plans for the rest of the weekend?' she asked as she dislodged Rascal from her favourite armchair.

'I think we really should attempt to speak to Micah.' Matt frowned as he spoke, and she could see the idea didn't appeal to her husband any more than it did to Kitty herself. He set the paper aside.

'I'm afraid you're right, but I think we need to choose a time when he is less likely to fly off the handle,' Kitty agreed. She had been having exactly the same thoughts.

'Norma Blake mentioned that Micah sometimes attends the church on Sunday mornings.' Matt looked thoughtful.

'I suppose it depends if he goes to the public house again tonight,' Kitty said. If the villagers all seemed to think he had killed his father he might not feel like facing them all at the church.

'Tomorrow morning would still be a good time I think. He has to attend to his animals and if he is hungover he is more likely to be peaceable.' Matt looked at her for agreement.

'I suppose so. If he does attend the church service, he will have to behave, at least whilst there. If we don't find him at the farm, then we can drive to the church and wait for them all to come out.' Kitty thought if Micah was still spoiling for a fight with the other Blakes, then heading him off after the service might do them all a favour.

'That's agreed then, we shall try to talk to Micah in the morning.' Matt picked up the newspaper he had put down while he had been talking to Kitty and prepared to return to his crossword.

'I wonder what our friend Inspector Lewis is up to?' Kitty asked.

Matt chuckled. 'Who knows. He certainly appears to have unleashed chaos after he told Micah about the terms of his father's will.'

There seemed to be little else they could do on the investigation until they had spoken to Micah. The rest of their afternoon and evening passed peacefully, and Kitty retired to bed hoping that things would go smoothly the next day.

The church bells were ringing the following morning when Kitty and Matt set off once more for Wassail Farm. It was another crisp and sunny autumn day and more of the leaves on the trees had started to turn.

'Let us hope we find Micah in an amenable mood,' Kitty said as she pulled to a halt at the entrance to the farm.

'Well, I have no desire to be chased off with a shotgun,' Matt agreed as he joined her at the farm gate.

The farmhouse door stood open and there was no sign of the dogs. The scrawny chickens were pecking and scratching in the dust near the doorway much as they had been when Kitty had visited the first day.

Matt pulled on the iron pull to clang the angel bell that hung from a rusty bracket near the door.

After a moment, Abigail appeared, her hands dusty with flour and an anxious expression on her thin face.

'Good morning, Miss West, we hoped to speak to Micah if he is around?' Matt lifted his hat politely to the girl.

The girl's posture seemed to relax slightly when she recognised them, and Kitty wondered who she had thought might be at the door.

'Micah is on the back field with the dogs. I'm expecting him down in a minute for his cup of tea. Would you care to come in and wait?' Abigail offered.

They wiped their feet on the tatty mat inside the front door and followed the girl as she showed them into a room that was clearly little used.

'Please take a seat and I'll just go and get the kettle on.' Abigail slipped away leaving Kitty and Matt inside the long, gloomy room with its low-beamed ceiling and old-fashioned heavy furnishings. Kitty took a seat on the tapestry-upholstered chair beside the fireplace. A fire had been laid in the grate but was unlit.

In the light coming through the small lead-pane windows which were set deep in the thick walls she could tell that Wassail Farm was unused to receiving callers, at least not ones that would be shown to the parlour. The room was clean and tidy but had the air of being little used.

After a few minutes, Abigail returned carefully carrying a wooden tray laden with tea things. She placed it down on the table.

'I think as Micah is coming, I just saw the dogs, so I'll let him know as you'm here,' she said and scurried away again.

'She reminds me of a frightened little mouse.' Matt watched her leave.

Kitty agreed, but even mice could bite. Had Titus pushed the housekeeper too far? Could she have been responsible for his death? She heard the low rumble of a man's voice emanating from the direction of the kitchen and guessed Micah had returned for his mid-morning cup of tea.

A minute or so later the door to the parlour opened once more and Micah entered. Matt stood and extended his hand to greet him. 'I hope this isn't a bad time of day for us to call. I appreciate you must be very busy now since the loss of your father.'

''Tis all right.' Micah nodded a greeting to Kitty and took a seat on the chair opposite her. She noticed he had removed his boots, and his big toe was protruding through a hole in his sock.

Abigail hovered anxiously in the doorway as if uncertain if she should stay or return to the kitchen.

'Shall I be mother?' Kitty offered, placing her hand on the handle of the brown china teapot.

Micah nodded his consent and Kitty saw the young housekeeper slip back outside the room as if anxious to get away. Kitty set about serving the tea, while Matt asked their host how he was faring since the unpleasant demise of his father.

'Not so good, to be honest, Captain Bryant,' Micah admitted as he accepted his cup of tea from Kitty, the dainty china cup incongruous in his large hand. 'I suppose you'll have heard how I've been done an injustice?'

'You mean the will?' Matt asked.

Micah scowled. ''Tisn't right. Wassail Farm should be mine and then there is that business of Father's money. I've an appointment at that fancy solicitor's where our Adam works on Tuesday afternoon to get to the rights of it all.'

'I believe there was some talk of a trust?' Kitty handed a cup of tea to Matt.

'That's what the police inspector were saying but I don't know as that's right till I see it or hear for myself. It struck me as if there is such a thing and Father were only entitled to his half of the farm, well then, surely if Uncle Hedley is still alive he would have his half and us lads would have the other half split into three. Or it might be as we lads have no claim at all just yet.

I might as well give the place to Uncle Hedley outright.' Micah's expression darkened.

'It does sound terribly complicated,' Kitty said soothingly.

Micah nodded, clearly brooding on the matter. 'What can I do for you both?' he asked suddenly, looking first at Kitty and then at Matt.

'Our purpose in calling was twofold,' Kitty said. 'First, I wanted to ask how you were doing. It was such a horrible shock when we found your father.'

'Thank you, that is a kind thought.' Micah looked directly at her and blinked. 'You'm one of the only people who has given me a kind word since he died. I know what he was like but even so...' His voice tailed away.

Kitty felt a little guilty about their true purpose for the visit so plunged on. 'The other reason for calling is we have been asked by your aunt Norma to investigate alongside the police to find who did this.'

Matt took a business card from his jacket pocket and handed it to Micah. The farmer studied it for a moment, his brow furrowing as he took in the information.

'We didn't want you to feel that there were matters afoot that you didn't know about. We felt sure that you would be as anxious as the rest of the family to clear your name and find out who really killed your father,' Kitty added quickly.

She had given some thought on the drive over to the farm of how best to present Norma's commissioning of their services in a good light to Micah.

'Private investigators, eh? Now why would dear old Aunt Norma do that? 'Tisn't for my benefit, that's for certain. It would suit all their purposes if they could find a way to pin this on me. The farm would definitely be Saul's and Uncle Hedley's then. Adam never wanted any part of it. He would give his part to Saul.' Micah sounded thoughtful.

'I think your aunt is sensitive to people raking up the past,' Kitty said.

'Or afeared of what might come out about the present,' Micah muttered darkly. He set down his empty cup and slipped Matt's card inside the breast pocket of his battered tweed jacket.

'The present?' Kitty asked mildly as she refilled his cup with the last of the tea from the pot.

Micah looked at her from under his thick dark brows before he added milk to his tea. 'Aye. I know as my aunt's been coming around here lately to see Father. Sneaking in when she thought as Abigail was busy or out and she thought as I were working up on the top field.'

'You saw her?' Matt asked, leaning forward slightly in his seat.

'Aye, a couple of times. There's an old path that leads from Blossomdown to Wassail through the orchards. There's a stile there. I reckon as she thought as no one would know she had been a nigh,' Micah said, before draining his second cup of tea.

'Did you say anything to your father about it? Or ask him any questions?' Matt asked.

Micah snorted. 'It would be a braver man than me to ask Father about anything like that. No, I just tucked it way in here.' He tapped the side of his head with his forefinger. 'Just in case, like.'

Kitty wondered exactly what he meant by that.

CHAPTER TWELVE

'Do you know some people called Pickering? From the livery stables next door?' Matt asked, changing the subject.

'Aye, they bought the place a few years back round about when Adam moved out. What of them?' Micah asked.

'We heard they and your father had been having some kind of dispute over the land. Something about grazing rights and maintaining the field boundaries?' Kitty said.

'I know as Father were annoyed with them, he said as they'd let their horses get out and into the crops the one day. Trampled all the wheat,' Micah said. 'The walls were damaged. Those are the ones as I've been putting right up near the woods.'

Kitty glanced at Matt. 'The Pickerings said that your father had been libelling them in the village. That he had driven off some of the people who had been boarding their horses at the stables.'

Micah sighed. 'It sounds like something Father would do. He used to be ranting on all the while about this, that and t'other. A lot of the time I didn't pay him no mind. It wore you down else. I've not had much to do with the Pickerings except when I've been repairing the fences and the walls.'

Kitty could see that ignoring his father's rages had been a survival tactic for Micah. Living with Titus Blake had not been an easy life for anyone it seemed.

'Now that the shock of the murder has worn off a little, who do you think is most likely to have killed your father?' Matt asked. 'You knew him better perhaps than anyone. Is there someone at all that stands out in any way?'

Micah scratched his chin through his bushy beard. 'It's hard to say. Uncle Hedley and him were at loggerheads over the field but I can't see it somehow. Uncle Hedley has a different temperament to Father. He's more likely to talk you to death or go after you in a legal battle. Aunt Norma could have done it. She might seem all cosy-like but she has a terrible temper when she's riled up. I wish as I could point somebody out to you. I know as people think it were me that murdered him.'

'That must be very hard,' Kitty said. She wasn't sure what else to say. Micah could well have murdered his father. He had the means, motive and the opportunity. There again, so it appeared did a lot of other people.

'It is. I'm the first to admit as I have faults aplenty, Mrs Bryant, but I didn't kill my father. Maybe as Aunt Norma has the right idea for once asking you to investigate. I'd like my name cleared,' Micah said.

'Thank you for seeing us this morning. We'll be in touch if we find anything useful,' Kitty said.

Micah stood and showed them out of the farmhouse. There was no sign of Abigail and Kitty guessed she must still be hard at work in the kitchen.

'What do you think?' Kitty asked Matt as she turned her car around ready to drive back along the lane.

'I don't know. It's interesting what he said about Norma

Blake being capable of murder. He seemed much calmer than I'd expected too, about it all.' Matt glanced across at Kitty.

'He did, didn't he? And, yes, it was intriguing his thoughts on Norma.' Kitty spied a black car heading towards them on the narrow road and tucked her car into one of the passing places so the other vehicle could get by.

To her dismay as the car drew closer, she realised it was driven by Inspector Lewis. He pulled level with her and wound down his window.

'Mrs Bryant, Captain Bryant, I do hope you aren't out here interfering in the investigation?' He looked accusingly at Kitty.

'Inspector, you are already aware that Mrs Blake has employed us to clear her family's name in Mr Blake's murder.' Kitty did her best to sound pleasant and not let him get under her skin.

'Oh well, no need to worry your pretty head about that, Mrs Bryant. I fully expect to make an arrest very soon.' The inspector looked pleased with himself as he spoke.

'That is good news.' Kitty knew he was unlikely to share any new evidence he had come across with them. She wondered who he thought was guilty.

'Yes, indeed. That's why it's always best to let the police handle serious cases such as this. You amateurs can always look for missing pets or handle the divorce cases.' Inspector Lewis chuckled.

'We'll bear that in mind.' Kitty forced a smile. She could quite happily have climbed out of her car and smacked him but that wouldn't do them any favours.

The inspector drove off along the lane in the direction of Blossomdown and Wassail Farms looking very pleased with himself.

'That man is the very limit!' Kitty accidentally crunched her gears as she went to pull away.

Matt laughed. 'He is quite dreadful. Well done for not rising to him, darling. I wonder who he intends to arrest?'

Kitty gave an unladylike snort of derision. 'Ten to one it will be the wrong person.'

'Probably, he does have form for that. I wonder if he has some evidence that we don't?' Matt said as Kitty turned her car onto Windy Corner.

'It's possible I suppose, he does love to go ferreting about,' Kitty said sourly.

Matt gave her an amused glance as she pulled to a stop on their driveway.

'Very well, I love to ask questions, too,' she admitted as he got out of her car. 'It's just that man really annoys me.'

'Well, we shall just have to wait and see if an arrest is forthcoming and what evidence there is for that,' Matt said. 'Until then we should just carry on as planned, looking for our own evidence to build a case.'

Kitty sighed as he unlocked the front door and waited for her to enter the house first. 'Does that mean we are still going riding tomorrow?'

'Absolutely,' Matt confirmed.

* * *

There was nothing in the morning paper the next day about any arrest being made in the case. The murder still occupied the front page accompanied by a photograph of Titus Blake, which had obviously been taken some years ago. Matt wondered who had supplied it.

There had also been no messages or telephone calls either from the Blakes or from Chief Inspector Greville to say that there had been a significant development. All of which made Matt think that perhaps the inspector had not been as confident in his evidence as he had seemed when he had spoken to them the day before.

Kitty had dug through her wardrobe and had rooted out some clothes that would be suitable for riding. Matt had been to the library and had looked at some of the local maps to get a sense of where the boundaries for the various farms lay.

Hopefully on horseback they would have a higher vantage point and would get a better sense of how the land was divided, especially near the areas that seemed to be causing so much tension between the two farms and the livery stables.

After a light lunch, and having walked Bertie, they left him in the care of Mrs Smith and set off for the stables. The weather at least was still holding bright and sunny with a light breeze, although the leaves on the trees lining the lanes were now starting to fall, drifting onto the verges.

Mrs Pickering was waiting for them when they arrived. Two of the horses they had met previously were saddled up and in the yard. Kitty was to ride Bramble and Matt was to ride Shadow. Mrs Pickering would accompany them on a black horse with a white blaze on her nose who she introduced as Arrow.

'Now then, I think since you said you were both a little rusty, perhaps a ride through the fields today to the woods might be pleasant. I shall, of course, accompany you,' Mrs Pickering said, holding the reins of Kitty's horse so that Kitty could mount.

'That sounds splendid,' Matt agreed.

To her credit, Kitty managed to get astride Bramble surprisingly gracefully since she said she hadn't been on horseback for quite some time. Matt mounted his own horse and then Mrs Pickering mounted Arrow ready to lead them on the trek.

He wondered where Mr Pickering was. They hadn't yet met him, but everyone had referred to the Pickerings as a couple running the business together. Mrs Pickering cast her expert eye over their seating position on the saddle and checked they were holding the reins correctly and they set off.

Mrs Pickering took the lead and their horses fell in behind her as they walked past the end of the farmyard and into a field that ran up hill behind the stable block. The air felt fresh and clear against the skin of his face and Matt started to relax, once he was assured that Kitty too was beginning to enjoy herself.

They crossed the field to follow a route alongside a drystone wall that curved up the hill towards a small area of woodland in the distance.

'Is this the boundary with Wassail Farm?' Matt asked, when his horse was near enough to Mrs Pickering's to hold a conversation.

'Yes, this is the one Mr Blake kept insisting we had damaged. He said we had failed to maintain our share and our horses had damaged his wheat crop. Since he often has his cows in here and they rub against the stones I think he is the one who caused the damage.' Mrs Pickering pointed the end of her riding crop over the wall to indicate the livestock grazing in the field.

Matt could see the next field along had been recently ploughed and it seemed some kind of cover crop had been planted. They were riding now along the crest of the hill, and they paused to look back down towards the farms.

Wassail Farm was clearly visible and Matt saw Abigail had pegged out lines of washing. He could also see the orchards, some of which must belong to Wassail Farm and the much larger ones, he assumed, must belong to Blossomdown. He thought he could just make out a narrow rabbit path running through the trees towards a stile set in the boundary wall between the farms.

This must be the path that Micah had mentioned yesterday. He wondered who else knew of the path and used it, besides Norma Blake. Someone could easily have gone from Blossom-down on the day Titus was murdered and no one would be any the wiser, unless they too had been riding along this path and looking down the hill.

Mrs Pickering urged her horse on, and they followed her along a track and into the cool shade of a small wood. The boundary between the stables land and Wassail Farm seemed less distinct at this point.

'This is very pretty,' Kitty said, looking around at the clumps of bracken that carpeted the ground either side of the track.

'There are bluebells and wild garlic here in the spring,' Mrs Pickering said.

The sound of birdsong was louder too inside the wood and the dappled light filtering through the trees was pleasant. A few golden leaves dropped down from above them as the horses plodded along the track.

Mrs Pickering suddenly pulled her horse to a stop. 'Well, really!' she remarked crossly.

Matt reined his horse in to stand beside hers and looked across to see what had caused her to sound so annoyed. Through the trees he could make out the shape of a man on the ground beneath a large oak tree.

'Is that Micah Blake?' he asked.

'He has no business to be in this area of the woods. Especially if he is laying some more of those dreadful rabbit snares that he uses.' Mrs Pickering looked very distressed.

'What is it?' Kitty had caught them up and leaned forward on her horse to see what was happening.

There was something about the way that Micah was positioned on the ground that concerned Matt. The man hadn't moved, even though he must have heard the horses approaching through the woodland.

'I think something is wrong.' He dismounted and handed the reins of his horse to Mrs Pickering.

'Matt, be careful,' he heard Kitty call after him as he made his way across the woodland to where Micah was lying.

As he drew closer, he could see that something was very wrong indeed. Micah's left foot appeared to be caught in an old steel-toothed trap. The kind poachers used to use some years ago to snare animals. The farmer lay face down on the coarse grass and bracken, his shotgun at his side.

A pool of blood had oozed stickily from his head and Matt swallowed hard. At first sight it looked as if Micah had tripped in his own trap and fallen, shooting himself in the face with his shotgun. There was no doubt that the man was dead.

'Stay there. I'm coming back,' Matt called across to where the two women and the horses were waiting.

He took one last look at the scene. For all the world it looked at first glance as if it were some kind of terrible accident and yet it also felt wrong. Another couple of wire snares lay nearby along with some strong brown sacks. The injuries to Micah's face were consistent with a shotgun blast but the position of the gun was wrong for it to be accidental.

The gun would have been under Micah's body and there would have been blood on the barrel. He wasn't sure but he suspected the angle of the shot was not quite right to be an accident either.

He hurried back over to where Kitty and Mrs Pickering were waiting.

'I'm afraid we need to go back and get the police. There has been a terrible accident. Micah Blake is dead.' Matt put his boot in the stirrup and remounted his horse. He took the reins back from Mrs Pickering who stared at him with a stunned expression on her face.

'Dead?' She looked at Matt and then at Kitty.

'I'm afraid so,' Matt confirmed.

'What's happened?' Kitty asked, looking towards Micah's body.

For a moment Matt thought she was about to try to ride a little closer to take a look for herself.

'I'll explain on the way down. Mrs Pickering can you guide us on the quickest way back to the stables?' he asked.

'Yes, of course, if you are confident enough to canter, we can go this way.' She waited for them to nod and turned her horse to follow another path out of the wood.

'What's happened?' Kitty asked as they headed towards the open pastureland.

'Micah's foot is in a trap and his shotgun has been fired at his head. It has been set up to appear like an accident, but I fear it's another murder,' Matt explained hurriedly, after allowing Mrs Pickering to get further ahead out of earshot.

Kitty's face paled. 'Oh dear.'

Once on the field, Mrs Pickering nudged her horse into a canter and Kitty and Matt's mounts followed suit. There was no more opportunity for any kind of conversation until they were once more at the bottom of the hill at the gate leading from the field into the stable yard.

Mrs Pickering dismounted at the gate and Matt did the same, holding his horse's reins loosely while he assisted Kitty to follow through the gate.

'May I use your telephone?' Matt asked the stable owner as she closed the gate behind them and prepared to lead the horses into the yard.

Mrs Pickering nodded and pointed to the shed that she used as an office. 'It should be open. I'll just get my husband.'

Kitty dismounted somewhat stiffly from her horse and followed Mrs Pickering into the yard, while the woman bellowed into the open front door of the farmhouse.

'Reginald! We have a situation.'

Kitty's horse jibbed on the rein, letting out a snicker and whinny at being startled.

Matt hurried to the hut and dialled the number for Torquay

Police Station. Once connected he asked for Chief Inspector Greville.

'Captain Bryant, good afternoon,' the chief inspector greeted him cheerfully.

'I'm afraid we have another murder, sir. Micah Blake is dead.' Matt quickly explained the circumstances and what he'd seen in the woods.

There was muttering and an unintelligible oath at the other end of the line before the chief inspector gathered himself. 'I'm on my way and I'll send for Inspector Lewis.'

Matt replaced the receiver and went to join Kitty. Mrs Pickering had tied the horses up outside their stables and was in the process of removing their tack. A man of a similar age with a stiff military bearing was assisting her and Kitty.

'The police are on their way,' Matt said.

The man straightened up from where he had been unfastening a girth strap on the saddle and Matt could see his face was badly scarred and he was missing an eye.

The man extended his hand. 'Captain Bryant, Reginald Pickering. My wife was telling me that you found Micah Blake dead in the woods?'

Matt shook the man's hand. 'Yes, I'm afraid so. It looks like foul play. The chief inspector is on his way here now.'

The other man inclined his head, acknowledging the news. 'Worrying, very worrying.'

'I'll turn the horses out into the field. The trough is full so they can have a drink. We had better go inside while we wait for the police.' Mrs Pickering took charge of the animals and sent them off into the nearby field with her husband's aid.

Matt placed his arm around Kitty's waist. 'This is not how I envisaged spending this afternoon.'

'No,' she replied. 'It's a rather worrying development.'

CHAPTER THIRTEEN

Kitty took advantage of Mr and Mrs Pickering's brief absence out of earshot to press Matt on why he didn't feel Micah's death was accidental.

'He was shot in the face, and it was made to look as if the gun had gone off accidentally, but the position of the weapon was wrong for the entry wound. I'm sure Doctor Carter will agree when he gets here,' Matt spoke hurriedly in a low tone. 'Either someone else had disturbed the scene or he was murdered, and it's been set up to look like an accident.'

The Pickerings came to join them. Mrs Pickering marching ahead of her husband who followed after her with a stiff gait, as if his injuries extended beyond his face. Kitty could only assume they were probably from his war service. She had seen many men like Mr Pickering who had returned to civilian life bearing terrible scars. Some like Mr Pickering's were physical and clearly visible. Others, like Matt's, were more hidden.

'Come into the house.' Mrs Pickering led the way into a large kitchen. A marmalade cat was asleep on a rocking chair in a pool of sunlight. The room was clean but full of the detritus of day-to-day life. Packets of seeds next to a newspaper folded on the dresser. The headlines about the murder on the farm next door clearly visible.

Mr Pickering went to the sink to wash his hands and to fill the kettle.

Mrs Pickering showed them to a large square scrubbed pine table surrounded by four matching chairs. She moved a couple of used crockery cups from the tabletop.

'Please have a seat.' She joined her husband at the sink to wash her hands, before joining them at the table. Mr Pickering focused on preparing a tray of fresh teacups.

'What exactly did you see, Captain Bryant?' Mr Pickering asked once the kettle was boiled, and the tea things deposited on the table before them.

'Micah Blake had caught his foot in what appeared to be one of his own traps, the old-fashioned kind. His gun had gone off, fatally injuring him,' Matt said.

Mrs Pickering shuddered, and Kitty also felt a shiver run along her spine.

'An accident, do you think, or foul play?' Mr Pickering asked as he poured the tea. 'So soon after his father's murder? You mentioned, I think, that you thought it was more likely to be murder, Captain Bryant?'

Matt took a business card from his pocket and presented it to Mr Pickering. Mrs Pickering leaned in to read it. Her gaze sharpened.

'Is that why you booked a ride today? Are you investigating Titus Blake's death?' she asked.

'Mrs Norma Blake has asked us to assist the police as she is keen to clear her family's name of any wrongdoing. The view from the back of a horse can be helpful when you are trying to understand difficult terrain.' Matt looked at Mr Pickering.

Kitty could see the other man understood the subtext of what Matt was saying. 'That's very true.'

Mrs Pickering, however, was clearly quite put out. 'I think

you could have been more open about your reasons for booking a hack,' she said.

'It was very difficult. Obviously, we do have to be quite discreet as our client's confidentiality is very important. If not for discovering Micah Blake today, then we would have had no reason to disclose our involvement with the case. We were both enjoying the ride and we were truthful when we said it had been some time since we had been on horseback,' Kitty tried to reassure the woman.

Mrs Pickering did appear slightly mollified when Kitty had said they had been enjoying the ride.

'I can't understand it at all. First Titus and now Micah. I know this will sound dreadful, but I had been thinking that Micah was probably responsible for murdering his father. What with knowing them both and reading the paper this morning.' Her gaze darted towards the newspaper on the dresser. 'Well, I said to Reginald over breakfast that it was the most likely thing to have happened.'

Kitty sipped her tea from one of the Pickerings' collection of mismatched china. The warm liquid helped to calm her nerves from the afternoon's discovery.

'I think many people probably had the same idea,' Kitty said.

Outside in the yard they heard the arrival of a motor vehicle.

'I expect that may be the police.' Matt rose from the table and hurried outside with Mrs Pickering hard on his heels.

Kitty and Mr Pickering followed more slowly.

As soon as she reached the door, Kitty saw the car was in fact the sporty little racing-green model driven by Doctor Carter. The doctor greeted them cheerfully as he lifted his medical bag from the passenger seat and clambered out of the car.

'Good afternoon. Got another one for me, I hear, Captain

Bryant, Mrs Bryant.' The doctor raised his hat to Mrs Pickering and Kitty, while Kitty introduced the Pickerings to him.

'I'm afraid so, Doctor. He's up in the woods and it's a bit of a hike from here. I think we probably need to wait for Chief Inspector Greville and Inspector Lewis to arrive,' Matt said.

'Jolly good. I passed Inspector Lewis on my way here. I presume he'll be arriving in a minute or two.' Doctor Carter seemed unperturbed at the idea of hiking up the hills into the woods.

Sure enough, he had scarcely finished speaking when a black police car pulled into the yard next to Kitty and the doctor's cars. Inspector Lewis had a very sour expression on his face as he got out of his vehicle. A uniformed constable was at his side.

'Ha, Lewis! Thought I passed you coming out of Blossom-down Farm.' Doctor Carter clapped his police colleague on his back, while Matt introduced Mr and Mrs Pickering to the some-what surly policeman.

'Mr Pickering, Mrs Pickering.' He nodded to the couple before turning to Matt and Kitty. 'I was hoping to have this case wrapped up today. Then I had a telephone call while I was at Blossomdown telling me to come here. The chief inspector said something about another murder?' Inspector Lewis looked at Kitty as if he held her personally responsible.

'That's right. I'm afraid Micah Blake is dead,' Kitty said.

Another black police vehicle crunched its way into the yard and filled the last remaining spot. Chief Inspector Greville, accompanied by another uniformed policeman, came to join them.

'I see everyone is here. Captain Bryant, perhaps you might be so good as to lead us to where you found Micah Blake,' the chief inspector said once he too had met the Pickerings.

'It might be helpful, sir, if Mrs Pickering could accompany us. She knows the lie of the land much better than I do and can probably show us the quickest and easiest way to reach where Micah is lying,' Matt suggested.

'Mrs Pickering?' the chief inspector asked, looking at the stable owner.

'Of course,' the woman agreed. 'There is a more direct route, although it's a bit steep.'

'Then, please lead on,' Chief Inspector Greville said. 'Mrs Bryant, perhaps you and Mr Pickering might wait here for us? We shall be back as soon as possible.'

'Of course,' Mr Pickering answered on behalf of both of them as his wife led the small, oddly assorted party out through the gate into the horses' field once more.

'Shall we adjourn inside, Mrs Bryant?' Mr Pickering suggested.

'Thank you.' Kitty suppressed a sigh as she resigned herself to being sidelined once more. Still, she had to admit to herself that her ride had physically taken more out of her than she realised.

She was certainly going to feel quite stiff and achy tomorrow. Riding had used muscles that she hadn't used for quite some time. In a way she was relieved she was being spared the hike back up the hill, even if she did feel as if she was missing out.

* * *

Matt sensed there was tension between Chief Inspector Greville and Inspector Lewis on the trek back up the hillside to the woods. Neither man spoke much, and both the constables were silent. Mrs Pickering had taken them on a much more direct route that, while suitable for humans, would have been dangerous on horseback.

Doctor Carter, as usual, appeared unperturbed by the whole affair and chatted amicably to Mrs Pickering about the stables and the horses all the way to the woods. They paused at the start of the trees to regain their breath. Matt looked back down the valley and saw that Abigail had taken in her washing. A thin plume of smoke came from Wassail Farm's chimney, pale grey against the clear blue sky.

All of their group fell silent as they entered the shade of the trees and followed the path they had ridden on horseback. The marks of the horses' hooves showing clearly in the leaf mould under the bracken at the edge of the path.

'Over there.' Matt indicated as soon as he caught a glimpse of Micah's body lying exactly as he had left it.

'Wait here, please.' Inspector Lewis looked at Matt and Mrs Pickering.

'Who approached the body?' Chief Inspector Greville asked.

'Just me, sir. I dismounted and went to check on him. I took care not to move anything or disturb the ground,' Matt said.

Chief Inspector Greville and Inspector Lewis went over first, looking carefully for any clues around the body, before permitting Doctor Carter to come over to them. Matt waited with Mrs Pickering on the path where they had stopped with the horses. The two constables also stood by waiting for instructions.

Mrs Pickering looked uncomfortable, and Matt felt quite sorry for her. This was not an unusual event for him, but for the stable owner it had to be very distressing.

After a few minutes, Chief Inspector Greville straightened up from where he had been crouched over Micah's body and came over to them.

'It seems you were correct, Captain Bryant. It's murder all right, although someone has tried to make it look like an accident.'

Mrs Pickering looked as if she were about to faint, and Matt placed his arm around her to guide her to a nearby fallen log so she could sit down.

'I was afraid that might be the case. The entry point of the gunshot wound appeared wrong compared with how he would have been carrying the gun,' Matt said as he and the chief inspector moved out of earshot of Mrs Pickering, who appeared to be recovering herself now she was seated.

'Exactly so. Doctor Carter is also of the opinion that Mr Blake's leg was placed in the trap after he had been shot.' The chief inspector glanced over at Mrs Pickering. 'Perhaps if you could accompany this lady back to her home. I'll meet you there shortly.'

Matt glanced over to where the doctor and the constables were huddled with Inspector Lewis over Micah's body. 'Of course, Chief Inspector.'

Mrs Pickering appeared only too relieved to accept Matt's arm for support as they started back down the hillside to the stables.

'You must think me quite feeble, Captain Bryant, but this is all such a shock,' Mrs Pickering said.

'Not at all. It's quite horrific, especially coming so soon after Titus Blake's murder,' Matt assured her.

'Reginald and I, we really did think that it must have been Micah who killed his father but now, well, I don't know what to think.' Mrs Pickering gave him a worried glance. 'What if we are not safe, either? What if whoever is doing this has something against all of us who own land here?'

'Has anyone else, other than Titus, ever threatened you? Or tried to purchase your stables?' Matt asked.

'Well, no, we've been quite settled here. Reginald suffered so much after the war, his injuries you know, we wanted somewhere out of the way where we could live quietly.' A tear ran down Mrs Pickering's cheek and she released her hold on Matt's arm to dash it away.

Matt understood how she and her husband must have felt. They had purchased the stables and were working hard to build a business. Mrs Pickering as the public face and her husband quietly working in the background. Now the murders would inevitably draw attention on them and could potentially ruin everything they had been striving for.

'I'm sure the police will make an arrest very soon. Inspector Lewis appeared fairly confident yesterday.' Matt wondered if that was still the case after today's murder. He had a feeling from the inspector's reaction when he had arrived at the stables that Micah might have been his main suspect.

Mrs Pickering sniffed and fumbled in her pocket for a handkerchief as they reached the bottom gate behind the farmhouse.

'Thank you, Captain Bryant, you have been very kind.' She glanced around at where the horses they had ridden a few hours earlier were now roaming contentedly around the field. 'Oh dear! The animals!'

Matt looked at her not at first understanding her meaning.

'At Wassail Farm, Captain Bryant. Poor Abigail won't know that something has happened to Micah and the cows will be due to be fetched down soon for milking,' Mrs Pickering said.

'Wassail Farm has no telephone. I think if I use your telephone again, I can let Hedley Blake know that someone needs to go there to assist. He has a cowman, Jim, I think his name is. Maybe he can sort them out for now,' Matt suggested.

He hoped the chief inspector wouldn't feel he was compromising their investigation by contacting Blossomdown, but he agreed with Mrs Pickering. The animals' well-being must come first.

He made his way to the office, while Mrs Pickering went to join Kitty and Mr Pickering inside the farmhouse. Norma Blake answered the telephone when the call was connected.

'Hello, Mrs Blake, this is Captain Bryant. I'm at Tillycombe Stables, the Pickerings' place. Something has arisen at Wassail

Farm which I feel necessitates your husband's assistance.' Matt chose his words carefully.

'Hedley? At Wassail Farm?' Norma sounded bewildered.

'I'm not at liberty to disclose what is happening but the animals will need attention there and I wondered if your husband could spare Jim, the cowman, to look after the cows?' Matt asked.

'Has Micah been arrested?' Mrs Blake asked, a breathless note creeping into her voice.

'No, but he is unable to attend to the animals and obviously Miss West will not be able to care for them.' As he spoke, Matt wondered what Abigail would do once she knew Micah was dead. She had nowhere to go, no family to turn to.

'I can see if someone is free to go around there.' Norma sounded uncertain.

'If you would be so good, Mrs Blake, it would be very helpful. As soon as we are able, Kitty and I will come and explain. Or you may have a visit from the chief inspector.' Matt thought it only fair to mention that the police would definitely wish to speak to everyone at Blossomdown.

'Oh dear, right. I'll arrange matters.' Norma rang off and Matt replaced the telephone receiver hoping he had done the right thing.

Still, the animals had to be tended and if his call alerted a potential killer to start preparing an alibi, well that couldn't be helped.

CHAPTER FOURTEEN

Kitty was relieved when Matt came in from the yard to join her and the Pickerings at the kitchen table.

'I've asked Blossomdown to send someone to care for Wassail's animals,' Matt said as he took his place.

'Thank you. I wonder what young Abigail will do now?' Mrs Pickering looked concerned. 'It's surely not safe for a young woman on her own when both the occupants of the house have been murdered.'

'She has no family to go to. I suppose she will be able to remain at Wassail Farm until everything is sorted out. I agree though, it's not a nice thing for a young woman to be alone with a murderer on the loose.' Mr Pickering looked at his wife.

'She would be welcome here if she wanted to stay. We have a spare room,' Mrs Pickering said.

'That's very kind of you. I'm sure she will appreciate having somewhere to go if she doesn't wish to remain at Wassail Farm.' Kitty wondered what Abigail would decide to do.

Wassail Farm would belong to Saul and Adam now. Unless, of course, Micah had been correct and half of the farm belonged to Hedley still. The business of how the trust worked still seemed very unclear. Perhaps Saul would move back and take over running the place. Adam had made it clear that he had no interest in it.

Kitty's mind raced with a hundred questions as they patiently waited for some members of the police party to return to the farmhouse. She longed to ask Matt about what the police had said and what Doctor Carter may have found.

The presence of the Pickerings meant she was forced to curb her inquisitiveness and make polite conversation, whilst refusing more cups of tea. After what felt like an endless time there was a knock on the door of the farmhouse and Chief Inspector Greville appeared, wiping his feet on the mat before entering the kitchen.

His face was rosy from walking down the hill and his moustache was limp from the heat of his exertions. 'Thank you all for your patience. The doctor will be down shortly along with Inspector Lewis. May I use your telephone, Mr Pickering, to arrange for Mr Blake's body to be removed from the woods?'

'Certainly, Chief Inspector. Let me show you where it is located.' Mr Pickering went out with the chief inspector to show him the wooden hut that the stables used as their office.

He was back moments later accompanied by the plump, congenial figure of Doctor Carter.

'Just popping in to say cheerio. The police have everything in hand now. I expect I shall see you both again soon,' he remarked affably to Matt and Kitty.

Kitty rather hoped he wouldn't, at least not professionally. Socially, she enjoyed Doctor Carter and Mrs Carter's company. She said goodbye to the doctor and waited for the chief inspector to return.

Mrs Pickering had just suggested more tea yet again, when the policeman re-entered the kitchen.

'That's all done. Now if I may ask you all a few questions about the events of today?' Chief Inspector Greville took out his trusty notebook and pulled a spare chair up to the table. The marmalade cat gave him a sour look and shot outside to the farmyard.

Mr and Mrs Pickering assured him they had been busy at the stable all morning. Mr Pickering had mucked out the stalls and cleaned the tack. Mrs Pickering had taught two private lessons. They had eaten lunch and then prepared the horses for Matt and Kitty's hack.

They hadn't seen anything of Micah Blake and hadn't gone beyond the yard and the small exercise area behind the stable where they gave their lessons.

'It was quite a busy morning,' Mrs Pickering explained as she mentioned that a feed supplier had called in and seen them both, verifying their alibis.

The chief inspector then led them all through the timeline of starting the hack up until the moment they had discovered Micah Blake's body.

'And none of you saw or heard anything while you were riding that struck you as odd or suspicious?' The policeman looked around the table as he posed his question.

All of them shook their heads. Up until the time they had seen Micah's body on the floor of the wood it had been quite a pleasant ride.

'We didn't see anyone else and it was all very lovely, until we found Micah's body,' Kitty said.

'And you remained here while the others rode out, Mr Pickering?' the chief inspector asked.

'Yes. I was quite tired after the morning's work. You may have noticed, Chief Inspector, that I am not a strong man. I usually need to rest each afternoon for a few hours. Running a stables is hard on the body.'

Mrs Pickering reached for her husband's hand and gave it a tender squeeze as he answered the chief inspector.

He had just finished his questions when Inspector Lewis

arrived. The inspector also looked hot and bothered after his scramble down the hillside. Kitty suspected he was probably annoyed that his senior had already interviewed the Pickerings.

'Ah, Inspector Lewis, just in time. I've arranged for Micah Blake's body to be collected from the woods. Perhaps you could remain here to tell the men where to go when they arrive?' Chief Inspector Greville asked.

'Yes, sir.' Inspector Lewis sounded a little sulky.

'I think I need to go to Wassail Farm to speak to Miss West and then on to Blossomdown to speak to the Blakes. Perhaps you can join me there when you've finished here,' the chief inspector continued. 'If Mr and Mrs Pickering will allow us to trespass on their hospitality for a little longer?' He looked at the Pickerings, who both nodded their agreement.

'That's splendid, thank you. I'm so sorry you have been caught up in this dreadful event. I can assure you both, however, that we will be doing our utmost to catch whoever has committed these crimes.'

The chief inspector rose from his seat. 'Mrs Bryant, may I ask that you and Captain Bryant accompany me? I'm sure Miss West might find some comfort in having another female present when I tell her about Micah Blake's death. I expect you will also wish to update your client, Mrs Norma Blake, afterwards.' He glanced at Inspector Lewis as he spoke.

Kitty could see Inspector Lewis was not at all pleased but could do nothing about it. 'Of course, Chief Inspector. We would be happy to assist.'

She and Matt accompanied the chief inspector out into the yard. Once outside, before they set off for Wassail Farm, Matt quickly told the chief inspector about Titus Blake's feud with the Pickerings. He also told him that he had asked Blossomdown Farm to care for Micah's animals but had not said why.

'Hmm, thank you, Captain Bryant. You are quite right, of course, the welfare of the farm animals must come first. Let's go and see Miss West and find out what she knows.' The chief inspector sounded thoughtful as he got into his car.

Kitty got behind the steering wheel of her own car and started the engine ready to follow the policeman to Wassail Farm.

'I wonder how Abigail will take the news of Micah's death?' Kitty asked as she turned out into the lane and followed behind the black police car.

'I don't know. It will be very strange for her not to have to answer to either Titus or Micah,' Matt said.

Kitty thought that if she were in Abigail's shoes she would be relieved to be free of Micah and Titus, but terrified that she might also be on the killer's list. Unless, of course, she was the murderer.

A moment later they pulled up next to Chief Inspector Greville's car in front of Wassail Farm. The door of the house stood open, and Abigail was outside in the yard talking to the man Kitty recognised as Jim, Blossomdown's cowman.

'Chief Inspector, Captain Bryant, Mrs Bryant, whatever is going on? Jim says as he's been asked to see to Micah's cows. Only Micah didn't come back for his afternoon cup of tea and the dogs have been a whining and sulking about all day. I've had to fasten them up.' Abigail looked completely bewildered.

The two collie dogs were tethered on long metal chains near the barn. They had immediately begun to bark as they had stepped out of the cars, only ceasing when Abigail had told them to hush.

'I think it best if we speak to you privately, Miss West, perhaps inside the farmhouse?' Chief Inspector Greville suggested.

Jim immediately looked interested in this suggestion but touched his cap and excused himself to fetch the cows to be milked. Abigail led the way inside the farmhouse where they all took a seat at the kitchen table, except Abigail herself who stood somewhat uncertainly looking at them all.

Kitty noticed the girl had her hands buried deep inside the large pocket on the front of her white apron and was twisting the material into bunches between her fingers.

'What's going on? Where's Micah?' Abigail asked.

'I'm afraid I have to tell you that Micah Blake is dead. Captain and Mrs Bryant found his body a little while ago in the woods at the top of the hill.' Chief Inspector Greville kept his gaze fixed on the housekeeper as he spoke.

The girl's knees sagged, and she moved forward to sit down heavily on one of the vacant pine kitchen chairs. 'Micah dead? But, how? I don't understand.' She looked at Matt and Kitty as if expecting them to contradict what the chief inspector had just said.

'When did you last see Micah today?' Kitty asked.

Abigail blinked. 'This morning at around eleven. He came for his morning tea and to check the post as normal. I was up to my eyes doing the weekly wash. He said he was going to try and get the fox that had been taking the chickens. I gave him a packet of meat paste sandwiches wrapped in greaseproof paper and he left the dogs here.'

'When did you expect him back?' Matt asked.

'Well, now. There would be the pigs to see to. Then he would come about three or four o'clock for a cup of tea, then he would do the milking. Then he would usually take the dogs to go and check on some of the fields afore coming back for supper.' Abigail sounded completely bewildered as she answered their questions about her employer's routine.

'Did he take his shotgun with him when he left?' Chief Inspector Greville had been discreetly taking notes once more in his book.

The furrow on Abigail's brow deepened. 'No, I don't reckon as he did. He just took some of the snares and his sandwiches.'

'Where did he keep his gun?' the chief inspector asked.

'There's a special cupboard in the hall. Titus and Micah both had guns as they keep there. There's a spare key to it here in the dresser.' Abigail rose and crossed over to a pine dresser. She opened one of the drawers and rummaged amongst the contents until she took out a small metal keyring with a selection of keys on it. She gave them to Chief Inspector Greville.

He got up and went out into the hall. After a moment, he returned to the kitchen. 'How many guns are usually in the cupboard, Miss West?'

'Just the two. Micah's and Titus's. Saul took his to Blossom-down when he left home, and Adam never had one of his own.' The girl had seated herself back down.

Kitty looked at the policeman.

'There is only one gun there now,' he said. 'You didn't see Micah taking the gun? You are certain of that, Miss West?'

'Yes, I'm sure. I give him his sandwiches and he complained as they were meat paste. He took up those dratted snares and said he'd be back once he'd laid his traps. He didn't go into the hall, I'd stake my life on it,' the girl said.

'These snares, what kind were they?' Matt asked.

'Horrid wire things, he used to use them mostly for rabbits, but he had been after this fox for ages and couldn't get him so said he would set some traps.' Abigail shrugged.

Kitty looked at her husband. From what he and the chief inspector had said the trap around Micah's foot had been different to the ones the farmer had been carrying. It was older with nasty steel jaws, much larger than the smaller rabbit snares.

'Has anyone been to the farm today?' the chief inspector asked.

Abigail shook her head, a stray strand of soft brown hair breaking loose from her ponytail to fall against her cheek. 'No, sir, only the milk collection early on. The last visitors here were on Sunday evening. Adam and Saul came by to see Micah to talk about the farm.'

'And where were you today, Miss West?' Chief Inspector Greville asked.

Abigail looked at him. 'Well, here, doing the washing.'

'And you didn't see anyone at all who can verify that? You didn't leave the farm at all for any reason?' the policeman persisted.

'No, getting the washing done on a farm takes a lot of work. I was up at half past five to light the fire under the copper and change the beds. Then I done the mangling, pegged it out as well as doing all my other jobs. I was in and out all day.' The girl gave the policeman a look that implied that he clearly had little idea what her workload entailed.

'You peg the washing behind the farmhouse?' Kitty asked.

They had seen the lines of washing from their viewpoint on the hill before they had discovered Micah's body in the wood.

'Yes, it gets less dusty out there while it's drying and catches the breeze,' Abigail said.

'Where were the dogs while you were hanging out the wash?' Kitty asked.

'Under my feet to start with and then I chained them up so I could get on. 'Tis funny you asked that though, because they started barking and whining just after lunch but when I came around the front there weren't anyone there. I thought as someone might have come to try and buy some cider, not knowing about Mr Blake being killed.' Abigail's eyes widened. 'You think as someone did come by while I were busy out back?'

It was clear the idea had terrified the girl. Her face had paled, and she looked as if she were about to faint.

'It is obviously something we must consider, Miss West. It may have been Micah himself, of course, come back for his gun,' Chief Inspector Greville soothed.

Abigail appeared a little reassured by this. 'It might, but he would usually have passed me if he were coming off the field. Unless he came by the lane and went in that way.' The logistics seemed to puzzle her.

'I suppose other people may have known where the keys to the gun cabinet were kept?' Kitty asked.

'Well, yes, Saul, Adam, even Hedley Blake would have known. Them keys have been kept in the dresser drawer for years and years. It's an old cabinet, been used since Titus and Hedley were boys, I reckon,' Abigail said.

This didn't sound good. Either Micah may have returned to collect his gun himself, or it seemed possible that one of their other main suspects may have come and taken it from the cabinet. She wondered if Doctor Carter had indicated a possible time of death for Micah. This would be crucial when they tried to discover where everyone was when Micah was killed.

She didn't recall Matt or the police saying Micah still had his lunch with him so she supposed he must have been murdered sometime between one and three o'clock when they had found him.

'Thank you, Miss West, you've been extremely helpful.' Chief Inspector Greville closed his notebook and prepared to leave.

'If you don't mind, sir, but what happens now?' Abigail asked as the policeman stood up.

'Well, I have other people to interview and I'm hopeful that we can discover who has committed these murders quite quickly,' the chief inspector said.

Kitty could see he had misunderstood the young housekeeper's meaning. 'Do you mean what happens now to you personally, Miss West?' she asked in a gentle tone.

The girl nodded and Kitty saw her eyes were shimmering with unshed tears.

'Yes, I mean, I don't have nowhere to go, and the animals

here will need tending even if Jim comes and looks after the cows.' She bit her lip as she finished speaking.

'Would you feel safe being here alone?' Kitty asked. 'Mrs Pickering has said you may go and stay in their spare room, if you wish.'

'That is right kind of her, but it seems a terrible imposition. I have the chickens and the pigs, and somebody has to arrange the other things. The dogs would be with me, and I always lock up sound at night.' Abigail was clearly torn about what she should do.

'If you are happy to remain to take care of things here, Miss West, we are going to Blossomdown now so can ask them to come and speak to you about the next steps for Wassail Farm, since it will fall to Adam and Saul no doubt now to arrange matters,' the chief inspector said.

'Thank you, sir, that would be most helpful.' Abigail looked relieved, and Kitty and Matt said their goodbyes, before following the policeman back out into the yard.

CHAPTER FIFTEEN

'I hope she will be all right there by herself,' Kitty said as they walked to the cars. 'She is such a frail little thing.'

'But she must also be considered a suspect along with several other people,' Matt reminded her as he slid into the passenger seat of her car.

Since this mirrored her own earlier thoughts, Kitty conceded this was true as she restarted her car to follow the chief inspector to Blossomdown. Matt's earlier telephone call there would have no doubt sent ripples all around the Blake family about what could have happened to Micah.

Mrs Blake had the door to the farmhouse open as soon as the cars entered the yard. She was waiting on the step, anxiety written large across her pleasant features as they made their way towards her.

'Good afternoon, Chief Inspector, Captain Bryant, Mrs Bryant. We've been all agog ever since we received Captain Bryant's telephone call asking for help at Wassail Farm,' Mrs Blake explained, leading them into the drawing room where Hedley and Saul were already seated and waiting.

'We thought as we should be here,' Hedley explained, after

shaking hands with everyone. 'I thought as something bad must have happened if Jim's aid were needed with the cows.'

Kitty tucked herself quietly on a chair in the corner of the room, while Chief Inspector Greville took his place on the end of the sofa. He took out his notebook and flicked it open. Matt had found a seat near Kitty.

'I'm sorry to have to tell you all that Mr Micah Blake was found dead this afternoon in the woods at the top of the hill behind Wassail Farm,' the chief inspector said.

'Micah. Dead?' Saul looked stunned. 'How? An accident? Suicide?'

All of the members of the Blake family stared at the chief inspector.

'Murder.' The policeman's face was grave.

There were a few seconds of shocked silence before Hedley spoke. 'Murder? How?'

'It seems your nephew had taken some snares to trap a fox that had been taking chickens from Wassail Farm. While out in the wood he was shot at close range with his own shotgun, his foot placed in a steel trap and the scene made to look as if an accident had occurred.' The chief inspector stared at the assembled Blake family.

Saul looked as if he might be sick at hearing the chief inspector's description of how his older brother had been killed.

'You are certain that it wasn't an accident?' he asked. 'He didn't catch his foot and fall? It just seems so incredible coming so soon after what happened to Father.'

'We are quite sure, Mr Blake. The doctor confirmed our initial suspicions when he attended. I'm afraid your brother was murdered.'

'I don't understand at all. Why would Micah be killed? We had all been thinking that perhaps...' Norma's voice tailed away under the gaze of her husband and nephew.

'You had all thought that perhaps it was Micah who may

have killed his father?' Chief Inspector Greville finished Norma's sentence.

Bright red patches appeared on Norma's cheeks. Hedley shuffled his feet and sighed, while Saul looked at the floor.

'It seemed a natural supposition given how Micah and Titus were,' Hedley said. 'We didn't want to believe it was the case. It seems we were wrong.'

He sounded uncomfortable. Kitty could hardly blame this branch of the Blakes for suspecting Micah. There had been a history of a volatile relationship between Titus and his eldest son. It had probably suited them all to believe that Micah was responsible as it would have removed the spotlight from them. Had this been what Norma had hoped she and Matt would discover when she had engaged their services?

'I need to ask you where you were today from around eleven o'clock this morning onwards?' Chief Inspector Greville said, looking first at Hedley.

'I've been turning over the soil in the bottom field getting it ready for the winter crop. I only came back here when Norma came to fetch me after Captain Bryant's telephone call,' Hedley said.

'I was here all day. Mondays is a busy day for me. I had washing to do, and I also do my bookkeeping for the farm on Monday afternoons,' Norma said. 'I went and fetched Hedley from the field after I'd sent Jim down to Wassail Farm.'

'I was in the orchard scything the long grass and getting it ready to dry off before this good weather breaks,' Saul said.

'Did any of you see anyone else, talk to anyone, who can verify where you were during this time?' Chief Inspector Greville paused from his note-taking to look at them all.

There was a shaking of heads from all three of the Blakes.

'I understand from Miss West that you, Saul, visited Micah along with your other brother, Adam, yesterday evening at

Wassail Farm. What was the visit about?' the chief inspector asked.

The colour in Saul's already ruddy cheeks darkened to a deeper red and he fidgeted uncomfortably in his seat. 'Adam said as we should talk to Micah about the farm and Father's will. Micah had made an appointment with Mr Frasier to see about the trust. He told us he wasn't satisfied as it was clear about things.'

'Is this about his concern that the three of you had a share of half of the farm and your uncle had the other half?' Matt asked.

'Yes. He said it might be as we didn't actually get anything yet. It could be as everything went to Uncle Hedley, and we'd only get our third each when he was to pass on.' Saul looked even more uncomfortable.

'And you and Adam wanted to discuss this with him? Did Adam know more about the legalities of it all? He does work for the solicitor concerned in all of this,' Chief Inspector Greville asked.

'Adam said he could find out and there was no need for Micah to be concerned about things.' Saul sighed. 'Micah hates being told what to do, especially by Adam, he said he had made an appointment and would get to the bottom of it all. They've always rubbed one another up the wrong way those two. So, Micah started shouting and Adam tried to calm him down.'

'What happened then?' Kitty asked. She could picture the scene quite clearly.

'Micah started needling Adam about being hoity-toity and thinking as he was so clever with his book learning. Adam was trying to say as how Micah should stop being stubborn and just listen to him for once. I got fed up with the pair of them so went to the kitchen to get a drink and see Abigail. I knew the sound of them shouting would upset her,' Saul said.

'How was the matter resolved?' Matt asked.

Saul grimaced. 'Same way as Micah and Father used to deal

with everything. Micah banged into the kitchen and said he was getting his shotgun. Adam said as he'd had enough and was going. Adam left and I went just afterwards, once I'd seen as Micah had calmed down and Abigail was all right. I walked back along the lane as Adam had headed off in his car.'

'Did Micah take the gun from the cabinet during this argument?' Chief Inspector Greville asked.

Saul shook his head. 'No, he didn't get that far. It was just bluster.'

'But you and Adam know where the key to the guns is kept?' Matt asked.

Saul shrugged. 'Same place they was always kept, I suppose, in the dresser drawer. There was two keys. Father had one on him and the other was in the dresser.'

Hedley nodded. 'That's right, that's where my father used to keep them too.'

It seemed that none of the Blakes were concerned that they had all just admitted they knew how to gain access to the guns.

There was a knock at the front door, startling them all. Norma jumped to her feet and went to answer it. She returned accompanied by Inspector Lewis. She excused herself to put the kettle on to make tea, while Inspector Lewis took a place on the sofa.

'I presume everything is taken care of, Inspector?' Chief Inspector Greville asked, once his junior had seated himself.

'Yes, sir. Micah Blake has been moved and the constables have gone back about their business,' Inspector Lewis said.

'Thank you. We have already called at Wassail Farm and should hopefully be concluded here soon. Mr Adam Blake has yet to be informed of his brother's death. I think it might be as well if you can go to Totnes and see him in person. Also, can you get clarification on the issue of ownership of Wassail Farm from his employer. I know we have enquired about this already and Mr Frasier was intending to research it further. Micah believed that Mr Hedley Blake either owns half or all of the farm. It seems this business of how the trust is structured might be of importance,' Chief Inspector Greville said.

Inspector Lewis got to his feet once more, clearly slightly irked at being dispatched on another errand.

'Yes, sir.'

'And please ascertain where Adam Blake has been today around the time his brother was killed.' Chief Inspector Greville appeared oblivious to his colleague's annoyance.

'Very good.' The inspector took his leave to go to Totnes.

Mrs Blake returned a moment later carrying a heavy tray, which Saul rushed to assist her with.

'Has the other policeman gone? I'd put a cup for him, and I've put out some of my apple tartlets,' Norma said as she dispensed cups of tea to everyone.

Chief Inspector Greville's eyes lit up at the sight of baked goods and he happily helped himself to two of the apple and pastry tarts.

'These are very nice, Mrs Blake. I wonder if I might get your recipe for my wife?' he asked, spilling pastry crumbs down his brown striped tie.

Norma looked pleased at the compliment to her baking. 'Of course, Chief Inspector, I should be delighted. I use our own apples, of course, and I think that makes a difference.'

Kitty glanced at Matt to see him hiding a smile. She knew that she wouldn't be asking Mrs Blake for a recipe. Baking, indeed cooking, was not one of Kitty's skills. Although she did pride herself on being able to make a good omelette.

The chief inspector, having cleared the plate of the remaining apple tartlets, turned to Hedley Blake. 'Sir, do you know how the trust was set up in the division of the farm should either you or Titus pass on? You mentioned before that you believed a trust may have existed?'

Hedley shook his head. 'I'm sorry, I really don't know.

When my father passed away, I was married to Norma, and we were working here. Norma's parents were elderly and unwell, so it seemed only right to just let Titus run Wassail Farm. I don't think we ever even really discussed it. I forgot all about it until a few years later when Titus was married, and Micah was born.' The farmer frowned. His brow creased as he tried to recall events from several years ago. 'I think it was Micah's christening. Norma and I had bought him a silver mug and we gave it to Thora, Micah's mother. Titus had been wetting the baby's head by drinking a fair amount of cider. He said something about Micah being the next generation in the trust to inherit the farm.'

'I remember that. It struck us both as a funny thing to say. We knew that Hedley's father had left a will and we'd assumed as he'd left Wassail to Titus, knowing that Hedley would be set up here at Blossomdown.' Norma looked at her husband.

'That was when I asked at the solicitor's office, it was before the present Mr Frasier's time. He said the farm was in a trust to the male heirs. He was a very elderly man and suggested I speak to Titus about it all.' Hedley sighed. 'By then, Titus was becoming more belligerent by the day, so I never did anything more about it at the time. It's only now after Titus's murder that it's all coming back to me about it all.'

'And presumably when the dispute over the boundaries started?' the chief inspector said.

Hedley's face turned a plum colour. 'If I did own half of Wassail, then it added even more legitimacy to my rights to that field and the spring. It could be shared between the farms. But I never intended to cut off Wassail's access to the water.'

Chief Inspector Greville made more notes. Kitty wondered what Inspector Lewis would discover when he spoke to Adam Blake's employer about the trust. Did Adam know more about the legal niceties of it all than he had let on when he had called at their house?

'Did Micah Blake say anything to you and your brother about his plans to trap the fox when you saw him yesterday evening?' Chief Inspector Greville directed his question to Saul.

Saul scratched the side of his forehead with his finger. 'No, well, I don't know exactly. We started the night talking about the farm and how things were going. I think he did mention a fox, but I don't know as he said what he intended to do.'

'But this going into the woods placing traps would be something your brother did fairly regularly?' the policeman asked.

'Yes. Him and Father were fond of the snares. Cruel, I always think. Father had some really old metal-toothed things inside the barn hanging up on the beams at the back. Micah used the wire ones. We don't use them at all here.' Saul looked to his uncle for confirmation.

Hedley nodded. 'That's right. Micah and Titus would often set them for rabbits and such.'

It seemed to Kitty that they were not much further forward. All the Blakes had the means to kill Micah and it seemed the opportunity. They knew where the traps were kept and had motives too. One of them must be responsible, or was it more than one of them? They could all be working together, she supposed. It was very unsatisfactory.

Chief Inspector Greville seemed to feel the same way. He closed his notebook and returned it to the breast pocket of his coat, before taking his leave of the family and Matt and Kitty.

Matt would have left at the same time as the chief inspector, but Kitty wanted to speak to Norma Blake so pressed her hand on his arm when he would have stood.

Hedley and Saul both excused themselves to return to their work, leaving Norma busily tidying up the dirty tea things onto the tray.

'How are you feeling about all of this, Mrs Blake?' Kitty

asked in a sympathetic tone as she placed a floral-patterned china cake plate on the tray.

'Truth to tell, Mrs Bryant, I can't rightly take it all in.' Mrs Blake sat down heavily on one of the fireside chairs. 'I had convinced myself that Micah must have been responsible for Titus's death. Oh, don't get me wrong, I didn't want to believe it, he was my nephew, but it seemed the most likely thing.' The woman shook her head as if trying to clear her mind.

'And now?' Kitty asked.

'I just don't know. The way that policeman were asking questions he obviously thinks as one of us must have done it. But we had no need to though. Blossomdown is a good business and Saul has no cravings for a share of Wassail Farm,' Norma said.

'Mrs Blake, before he died Micah said he had seen you going through the orchard to Wassail Farm he thought to meet his father in secret.' Kitty tried to phrase Micah's words tactfully, but she wanted to know what the woman's explanation for her behaviour would be.

Norma's face crumpled and she pulled her handkerchief from her pocket and pressed it to her mouth with a trembling hand.

'Oh, that sounds so bad, but it's not what it sounds like at all.'

CHAPTER SIXTEEN

'Perhaps you could tell us what you were doing and who you were meeting there?' Kitty suggested.

Mrs Blake dabbed her eyes and blew her nose. 'I was meeting Abigail.'

Kitty's gaze met Matt's. The housekeeper hadn't said anything about Norma calling at Wassail Farm in secret to meet with her.

'Why were you meeting with Abigail? And why in secret?' Kitty asked.

Norma sniffed. 'It had to be in secret. Titus would have gone mad if he'd found out that I'd been to the farm. I didn't want Abigail to feel his wrath any more than she had done already, poor girl.'

'I can understand that, but what were you meeting her for?' Kitty sensed there was something important lying behind Norma's clandestine visits. It was a big risk for both women, knowing how much trouble it could stir up for them if they were discovered. 'And why did you go there? Why could she not come to you? Or you both meet in the village?'

'It all started by accident.' Norma dabbed her eyes again,

her hand trembling as she did so. 'If I tell you both you must promise to never, ever, tell Hedley any of this.' She looked anxiously at both Kitty and Matt.

'Of course,' Kitty assured her. 'If it's not relevant to the murders anything you tell us will be in confidence.'

'This all goes back years, to before I married Hedley. I was seventeen when Titus started courting me. I was a slip of a girl, my head full of romance and dreams of the future. This was before the war.' Norma paused to wipe her eyes once more.

'What happened?' Kitty asked in a gentle tone.

'Like I said I was a romantic girl. I used to love the picture house, Rudolph Valentino and all those films seemed to my foolish heart so, well, glamorous in a way. Titus was always a jealous man. I was a little afraid of him even then. He said that I didn't care for him, and I should prove that I was his girl as we were going to be wed.'

Kitty had a sick feeling in the pit of her stomach that she sensed where this story might be leading.

'We were engaged, after all. One thing begot another and he, well, he wouldn't take no for an answer. He forced himself on me one afternoon. He said as I should be grateful that I was going to be wed to him. No one else would want damaged goods.' Norma's lower lip trembled and tears spilled down her cheeks.

Kitty sucked in a breath. 'He raped you?' She placed her hand over Norma's.

The woman gave a brief affirmative nod. 'I was terrified and then when I realised as I was pregnant, I didn't know what to do, who to turn to. I didn't tell Titus. He would have forced me to marry him, and I'd already returned his ring. My parents would have died of shame. I kept it a secret. I wore baggy clothes, distanced myself from him, hoped it would all just go away. That was when Hedley first started to be kind to me. He didn't know, still doesn't know what Titus did.'

The woman's tears fell faster, dripping off her face onto her apron.

'I'm so sorry, that must have been a terrible time for you,' Kitty said. She couldn't imagine what the woman must have gone through, alone and frightened.

'I gave birth in the barn one night all on my own. Mother and Father were in bed. I often went outside at night to check on the poultry so no one would have thought anything of it. My baby was born dead, the cord was tight round his neck. A little boy, so beautiful and perfect but he never opened his eyes or took a breath. I didn't know what to do so I wrapped him in my cardigan and placed him in some old feed sacks, before hiding him under the hay.' Norma gulped and scrubbed at her face with her sodden handkerchief.

'Oh, you poor thing.' Kitty could see how traumatised Norma was even after all this time.

'I had to spy my chance to take him somewhere. I didn't want him thrown away like he was a piece of rubbish. I decided to take him to Wassail Farm. There was a spot I used to love not far from the farmhouse where there are two cherry trees. The blossoms were always so pretty in the spring. I buried him where no one would disturb the ground. I called him Sebastian. That was the name I was going to use if I had a son, so it had to be his name.' Norma blinked.

'And you go there to visit his grave?' Kitty guessed.

Norma nodded. 'I know it's daft and, well, I take a flower sometimes or just sneak over there and check as he's all right under the trees. Abigail noticed me. She notices lots of things that girl.' Norma's voice softened and Kitty could see that Norma was fond of the young housekeeper.

'Did you tell her about the baby?' Kitty asked.

Norma nodded. 'It all came out the one day, a couple of years ago. I knew as Titus beat the girl when he were in one of his tempers, but I was there the one afternoon and she was in a terrible state. He'd forced himself on her. It was like history repeating itself all over again. There was nothing I could do. No use going to the police, and she wouldn't come back to Blossomdown with me, even though I begged her. She was afraid of what might happen and, well, it was all such a mess.' Norma looked at Kitty. 'You understand.'

'Yes, yes, I do.' Kitty could picture the scene all too well. Poor Norma and poor Abigail.

'I told her about Sebastian and how it had happened to me. I helped her get herself straight. She moved out of her bedroom at the farm to sleep by the fire in the kitchen. It was safer. She could run out the back door if he come at her again and there was fire irons to hand. I think she kept a knife under her pillow for a long time,' Norma said.

'So, you started calling on her regularly?' Kitty asked.

'Yes, I'd take her a few bits and pieces. A ribbon for her hair, some salve for her bruises, some bath salts. Just little things to help her. She had nothing. Even the clothes she had were Titus's wife's things cut down to fit her. Titus never gave her enough wages for her to buy anything for herself. She would try and save what she could. I keep her money here for her so he could never lay his hands on it.' Norma's voice broke as she spoke.

'It must have been very difficult for both of you,' Kitty said.

'I'm worried about her, Mrs Bryant. Will she be all right there by herself? I know she's got the dogs and she's a sensible girl, but whoever killed Micah and Titus is still on the loose. She could come here if she wanted. Hedley wouldn't object and I know as Saul is sweet on her.' A small smile lifted the corners of Norma's mouth for the first time that afternoon. 'Though he thinks as we've not noticed.'

'Does Saul know what his father did to you, or to Abigail?' Kitty asked.

A look of fear crossed the older woman's face. 'No, and he

must never know. Neither him nor Hedley. Mrs Bryant, swear you will not say anything.' Norma pressed hard on Kitty's hand.

'Anything you have told me is in confidence. If it is not relevant to Micah or Titus's deaths, then you may be assured it will go no further. Abigail says she needs to stay at Wassail Farm for the animals. She has the dogs with her as you said. Mrs Pickering has also offered her a room if she wishes to go there,' Kitty said.

'That's kind of them.' Norma scrubbed at her face once more with her handkerchief, before returning it to her apron pocket.

She seemed reassured by Kitty's promise. 'Dear me, what must you think of me. I just don't want Hedley to know about this. I couldn't bear to live with the shame of him thinking less of me. I've always blamed myself for us not being blessed with children of our own. I know it must be my fault. I think maybe it's a punishment on me for what happened to Sebastian.'

'You mustn't think that.' Kitty squeezed the older woman's hand. 'You were a young girl who went through the most horrific ordeal all alone and unsupported.'

'Thank you, Mrs Bryant. You've been very kind and understanding,' Norma said as she extracted her hand from Kitty's. 'Now, forgive me, but I need to shake my feathers or Hedley and Saul will be coming back to find there's no supper ready.' The woman seemed anxious and embarrassed after her confession.

'Of course, we should go too. There is a lot for us to consider,' Kitty said, getting to her feet. She guessed that Norma needed some time by herself to recover from what she had just told them.

Matt uncurled himself from where he had been sitting as quietly and unobtrusively as possible in the corner while Norma had been confiding in Kitty.

They saw themselves out of the farmhouse, while Norma

took herself off to the kitchen to prepare the evening meal and to splash cold water on her face.

'Whew, that was a lot. What a dreadful man and what a lot of damage he caused,' Kitty said as she slipped behind the steering wheel of her car.

'We shall have to talk to Abigail about what Norma has told us.' Matt sounded thoughtful as Kitty started up the car.

'I suppose so. The more we learn about Titus Blake the less surprised I am that he was murdered. The biggest mystery is why no one did it sooner,' Kitty said, crashing her gears as she slowed down for a corner.

'Indeed. He was a truly terrible man. The puzzle though is why has Micah been murdered?' Matt said.

'I don't know. There seems to be such a tangle of possibilities,' Kitty said as she headed towards the common.

'There is always a possibility that Norma and Abigail are working together. They could have killed Titus and then if Micah had started to become suspicious, killed him too,' Matt suggested.

Kitty considered this as she pulled her car to a halt outside their house. 'True. They could have become aware that Micah had seen Norma sneaking into Wassail Farm. He thought it was to see Titus, but they may have realised that having got rid of his father he could mention this to the police.'

Matt got out of the car and found the key ready to unlock the front door. 'That would make sense. Norma could have hired us to try and discover what we and the police had found out about the murders. To keep both her and Abigail one step ahead of us.'

Kitty followed him to the front step. 'It's a good point. I hope it's not the case though. Listening to that story this afternoon was quite harrowing.' She knew she had to keep an impartial outlook and review any evidence they found objectively. Even so, it would have taken someone with a much harder heart than hers not to feel for Abigail and Norma.

Matt smiled sympathetically at her as he inserted the key in the front door lock. 'I know what you mean. They are both strong candidates for committing the murders though, either singly or together.'

He opened the front door as he spoke, and a slight breeze sent a small collection of white feathers whirling past them out onto the front step.

'Oh no!' Kitty said, peering around Matt to see what appeared to be a snowstorm of feathers on top of the tiles of the hall floor.

'Bertie!' Matt called as he entered the house looking for the culprit.

'Mrs Smith must have gone home, and he's found something to destroy while we've been out.' Kitty followed Matt inside the hall, pausing briefly to remove her hat and hang it on one of the hooks.

It had been a little while since Bertie had done anything really naughty, but it was clear that in their absence the dog had got into mischief. Bertie was soon located in the kitchen lying in front of the range with Rascal curled up next to him.

'You naughty dog. What have you destroyed this time?' Kitty asked when she spotted a fragment of telltale white down clinging to the corner of the dog's mouth.

Matt went into the drawing room and emerged with the remains of one of the new cushions Kitty had bought only the week before to brighten the room.

'Oh no.' Kitty viewed the ruined cushion with dismay.

Matt handed it to her.

'I think it can be saved. I'll have to ask Alice if she can salvage it. In the meantime, we had better get these feathers up and keep them in case it can be made good.' Kitty looked at the heaps of down lying like snow on the floor. 'I'll fetch the dustpan and brush.'

'I'll take Bertie out for a walk and see if I can get him to lose some of this energy.' Matt picked up the dog's leash from the hall stand and Bertie slunk around Kitty to stand next to Matt. His tail was between his legs.

Kitty shook her head in mock despair. 'Oh, Bertie! What shall we do with you?'

She had scarcely finished gathering up the last trace of the scattered feathers when there was a clattering outside the house. It sounded as if one of the new small tractors that some of the local farms had started to use had pulled to a stop in front of the drive.

Before Kitty had time to investigate there was a smart rapping at her front door. She replaced the dustpan and brush inside her cleaning closet and went to see who it could be. She opened the door to find a woman standing on the doorstep. She was sturdily built and dressed in dark-green coveralls, her brown hair caught back in a neat bun at the nape of her neck. A few grey hairs shone in the late afternoon sunlight and her cheeks were rosy with the signs of someone used to being outdoors.

Kitty didn't recognise her. 'Hello, may I help you?'

'Mrs Kitty Bryant?' the woman asked.

'Yes, that's me.' Kitty was bemused about who the woman might be.

'My name is Dora Bird. I had to come and find you to ask if what I've just heard in the village is true? Is Micah Blake dead?' Kitty realised the woman was trembling as she spoke, and her eyes seemed to hold a desperate plea.

'I think, perhaps, you should come inside, Miss Bird,' Kitty suggested.

'Mrs Bird, I'm a widow,' the woman said as she followed Kitty into the hall, taking care to leave her boots at the entrance.

'I beg your pardon, Mrs Bird.' Kitty led her into the drawing room where the woman perched herself carefully on the edge of one of the black leather seats.

'I didn't know what to do. I heard as the police had been to the woods at the top of Wassail Farm and the Pickerings' place. My farm lies behind the wood on the other side. Your name and your husband's name were mentioned so I asked for directions and came straight here.' There was a catch in the woman's voice as she spoke.

'Forgive me for asking, Mrs Bird, but you seem very distressed about this news,' Kitty said.

'Just please tell me if it's true,' the woman asked.

Kitty nodded. 'I'm afraid it is. Micah was in the woods, he'd been shot.'

Colour leached from the woman's cheeks and Kitty thought she was about to faint. 'Mrs Bird, are you all right? Can I ask why you are so affected by Micah's death?'

The woman reached inside the neck of her coveralls and pulled out a fine gold chain. On the end of the chain Kitty saw a ring set with three small diamonds.

'I'm Micah's fiancée.'

CHAPTER SEVENTEEN

Kitty stared at the ring and then at Dora for a moment, completely thrown by this unexpected turn of events. This was such a shocking revelation.

'Forgive me, Mrs Bird, for being so taken aback. I was unaware that Micah Blake was engaged to be married,' Kitty said once she'd recovered herself.

Dora released her hold on the chain and dropped her hands onto her lap. 'It was a secret. Micah proposed a few months ago. This was his late mother's ring.'

'Oh, my dear, I'm so, so sorry. It must have been a dreadful shock hearing the news of his death in the village like that,' Kitty said.

Dora nodded miserably. 'I couldn't believe it. I thought it had to be a lie. Micah was such a big, strong man. He'd been to see me late last night after his brothers had gone home. With his father gone we could start to make some plans and now...' She burst into tears.

'I think I should go and put the kettle on,' Kitty said and hurried into the kitchen to get a tea tray ready. Hopefully it would give Dora a little time to recover her composure. She would have offered brandy but the woman had arrived by tractor.

She returned a few minutes later bearing a tea tray and was thankful that Dora, although red eyed and nosed, seemed somewhat calmer.

'Why don't you tell me all about you and Micah,' Kitty invited as she set the cups out for the two of them and decided a tiny splash of brandy probably wouldn't go amiss.

'Like I told you, Mrs Bryant, I'm a widow. My husband died about four years ago now and I manage our farm on my own. There's just me and my son, Freddie. He's twelve and a good lad. My farm isn't very big, and I manage most things all right by myself but about twelve months ago I had a problem I couldn't fix. I ran into Micah up in the woods. I knew his reputation, but he was polite to me, and he came back and gave me a hand.' Dora sniffed and wiped her nose with a grubby-looking handkerchief.

'And that was when it started?' Kitty asked, adding milk to their tea.

Dora nodded. 'He came to call a few times to see how the repair he'd made was holding up and we got talking. He took an interest in Freddie. He'd show him things about farming, teaching him. I started to look forward to his visits. We'd have a bite of supper together and, well, it went on from there.' Dora accepted the cup of tea from Kitty.

'I presume Micah didn't want his father to know about you?'

'Titus would have caused trouble. There was no doubt about that, especially if he thought Micah might leave Wassail to live with me. I know as Micah had a reputation too but when he was away from his father and Wassail Farm, he was a different man. He was kind to me and good to my boy. He asked me to marry him, and I agreed.' Dora's eyes misted as she spoke.

Kitty waited for the woman to recover to finish her story.

Dora sipped her tea and composed herself enough to continue. 'He wanted me to know as his intentions were honourable. He said he would inherit Wassail Farm when his father passed on so until then he had to stop and work for him. I told him to just leave and come and live with me and Freddie, we could make a go of it on my land. I wish he'd have listened.' She shook her head sorrowfully.

'Why did he insist on staying?' Kitty asked.

'His father wouldn't have given us any peace and Wassail was too much for one man to run it without help. His father's temper and drinking was getting worse. He thought if we waited it out for a few months, the way Titus's health was heading, well, then he'd inherit Wassail and we could live there.' Dora sighed.

'Titus's murder must have been a terrible shock,' Kitty said.

Dora nodded. 'It were. It shook me and Micah up no end. He didn't know what had happened.'

'And neither of you knew who might have killed Titus?' Kitty asked. It was clear that Dora had not suspected Micah of murdering his father even if others had not been so charitable.

Dora looked bewildered. 'Lots of people disliked Titus, and with good reason, but to kill a man is something else.'

'You know there were rumours in the village that Micah may have killed him?' Kitty decided to bite the bullet and be upfront. Dora must have heard the talk, so she wanted to know why Dora had been so certain her beloved was innocent.

'Aye, I heard them but I knew he hadn't. That day Micah was up mending the wall on the top field. I was with him over the lunchtime. I took him up some food and a drink,' Dora said.

'So, Micah had you as an alibi but he never said.' Kitty frowned as she spoke.

'He didn't want my name brought into anything. Like I said to you, Mrs Bryant, he loved me, and he was good to me. If he had been arrested, I would have gone to the police right away. It left us in a fix really. The police might have thought us being engaged added to a reason for Micah to kill his father and my saying he'd been with me wouldn't have carried no weight,' Dora said.

'Do you know of anyone who may have wanted to harm Micah?' Kitty asked.

A tear rolled down Dora's cheek. 'No. He could be loud and blustery, especially if the drink was in him, but for all of that he wasn't a man as made enemies, not like his father.'

Kitty sipped her tea. 'Did Micah ever say anything about him suspecting anyone?' she asked.

That was one of the few reasons that she could think of why Micah might have been murdered. If Micah had seen something or heard something that could betray his father's killer, that person could have wanted to silence him.

Dora shook her head once more. 'No, we talked it over who could have done it, but he didn't have any firm idea at all. I mean there were rows in their family and Titus had upset a good many folks in the village as well over one thing and another, but there was no one incident as we could think of to point to anyone in particular.' Dora finished her tea and set her cup back down carefully on the tray.

'I see. Thank you, Dora. I am truly sorry for your loss,' Kitty said before finishing her own drink.

'We were going to set a wedding date after Micah had been to see that solicitor in Totnes. He wanted to be sure how things stood with the farm. If he was right and Wassail was to go to Hedley, then he intended to leave and come to me. We'd bring our wedding plans forward. Originally, we had thought around Christmas would be good when the farm work was a bit less heavy. Now it'll be his funeral as I'll be going to.' Dora's lip trembled as she spoke.

'I really am sorry,' Kitty repeated. She could see how distressed the woman was.

'Freddie will be devastated.' Dora blinked and took out her handkerchief once more to wipe her eyes. 'He was fond of Micah. Now 'twill be just the two of us again.'

'Will you be all right?' Kitty asked.

Dora gave a small shrug. 'I have to be, Mrs Bryant, I don't have no choice.' She slipped the ring and chain back inside her overalls. 'I'd best be off. I've a lot to do and I need to tell Freddie what's happened before he finds out from somebody else.'

'Of course.' Kitty rose to show the woman out.

Dora pulled on her boots at the front step and prepared to depart. 'They will catch whoever's done this, won't they, Mrs Bryant?'

'I'm sure the police will do everything they can, as will Matt and I,' she promised.

'Micah said as Mrs Blake had employed you to look into things. Do it for me and Freddie as well, Mrs Bryant,' Dora said.

'We'll do our best,' Kitty assured her.

She watched the woman walk up the drive and climb up onto her tractor to set off back to her farm.

The case was becoming more and more complicated. It was clear that Dora had a different view of Micah than anyone else in his family had. Indeed, her view was different to others in the village. Kitty sighed, she was still no further forward either in discovering who could have had a motive for killing Micah.

She cleared away the tea things and wandered back into the drawing room to wait for Matt and Bertie to return. She was keen to discover what her husband would make of this latest turn of events.

She heard his key in the lock some ten or so minutes later.

* * *

Matt removed Bertie's leash and sent the spaniel off to get a drink of water from his dish in the kitchen.

'Matt, I have had the most astonishing visitor while you were out.' Kitty almost hauled him into the drawing room in her excitement to tell him the news.

'That is most unexpected,' he said, having heard his wife's breathless recitation of Dora Bird's visit. 'Micah Blake was secretly engaged, and no one knew.' He gave a low whistle of surprise.

'I know. I couldn't believe it. She showed me the ring and said it had been his mother's. She also said she had been with him when Titus was murdered.' Kitty looked at Matt.

'An alibi for a dead man. I suppose Micah could have been working with someone else,' Matt said.

'You mean he could have killed his father and then the other person killed Micah? I suppose that is still possible,' Kitty agreed. 'I felt so sorry for the poor woman. She seems to be the one person so far who is genuinely grieving for Micah. Even when we were at the Blakes' house earlier, they just seemed, I don't know, annoyed that Micah was dead.'

'Yes, I thought the same thing. It had suited all of them to cast Micah in the role of having murdered his father. I wonder how Adam Blake has taken the news of his brother's death. Those two were often at loggerheads it seems,' Matt said.

'Saul didn't seem unduly upset about his brother either. He was more bothered that Abigail was alone in the farmhouse now.' Kitty smiled as Rascal strolled into the room to rub against her legs, purring as he did so.

'Secret babies, secret engagements, I wonder what other skeletons will tumble out of the Blakes' cupboards over the next few days,' Matt mused, watching as Kitty bent to stroke her cat.

'I'm sure there will be more revelations to come,' Kitty said as she leaned back in her chair. 'I don't suppose Micah will have left a will?'

'Unlikely, I would have thought but you never know. His share of the farm will revert to Adam and Saul I expect.' Matt thought Kitty made a good point. He wished they could have accompanied Inspector Lewis to Totnes to talk to the youngest of the Blake brothers.

'And then there is Hedley. All of this history with Norma and Titus and he doesn't seem to know much about it at all, except that Norma chose him instead of his brother.' Kitty looked at Matt.

'Yes, I'd quite like a good chat with Hedley to find out his take on everything. He has quite strong motives for murdering his brother, especially if we discover he did know what happened to Norma all those years ago.' Matt could see that Hedley could well have wished his sibling dead.

'What about Micah?' Kitty asked.

'If Hedley did it you mean? Well, Micah was intent on talking to the solicitor to get to the bottom of the trust to find out who actually inherited the farm. Does it all go to Hedley now? Or do the remaining two brothers inherit? Or is it shared? Hedley would have a stake in knowing the outcome too.' Matt frowned. 'I think that's definitely something we need to find out. Different trusts can have all kinds of odd rules regarding inheritances.'

'I wonder how much Adam knows,' Kitty mused. 'He works in those offices, and he must have tried to discover the truth about who gets what. We know they had already been looking at the boundaries between the farms and he had seen the documents. Ownership and inheritance must have reared its head at some point, surely.'

Matt agreed with her. Did that give Adam a motive for murdering his father and older brother? He had said he wasn't interested in inheriting the farm, but was he being truthful?

Perhaps he was working with Saul, and the two brothers together had wished to oust Titus and Micah so Saul could move into Wassail farm, even potentially marrying Abigail? Adam had hated his father and there was no love lost between

Titus and Saul. But, apart from the argument yesterday, had Adam hated Micah enough to murder him?

Saul had moved out to Blossomdown to get away from his father and older brother. It was clear Hedley and Norma saw him as the natural person to take over there so did that give him a reason to want Titus and Micah dead? They posed no threat to him now, and he had no need to inherit Wassail Farm. The only motive Matt could see was Titus's treatment of Abigail and the potential for mistreatment from Micah. Or perhaps jealousy if Micah were alone with Abigail at the farmhouse.

If Saul hadn't known about his older brother's engagement to Dora, he might have feared that Micah could work his way into Abigail's affections. Abigail was a good housekeeper from what he had seen. Micah could have wanted to retain his home comforts given that no one knew of his relationship with Dora.

If his engagement had been known about then, perhaps, he might not have been killed? It was an interesting thought.

CHAPTER EIGHTEEN

The following morning dawned crisp and cool with bright blue skies and a distinct nip in the air. Kitty shivered and huddled into her woollen cardigan as she ate her breakfast.

'What are our plans for today?' she asked once she'd swallowed her last morsel of toast, ignoring Bertie's begging eyes from where he was sat under the table.

'I think we should try to find out what Inspector Lewis discovered when he spoke to Adam Blake yesterday. I would very much like to know the ins and outs of that trust and how it was impacted by Titus Blake's will,' Matt said, setting aside his teacup.

'I agree. I think somewhere in all of this must be the motive for why Micah was killed. Titus's death is slightly different. Lots of people hated him, many for seemingly good reason, but Micah's death is complicated.' Kitty dabbed at the corners of her lips with her linen napkin. 'I take it you will telephone the police station?'

Her husband grinned at her. 'You mean, I suppose, that I should be the one to speak to our friend Inspector Lewis?'

'I do try hard to be nice to him,' Kitty grumbled.

Matt chuckled. 'Very well, I'll see what I can find out. What are your plans?'

'First, I need to drop that cushion cover over to Alice to see if she can rescue it.' Kitty glared at the unrepentant Bertie. 'It won't take me long to pop into Paignton.'

'Very well, I'll see you back here shortly and hopefully I'll have found out more about the Blake trust by then,' Matt agreed affably.

Kitty kissed the top of his head and found her new red felt hat and matching leather handbag ready for the short drive to see Alice at her new business premises.

Alice had rented a small workshop at the back of a store-front on Winner Street. At the front of the shop, she displayed some of her custom-made children's wear along with some items she had bought in to sell. Undergarments and accessories for infants mainly, with some haberdashery items. The window displays always looked enticing and the pale-blue sign above the storefront bore the legend, *Miss A Miller: seamstress for all your sewing needs.*

At the back of the store she kept her bales of material, her machine, cutting table and selection of threads and fasteners. Changing cubicles, a large mirror and a couple of mannequins filled the rear of the space. She could pop out to serve customers and take orders, whilst fulfilling her repairs and commission work.

She had been kept busy ever since she had opened the shop. The endorsement from Kitty's cousin Lucy had added a certain cachet to her advertising and word of mouth about the quality of her work had soon spread.

To Kitty's delight the shop was quiet when she walked in the door. The brass bell on its coiled spring setting off a merry jingle to announce her entrance. Alice was busy cleaning the shelves in her haberdashery, tidying up reels of ribbon and lace trim and dusting as she went.

'Kitty, well this is a pleasure.' Her friend beamed at her as she climbed down from her step stool.

'I have a favour to ask. Bertie has been up to his old tricks again and I am not certain this can be saved.' Kitty drew the damaged cushion cover from her bag.

Alice smiled and tutted as she inspected the damage. 'I can do something with it, but I might have to alter it a bit. Did you save the filling?' she asked as a stray feather fluttered to the floor when she turned the cover inside out.

Kitty nodded. 'I did. I only got these cushions a week ago, wretched dog.'

'How was your horse ride?' Alice asked as she set the cushion cover to one side in her workshop. 'I heard a rumour that there had been another murder out that way? Is that right?'

'I'm afraid it is.' Kitty quickly told her friend what had happened the previous day during their outing.

Alice's eyebrows rose sharply when Kitty explained how Micah's body had been found. They were forced to break off the conversation for a moment while Alice served a young mother with some woollen vests for her infant.

Once the woman had gone Kitty continued her story, telling her friend about Norma's secret and Dora's engagement. She knew Alice wouldn't breathe a word to another soul and she always valued her friend's thoughts during their investigations.

'That's proper shocking. It all sounds very complicated. I can see what you mean about the older Mr Blake being killed but not so much the son. Do you think as the other two sons might be in danger?' Alice asked as she tidied her shelf from where she had taken out the baby vests.

'I don't know. You met the youngest son the other day,' Kitty said.

Alice's cheeks pinked slightly at the recollection. 'Oh yes. That's the one as you said worked for the solicitor?'

'Yes, Mr Adam Blake,' Kitty said. 'He says he wants nothing

to do with the farm at all and is happy to let his brothers take it all on.'

'I suppose if he's made a go of it in the law business then it might be better for him. I suppose if he's the youngest he probably reckoned as his share wouldn't ever be very much anyways.' Alice whisked her feather duster along the short glass-topped countertop.

'True,' Kitty said. She hadn't really thought much about that.

'What about the middle one? Saul, you said his name was? He could have wanted to get his own back on his father. He hated him enough to run away from home and you said you thought he was sweet on the housekeeper.' Alice finished her dusting.

'Yes, but he also stands to inherit Blossomdown and it's a much better proposition I think than Wassail Farm. Norma and Hedley wouldn't object to him marrying Abigail I don't think,' Kitty said.

Alice frowned. 'Well, if he found out what his father had done to his sweetheart, he would have motive aplenty. But then why kill his brother? Unless Micah had found out it was his brother and he had to stop him going to the police. It doesn't sound to me as if money is at the bottom of all this. Unless, of course, Captain Bryant manages to find something out from that Inspector Lewis. No, it's a bit like that film we saw a few weeks ago.' Her friend looked at her.

'Which one?' Kitty wasn't as into the world of movies and actors as Alice.

'The one about those two brothers who owned the cattle ranch,' Alice said. 'Perhaps that's why I'm thinking of it. They fell out over a woman to start with, didn't they? Then the one tried to get his own back and ended up shooting his brother.'

'You think a woman is behind this?' Kitty asked. 'I suppose Saul might have disliked Abigail being at the farmhouse with Titus and Micah, but it had been that way for years.'

'Things change though, don't they? I don't know, it all seems odd to me,' Alice said.

Kitty knew what she meant. She'd hoped Alice might shed some clarity on it all, but it sounded as if she too was stumped.

'I suppose I should get home and see if Matt has had any luck with Inspector Lewis. I'll see you tomorrow evening at the picture house?' Kitty said, making her way towards the door.

'I'm looking forward to it, and a nice fish supper afterwards,' Alice reminded her with a smile.

Kitty had a smile on her own face as she stepped into the street and closed the shop door behind her. She was so wrapped up in her own thoughts she walked straight into a gentleman walking swiftly along the pavement in the opposite direction.

'I do beg your pardon,' Kitty gasped as the man she had cannoned into steadied her. 'Oh, Mr Blake, what a surprise.'

Kitty wondered if Adam's ears had been burning earlier when she and her friend had been discussing him. He was certainly one of the last people she had expected to run into this morning.

'Mrs Bryant, I'm sure the fault is mine. I was preoccupied,' Adam responded politely.

'No, I assure you that I am equally to blame,' Kitty said. 'I had just called to see my friend Alice at her shop and wasn't looking where I was going.'

'I have just been at the undertakers. I offered to go on my uncle Hedley's behalf. We were arranging things for my father's funeral. Now it seems it will be a double service.' A cloud passed over Adam Blake's handsome face.

'I'm so sorry about your brother Micah. It must have been the most awful shock,' Kitty said sympathetically.

Adam swallowed and Kitty could see he appeared deeply affected. 'Do you have time for coffee, there is a small tea room just a couple of doors down?' Kitty suggested.

'Thank you, Mrs Bryant, that's most kind of you.' Adam fell into step beside her, and they walked further down the street to the tea room near where Kitty's car was parked.

The place was quiet as they entered with just a couple of elderly ladies seated at the window table taking tea. Kitty and Adam took a table near the back of the small space where they would be less likely to be disturbed or overheard should more customers come in.

A smartly dressed young girl in a black and white maid's outfit came and took their order and Kitty drew off her gloves, putting them on the table beside her place setting. If Matt had no joy with his telephone call to Inspector Lewis, then she hoped she might learn something of benefit from Adam Blake.

'My employer has given me some time off to assist my family,' Adam explained while they waited for the girl to return with their drinks.

'Were you at work when the police contacted you about Micah?' Kitty asked, knowing that was where Inspector Lewis had gone after leaving the Blakes' house.

Adam nodded, then waited until the waitress had set down the chrome coffee set and geometrically patterned china cups and saucers in front of them before continuing.

'Yes, I thought I should carry on working. It would be hypocritical of me to pretend I was mourning for my father. Shocking though that might seem,' he said once the young waitress had gone back to her other table.

'I understand your difficulty,' Kitty said as she poured coffee from the tall slim pot into their cups, before adding steamed milk from the matching jug. 'Your father did not have many friends it seems.'

Adam made a small scoffing noise. 'I would be surprised,

Mrs Bryant, if you found that Father had any friends. He had men he drank with at the public houses in Stoke Gabriel, but they were acquaintances at best.'

'So, there is no one that you know of who he may have confided in if he felt worried or threatened?' Kitty asked. This was something she hadn't considered before. If Titus may have mentioned something to a friend, then it could provide a valuable lead.

'No, there is no one. Father would brag and bluster when the drink was first in him. If he had too much, he would become argumentative and violent. We all learned as children to keep out of his way then, or it would be the worse for us. He got worse after Mother died. I think she always managed to rein him in but when she passed on, he grew more violent.' Adam gave a small, almost defeated, shrug of his shoulders.

'Was this around the time that Saul left to stay with your aunt and uncle?' Kitty asked.

Adam added sugar to his cup and stirred. 'Yes, Saul left about nine months after Mother passed on. He couldn't stand it anymore. Micah was older and could put up with Father's temper. Father knew too, that he couldn't really afford for Micah to up and go. I was too young to be of much help on the farm. I got a place at the solicitor's and my old schoolmaster helped me find lodgings with a family in Totnes so as soon as I was able, I left home too.'

'Saul said that you accompanied him to see Micah on Sunday evening at the farm.' Kitty kept her tone casual as she waited to hear what Adam had to say about the visit.

Adam set his teaspoon down in his saucer. 'Saul and I thought we should talk to Micah about the future of the farm. He'd made an appointment to see my employer. Something about some questions he had regarding the trust and Father's will.' The frown lines on Adam's brow deepened. 'I tried to tell him that it would make no difference what it said. The farm was to stay in the family and since I had no interest in farming and Saul was content at Blossomdown, then Wassail was pretty much his anyway. Although it was still a worry since Micah might not have run it properly if he'd followed Father's methods.'

'But this didn't satisfy him?' Kitty asked, after taking a sip of her coffee.

'No. Micah could be bull-headed like Father. He'd get something into his thick skull, and nothing would shake the idea from it.' A note of irritation had crept into Adam's voice.

'He thought that the trust meant that your uncle was, in fact, the owner of Wassail Farm, at least until his death and only then would it go to the three of you,' Kitty said.

'Yes, that or half was Uncle Hedley's and Father's portion was split three ways. He started going on about the land and how Uncle Hedley would do us down taking the water rights and that he had his own plans to expand the farm.' Adam shook his head.

Kitty guessed that Micah's expansion plans had included incorporating Dora's land into the property.

'Do you know how the trust is set up? Does it all fall to your uncle until he passes?' Kitty asked.

'I don't know. It would seem the likeliest thing, but trusts can be set up in different ways. It wasn't set out in a straightforward style. Micah even asked me if I knew how things would fall in the future, if any of us had children or adopted children.' Adam shook his head as he stared at the tiny bubbles clinging to the surface of his coffee around the edge of the cup. 'I mean, what kind of questions are those?'

Kitty guessed that Micah and Dora must have been thinking of Freddie and if Dora's farm were to be added to Wassail, if the lad's rights would be protected. No doubt they would also want to know if he could claim Wassail Farm or a share of it in the future, alongside any children Saul or Adam might have.

Adam sipped his coffee for a few minutes before speaking again. 'Why was Micah killed, Mrs Bryant? That's what's bothering me. Do you think someone has a grudge against our whole family? Are myself and Saul also in danger? Then there is Abigail. She's alone now at the farm and I know Saul will be worried about her staying there by herself.'

'I agree, it is concerning but there is no proof that someone is targeting all of your family. I take it that you and Saul or your aunt and uncle have received no threatening letters, or had any serious disagreements with anyone that would cause you to think they posed a threat?' Kitty asked.

'No, not that I'm aware of. I can't speak for Aunt Norma and Uncle Hedley, but I'm sure she would have told you if she had. Saul has never said anything either.' Adam gave her a wry smile. 'I'm sorry if I sound a little paranoid.'

Kitty returned his smile. 'It is understandable. I take it that Micah never said anything about anyone threatening him personally. Or having fallen out with anyone?'

'The only people he fell out with was when Father dragged him into one of his disputes. Micah was as stubborn as an ox and would argue with his own shadow if he had a drink in him, but he never made enemies the way Father did.' Adam drained his cup of coffee.

'Saul said that you and Micah argued on Sunday evening?' Kitty split the last of the coffee from the pot between their two cups.

'We did. Well, we all did. Saul had a sulk on because he went looking for Mother's jewellery box and it was gone. I reckon Father probably sold what there was in it. Not that there was much, her engagement ring, a cross and chain and a little silver bangle she'd had as a child for her christening.' Adam poured the steamed milk to top their cups up.

'What did Micah say?' Kitty knew very well where the engagement ring had gone. It was on a gold chain around Dora Bird's neck.

'He said as he didn't know and anyway the jewellery had been left to him as he was the eldest. Saul was cross and took himself off to the kitchen to see Abigail. I stayed and tried to talk to Micah about the farm. He insisted he wanted to get things straight with the solicitor. He said the money Father had left to Aunt Norma was owed to him in wages. If he didn't own the farm, then he wanted to know how he could challenge the will.' Adam looked deeply unhappy as he stirred more sugar into his cup.

'You left him on bad terms?' Kitty said.

'I told Saul I was going. I could see there was no talking to Micah when he was in that mood. He said as he had plans anyway. I took it to mean he intended to walk to the village pub. Saul said he'd stay with Abigail for a bit, so I left.' Adam finished his story and picked up his cup.

'Did Micah say anything about his plans for the following day?' Kitty asked.

Adam finished his fresh drink. 'No, he'd said earlier he wanted to deal with the fox but nothing definite.'

'I take it you and Saul knew where the guns were kept and the keys to the cabinet?' Kitty asked.

Adam smiled. 'That's what that police inspector asked too. Yes, we all knew. I think Blossomdown have a similar arrangement. I expect most of the farms hereabout are the same.' Adam fiddled with the teaspoon lying in the saucer beside his empty cup. 'Mrs Bryant, could the police be mistaken about Micah's death? I mean, his foot being in a trap and the shot from the gun to his face. It could have been a ghastly freak accident, couldn't it?'

Kitty finished her own drink and placed her cup carefully in its saucer. 'Matt didn't think so and the police and Doctor

Carter were of the same opinion. I'm afraid it was definitely murder, although perhaps someone hoped it would be taken as suicide.'

Adam considered her answer, his gaze locking with hers as if he needed to be satisfied that she was telling the truth. 'Then I hope they find who did it soon, Mrs Bryant, before anything else happens.'

CHAPTER NINETEEN

Inspector Lewis was unavailable when Matt first telephoned the police station. He was sorely tempted to just ask for the chief inspector but was mindful that he and Kitty should be at least seen to try to work with the annoying Yorkshireman.

Instead, he said he would try again in half an hour, or the inspector could telephone him on his return to the police station. He replaced the receiver and went back to the dining table to complete his morning crossword. The French doors were open, and the air outside had warmed up a little now the sun was higher in the sky.

Rascal was out in the garden stalking grasshoppers under the shade of the apple tree, while Bertie lay snoring peacefully in a pool of sunlight. Matt had scarcely solved two of the clues when the telephone rang. He hurried into the hall, calling to their housekeeper in the kitchen that he would take the call.

'Captain Bryant, good morning, the desk sergeant said you called. I presume you have some information for me about the case?' the inspector greeted him crisply.

'We have uncovered more information, yes. Much of it is highly sensitive and I'm not certain how relevant it might be to your enquiry,' Matt said. He knew they would have to share Norma's secret and the information about Dora's engagement at some point.

He just hoped the inspector would be discreet.

'I think I should be the judge of what's relevant or not, Captain Bryant,' Inspector Lewis replied.

Matt suppressed a sigh and decided to share Dora's engagement news first.

'So, Micah Blake had an alibi for his father's murder after all and the stupid woman has only come forward with this now that he's dead. Very convenient, if you ask me.' Inspector Lewis sounded most put out about Micah having an alibi.

Matt could only think that the policeman had been reluctant to let go of his theory that Micah had murdered his father, presumably with an accomplice.

'Did you manage to speak to Adam Blake and his employer yesterday?' Matt asked.

'Yes, Adam Blake appeared quite shocked when he learned his brother had been killed. He'd been out at various points during the day delivering court documents and going to the post and the stationers. Meaning he had opportunity,' Inspector Lewis said.

'He had an argument with Micah on the Sunday evening when he called at Wassail Farm with Saul Blake. That was reportedly about the future of the farm and its ownership. What did you discover about the structure of the trust?' Matt asked.

'That was a complicated affair. I was there till seven o'clock with Mr Frasier, the solicitor. He'd been doing some work on it ready for Micah's appointment today. It was worded most peculiarly, and it took some time to work through the legal phrases to get to the crux of the clauses.' Inspector Lewis sounded most unhappy.

'And who does Wassail Farm belong to now? And how does the inheritance work?' Matt asked.

'From what we could work out, when Hedley and Titus Blake's father died the farm went as expected to both sons equally. Hedley, it seems, was unaware of this and believed his father had willed the farm to Titus. Which apparently, he had, but of course the trust overruled his wishes. Then when Titus was killed, despite his will saying the three sons were to inherit as per the trust, that couldn't happen until Hedley passes on,' the inspector said.

'Then the farm is entirely Hedley's for now?' Matt asked.

'Yes, when Hedley passes it would have then gone to all three sons, but now Micah is dead it will go to Saul and Adam,' the inspector confirmed.

'So, Micah was right all along. He had no claim to Wassail Farm until his uncle dies. Hmm, interesting. Thank you, Inspector.' Matt decided he should keep Norma's secret for a little longer, at least until he and Kitty had verified it with Abigail West.

'The solicitor said he would make an appointment to go and see Hedley Blake to clear the matter up,' Inspector Lewis added. 'Is that all, Captain Bryant? Only I'm sure you'll appreciate that I'm a very busy man right now.'

'Of course, Inspector. I appreciate your time.' Matt replaced the receiver on the stand and wandered back to his newspaper deep in thought.

* * *

Kitty hurried into the house just before lunchtime. She found her husband in the dining room completing his daily puzzle.

'Hello, darling, you've been a while. Was Alice all right?' Matt asked.

'She's fine, and she thinks she can save my poor cushion. You'll never guess though who I bumped into?' Kitty said, eager to share her latest discoveries with Matt. She took a seat at the table.

Her husband listened carefully as she told him all about her chance encounter with Adam Blake and what he had said about his visit to see Micah on the Sunday evening.

'Very interesting indeed. I wonder why Saul was looking for his mother's jewellery? To propose to Abigail, perhaps? Jealousy of his brother could be a motive for murder.' Matt looked thoughtful.

'It's possible, but we don't know how Abigail feels about Saul. We noticed he seemed sweet on her before anyone else said anything. Now both Norma and Adam have confirmed it,' Kitty said. 'How did you get on talking to Inspector Lewis? Do we know about the trust?'

Matt told her what the inspector had said.

'And the solicitor is going to see Hedley to tell him about it all? I hope this won't put Hedley in any danger.' Kitty frowned. 'It may be that whoever is doing this has Wassail Farm as their end goal.'

'Do you think Saul or Adam are in the frame for the murders?' Matt asked.

'I rather think they have to be, although Saul's reasons seem clearer than Adam's. I suppose too that Hedley could also be responsible. He may know much more about the trust than he's been letting on. He definitely benefits financially,' Kitty said, leaning forward in her seat.

'If Abigail is as keen on Saul as he is on her, then that also gives her a motive. I would like to know if she knew about Micah's visits to Dora Bird,' Matt said.

'Then I think we should go to see her after lunch and hear what she has to say,' Kitty suggested. 'I'd also like to try and find Dora's farm just so we can see where it lies in relation to Wassail, Blossomdown and the Pickerings' stables.'

'I suppose too that we cannot entirely rule out the Picker-ings,' Matt said slowly.

Kitty sighed. 'I suppose so. They had quarrelled with both Titus and Micah. They could have set up the ride taking the route we followed so that we would discover the body.'

They paused for a sandwich lunch and took Bertie for a quick run over to the nearby common, before setting off for Wassail Farm once more. Kitty paused on the way at a roadside stall outside a cottage to purchase a bunch of late summer flowers.

Matt looked questioningly at her as she returned behind the wheel.

'I thought we could give them to Abigail as a friendly gesture. It looks much nicer than us simply turning up and firing questions at the girl,' Kitty said, thrusting the posy onto Matt's lap for him to carry while she drove.

Matt merely gave a small shake of his head and grinned at her. 'Using honey to trap our fly, eh?'

The dogs were loose in the yard as Kitty drove up to the farm gate. She didn't blame Abigail for allowing them to roam freely while a murderer was on the loose and the woman was alone at the farm.

She sounded the car horn so the girl would know someone was there and waited for her to come out to call the dogs to her. Abigail appeared through the open door of the farmhouse a minute later, drying her hands on her apron. She saw Kitty's car and called the two dogs, tethering them to the long, metal chains outside the barn.

Once the dogs were secured, Matt jumped out of the car and opened the gate, allowing Kitty to drive into the yard, before closing it once more.

'Captain Bryant, Mrs Bryant, how can I help you?' Abigail's

expression was wary as Kitty switched off her engine and got out of the car.

'We thought we would call and make sure you were all right after yesterday,' Kitty said. She picked up the posy from where Matt had left it on the passenger seat. 'These are for you, just a little something to cheer you up.' She presented the flowers to the girl.

Abigail stared at the posy of cottage garden blooms for a moment seemingly lost for words. A tear rolled down her cheek. 'Thank you, Mrs Bryant. Nobody hasn't ever give me flowers before,' the girl said, before quickly wiping her cheek. 'Come inside. I was just about to make a cup of tea.'

Kitty and Matt followed Abigail through into the kitchen. It was plain the girl had been ironing. The scent of freshly pressed clothes was in the air and a large wicker basket full of folded linen was beside the range. A black flat iron stood on a trivet beside a mister full of water.

They took a seat at the kitchen table while Abigail filled the kettle and set out some cups and saucers.

'Were you all right here last night by yourself?' Kitty asked.

The girl nodded as she placed a pressed-glass sugar bowl and a small, chipped china jug of milk on the table. 'It were strange and I'm glad as I had the dogs with me. They slept in here beside me and I made extra sure as I'd locked and bolted everything.'

'Mrs Pickering's offer is still open to stay at the stables and also Mrs Blake has said you would be welcome at Blossomdown too,' Kitty said as the girl spooned tea from a battered tin caddy into the teapot.

'I know, and that's right kind, but I have to think of the animals, even with Jim coming over to see to the cows. The milk has to be got ready early at the farm gate and the churns brought back in. Then there's the chickens and the pigs,' Abigail said.

'I'm sure the Blake family appreciates everything that you're doing,' Matt said.

Abigail lifted the now boiling kettle from the top of the range, wrapping a rag around the handle at the top so as not to burn herself. She poured the water onto the tea leaves in the pot and gave it a stir, before putting the lid on.

Once the kettle was put back safely and the tea was brewing, the girl found an old jam jar from under the kitchen sink and placed her posy in water, admiring the blooms as she did so. 'This was right kind of you both,' she said after putting it on the windowsill.

Kitty was glad such a small gesture appeared to have given the girl so much pleasure.

'It was nothing. We saw Norma Blake yesterday and she confided some things to us that I believe you are party to,' Kitty said once the tea had been poured through the metal strainer and the milk added.

'Oh.' Abigail immediately looked wary and a little scared.

'It's quite all right. You will not be betraying Norma's confidence if you speak to us. She has already told us about the journeys she makes in secret through the orchard to visit a particular spot here on the farm,' Kitty said.

Colour mounted in Abigail's cheeks. 'I noticed her coming and going when she thought as no one could see her. She would wait until Titus had gone up on the top fields, or she knew there was the livestock market and he was gone for the day. I wondered what she were doing so I followed her to see one day.'

'She said she would sit under the cherry trees, or would leave a flower or a token in a certain spot where it couldn't be seen,' Kitty said.

'I thought perhaps, at first, as she were coming to spy on the farm. She weren't coming for Titus as she was definitely avoiding him and not wanting to be seen,' Abigail explained.

'You said you followed her?' Matt said.

'She didn't see me, so I crept out the back door and followed along to see where she was going. She went around the bottom of the orchard on Wassail land until she come to the dip where there is two old cherry trees with a bit of a broken old wooden seat. I hid behind the raspberry canes and watched. She put a marigold on the grass close up to one of the trees and sat on the end of the bench for a minute. She took a little book out of her apron, and it looked like she were reading. I could see her lips moving but I couldn't hear what she was saying.' The house-keeper's brow creased as she tried to recall the events of the day.

'Did you confront her?' Kitty asked.

Abigail shook her head. 'No, not that day. I could see what she was doing weren't causing any harm and I thought it seemed private. It was none of my business. I went back to the farmhouse and a bit after I saw her sneaking back to get home to Blossomdown.'

'When did you talk to Norma about these visits and the purpose of them?' Kitty knew if she had been in Abigail's shoes she would have had to have said something. Her curiosity would have got the better of her.

'After that day I kept a special watch. She came by a couple more times, same sort of thing each time. Then one afternoon as she came, Titus came back from the market early and I was scared as she might bump into him. While he was in the yard bellowing at Micah, I run around and warned her to go. She looked terrified, thanked me and fled. There weren't no time that day to explain anything. I had scarce got back in the farm-house afore Titus come clumping inside demanding a cup of tea.' A shiver ran through the girl's slight frame as she told her story.

'What happened next?' Kitty asked in a gentle tone.

'The next time she came, it was autumn, the first bit of frost had been on the top field. It was the day Titus, well... She brought me a jar of honey from their bees, and we had a cup of tea together, then she told me about her baby.' Abigail's eyes were wet with tears.

'And together you've kept her secret ever since?' Kitty said.

The girl sniffed and nodded. 'Yes. It was nice to have someone as a friend. She understood what Titus was like and how hard it was living here, especially since the missus died and Adam and Saul moved out. She keeps my money for me. Titus would steal it back if he wanted coins for the pub.' Her pale cheeks had pinked a little as she mentioned Saul's name.

Kitty sipped her rapidly cooling tea. It seemed that Norma's story was true. It still could mean that the two women might have conspired together to rid themselves of Titus.

'How was Micah after his father's death?' Kitty asked.

Abigail bit her lip. 'He was sad. I think seeing his father like that in the press properly upset him. Then he was all, well, excited I suppose about finally inheriting the farm. He told me as we'd have a telephone and get electric put in.'

'And when he learned that there was a trust in place, and it might be that he wasn't to even get a share just yet?' Matt asked.

'He was angry and upset. He stomped about the place saying as it weren't fair after all the work as he done and what he'd put up with. He said he was going to see the solicitor to get to the bottom of things. He was prepared to challenge his father's will. He said he had plans for the future.' Abigail sighed as she spoke.

'Did he talk about his plans and what they involved?' Matt asked as he glanced at Kitty.

Abigail finished her cup of tea. 'Only about modernising the place. He said there would be big changes, decorating and making it nice. He asked me if I had any plans now that I'd got a bit of money and could move on if I wanted.'

Kitty's gaze locked with Matt's. Perhaps this could be a motive for Abigail and Norma to get rid of Micah. If he had wanted Abigail to move out, presumably once he had married Dora, there would be no place for the girl at Wassail Farm.

'I told him as I hadn't thought about it. It was all a bit sudden. Besides where would I go? I don't have any family. I was a foundling. I was left wrapped in old newspapers like a bundle of fish and chips in the porch of a church. The lady as does the flowers found me and took me to the orphanage. Even my name was because they named anyone like me as come in without no papers alphabetically. So, I was A and Abigail was next on the list. West was after the street where the church was. I'd have to look for another situation.' Abigail gave a small, resigned shrug of her skinny shoulders.

'Did you think that Micah wanted you to move out?' Matt asked.

Abigail gave him a startled look. 'You mean was he hinting? I don't know, I hadn't thought. Everything was so confusing when Titus was killed. I hadn't expected any money and well, as I said, Mrs Blake keeps what bit I've got saved up safe. I'd have had no home or job if Micah had turned me out.' The girl looked horrified at the thought. 'He never said that though. He was just making conversation.'

Kitty was not so sure. It sounded to her as if Micah was starting to prepare the ground ready to suggest that Abigail moved on before his wedding to Dora went ahead. If that was true, then Abigail would have had a reason to wish Micah dead.

CHAPTER TWENTY

Kitty could see from Matt's expression that his thoughts mirrored her own.

'Abigail, did you notice any changes in Micah over the last few months? You know, going out more? Seeming different to usual?' Matt asked.

Abigail looked puzzled for a moment, then her brow cleared. 'His father kept saying as Micah had a woman. He would tease him when he'd been drinking, and Micah would get angry and storm out of the house.'

'Did you think this was true?' Kitty asked. 'That Micah was courting?'

For the first time since they had been talking, Abigail seemed evasive, her gaze didn't meet Kitty's or Matt's. 'I don't know. He was out a lot more and his father said as he wasn't at the pub so much. I suppose he could have been.'

'Did Titus say who the woman was?' Matt asked.

Once again, Abigail's gaze skittered away. 'He would just say as he hadn't far to go to land in a nice warm bed.' The girl shuddered and swallowed. 'He was terrible crude at times.'

Kitty was pretty certain Abigail had known exactly who

Titus had been referring to and she would have worked out for herself who Micah's lady friend might be.

'What are your plans now?' Kitty asked. 'Matt was telling me that Inspector Lewis said that Wassail Farm will obviously go to a member of the Blake family. I assume they may simply incorporate it all into Blossomdown if Adam is uninterested in his future share of the inheritance from the trust.'

Abigail's eyes widened slightly at this. 'I don't know. I thought as I should stay until the animals was sorted out and then I suppose Mr Hedley or Norma would say what they thought as I should do.'

'What about Saul Blake?' Kitty asked, watching as colour flooded into Abigail's thin cheeks.

The girl rose from her seat and began to tidy the empty teacups onto the tray.

'I have offended you, I'm sorry. I got the impression that Saul was very fond of you.' Kitty worded things carefully.

The girl slowed her slightly frantic tidying and stilled for a moment, her shoulders drooping. 'Saul and I have been, well, talking about a future together but I'm a foundling and he is set to take over Blossomdown. Nobody knows who my people are. Chances are they weren't good people. Norma has always been kind to me, but I don't know if that would extend to me marrying Saul. Especially, well, after what happened to me with Titus.' The girl turned anguished eyes to Kitty.

'I think Norma thinks very highly of you. Would that be what you and Saul would like? To marry and perhaps take over Wassail Farm, until such time as he inherits Blossomdown as well?' Matt asked.

Abigail turned to face him. The spots of high colour still glowing on her cheeks. 'It sounds so mercenary put like that, but apart from the orphanage I've never had no other home apart from here and I'd be a good wife to Saul.'

'I'm sure you will be. Is that why Saul was looking for his

mother's jewellery when he and Adam called on Sunday evening? Did he intend to propose to you with his mother's ring?' Kitty looked at Matt as she spoke. She was certain Abigail had known of Saul's intentions.

'He was angry as the jewellery box was empty. The ring was gone. He said to me that Micah or Titus must have sold what was in there. He asked me if I was willing to wait and I said of course I was.' Abigail sat down heavily on one of the chairs before covering her face with her hands for a moment.

'Did you know the jewellery was missing?' Kitty asked as Abigail uncovered her face and seemed to recover her composure.

'No, the box was in Titus's room, and I never went in there after the missus died. I would ask him to strip his own sheets and leave them outside the door. I didn't know as Saul planned to give me his mother's ring.' She tilted her small chin upwards. 'Truth to tell, I'm glad it were gone. Even my clothes are mostly missus's cast-offs which I altered to fit me. I couldn't afford to buy new things, not on the money Titus paid. At least now if Saul does give me a ring it won't be a hand-me-down.'

Kitty could see the girl was speaking from the heart. She doubted that Abigail had ever had anything much new in her life. Everything the girl possessed was given to her or chosen by someone else. It was little wonder that Kitty's gift had moved the woman to tears.

'We should go and leave you to finish your chores. I hope things are settled for you soon,' Kitty told her.

'Please continue to be very careful until whoever killed Micah and Titus is caught,' Matt warned as he stood and pushed his chair back under the table.

'I will, sir, and thank you,' Abigail assured them.

She walked them out to the farmyard and once they were inside Kitty's car she freed the dogs from their chain, before walking down to secure the farm gate once Kitty had driven back onto the lane.

'Where next?' Matt asked as he settled back in the passenger seat.

'I think a little tour to see where Dora Bird's farm lies,' Kitty said, taking a different road to the one she usually took. 'It should be somewhere along here if as she said her land meets with the other farms on the top of that hillside where we found Micah.'

'That must be more towards Aish, the hamlet further down. I agree, we don't need to see Dora but understanding the geography would be useful,' Matt said.

The lane was narrow, and the lush autumn foliage was virtually brushing against the sides of her small red car. It was little more than a trackway. They reached a spot where they could pull to the side next to a field gate.

Matt stood up and leaned forward slightly with his hand resting on the top of the windscreen to steady himself as he took advantage of the higher position.

'I presume that must be Dora's place just along there. The land does rise behind her farm, and I can see the stand of trees where we found Micah,' Matt said.

'That all fits with what Dora told us then,' Kitty said.

'It certainly appears that way.' Matt sat back down and settled himself in the passenger seat once more.

'Dora too then could have had a motive to murder Titus if she wanted to marry Micah and merge the farms,' Kitty said.

'And killed her fiancé if he realised she was the murderer? It's possible I suppose,' Matt said.

'Unlikely though. She really seemed to love Micah, and she has her son to think of,' Kitty said.

Her curiosity on the matter satisfied, Kitty turned her car around in the narrow lane and they set off back down the road to rejoin the main route from Stoke Gabriel. They had not gone very far when Kitty pulled to the side to permit a laden horse-drawn farm cart to get past.

'Mrs Bryant, Captain Bryant.' Hedley Blake was driving the cart. He greeted them as he pulled level. 'Have you just been to Blossomdown?'

'No, sir, we've been checking out a few things elsewhere today,' Kitty said. 'I ran into your nephew, Adam, this morning, and he said he had been to make some of the funeral arrangements on your behalf.'

Hedley's ruddy face looked downcast. 'He did that. He's a good lad. I'm tied up with the farms and his employer has been so kind as to spare him a couple of days to help me out. The solicitor is calling on me in the morning to make clear how things stand with the trust and such. 'Tis a bad business.'

'It is indeed. Have the police called to see you at all lately?' Matt asked.

Hedley shook his head. 'No, only a telephone call from that Inspector Lewis to say as the solicitor were going to see us about the trust.'

The horse pulling the cart shook its head making the harness jingle. Kitty guessed it was impatient to be off and freed from its task.

'Let's hope whoever did this is caught soon. Do you know of anyone who may have wished to harm your nephew?' Matt asked.

Hedley scratched his chin as he thought about the matter. 'No, I can't say as I do really. None of this makes any sense to me. I wish they would catch whoever did this quickly though. It's Norma as I'm afeared for. 'Tis playing on her nerves, I think. She's as jumpy as a cat and that's not my wife.'

'Oh dear,' Kitty sympathised. She wondered why Norma was so nervous. It could simply be fear of her secret coming to light after all these years, or it could be that the woman knew something that she hadn't yet shared with anyone. Or, perhaps, she was directly involved in the murders.

'I need to sort out what is going to happen at Wassail Farm now too. I don't like that young girl being there on her own with a murderer about,' Hedley said.

'No, it must be quite a worry,' Matt agreed.

A delivery van had pulled up behind the cart while they had been talking so Hedley bid them goodbye and signalled his horse to continue on. Kitty waited patiently until both the cart and the van had passed her before pulling out once more into the now clear lane.

* * *

Matt could tell his wife was preoccupied as she drove them both back to their house. He sensed that she had hoped they would make some kind of breakthrough in the case after talking to so many different people. It was clear to him that unless the police had discovered an outsider, a disgruntled villager for example, the murders had to have been committed by one of the people they had already encountered.

No one else appeared to have a strong enough reason to murder Micah, certainly. Various people seemed to have motives, some stronger than others, especially in Titus's case. The motive for Micah's death seemed much less clear. He sensed this was what Kitty was grappling with.

It seemed there was little more progress that would be made that day. Once back at the house, and with Kitty's agreement, he changed and took his golf clubs to hit a few balls on the course. He often found being outdoors helped him to think.

The course, somewhat surprisingly considering the fine weather, was quiet. He made his round of nine holes in good time before deciding that was sufficient for the day and heading back inside to the bar. A swift drink to ease his parched throat and he would return home in time to change for dinner with Kitty.

The club house too was quiet and Samuel, the club steward, was whiling away his time by polishing the glasses behind the bar.

He stopped when Matt arrived and immediately came to serve him.

'Good afternoon, Captain Bryant. Another fine afternoon today.'

'It is indeed, Samuel, I thought more members would be playing,' Matt agreed, before ordering a pint of beer.

He took a seat on one of the leather-topped brass-legged stools at the bar.

'It was busy earlier today, sir. I think you've caught the lull,' Samuel confirmed as he pulled the pint and placed the glass in front of Matt.

Matt paid the man and took a sip of his drink. 'It's thirsty work out there, although I suppose this fine weather won't hold for much longer.'

'No, sir, I suppose not. Are you very busy in your line of work at the minute?' Samuel asked as he picked up a cloth to start cleaning the area around the beer pulls.

Matt knew the steward was very familiar with Matt's profession since he had shown an interest before in previous cases when they had been finished and the matters had gone to court.

'Enough to keep me out of trouble,' Matt said lightly.

'Those murders are bad over at Stoke Gabriel,' Samuel said.

'Titus and Micah Blake, you mean? Did you know them at all?' Matt knew that the steward was a local man, but he wasn't sure which village he lived in.

'Yes, sir, I did. I was born in Stoke Gabriel, although I live just down the road in Churston nowadays. I used to get my cider from Wassail Farm like a good many others I suppose.

Titus Blake wasn't a very nice man, used to cause a lot of trouble with one thing and another.' Samuel set about cleaning the bar top.

'Did you know the son, Micah, at all?' Matt asked.

'Yes, sir, used to see him about the place. Had a bit of a temper like his father, but generally he kept himself to himself.' Samuel leaned on the newly cleaned counter, clearly happy to take five minutes' break for a chat.

'I can understand why some people might have a grudge against Titus but why would Micah be killed?' Matt was interested to hear the steward's take on matters.

'A lot of people hereabouts thought that Micah had killed his father. No one would have blamed him the way the old man treated him. He didn't treat any of those lads very well,' Samuel said, his brow crinkling as he pondered the problem. 'Then, now Micah has been killed, that has started people worrying. I can only think as Micah knew who had done it, or had seen something that could set the police down the path to the killer.'

Matt murmured his agreement with Samuel's thoughts since they seemed to reflect his and Kitty's own ideas on the matter.

'Do you know the other sons, Saul and Adam?' Matt asked.

'Oh yes. Saul is a proper farmer. He's done well working with his uncle once he managed to get free of his father. He's courting Abigail West, the housekeeper at Wassail. I've seen them a couple of times in the lane when they thought as no one was about. I reckon they didn't want old Titus to find out. He'd not have been pleased if the girl had gone off elsewhere.' Samuel looked at Matt. 'The girl's been seen with some right bruises at times. Claimed as she bumped into a door, or fell over the dogs.'

Matt could hear the disapproval in Samuel's tone. The steward's testimony seemed to bear out what he had witnessed for himself.

'Do you think Hedley and Norma would be happy with Saul courting Abigail? He seems to be being groomed to take over at Blossomdown when his uncle steps down,' Matt said.

The steward's frown deepened. 'I reckon as they'd be happy enough. The lass works hard, and she knows how to run a farm.'

Matt sipped his pint. 'What about Adam, the youngest boy? He's left the farm behind, hasn't he?'

Samuel snorted. 'He were always the brains of the three of them. Very close to Saul after he saved his life when they were kids.'

'Saul saved Adam's life?' Matt wanted to be certain he had understood the man correctly.

'Aye. Saul would be about ten and Adam about eight. They'd gone swimming in the creek. Saul was always a good swimmer. Adam, not so much. Well, Adam got in trouble in the water and young Saul swam out and saved him, dragged him back to the shore. Titus were furious. Banned them all from swimming after that.' Samuel straightened up as if ready to continue with his bar duties.

'And now Adam works for a solicitor's firm in Totnes. He seems to be doing well for himself.' Matt finished his drink and placed the empty glass down on the counter.

'He'll always land on his feet that one. His old teacher helped get him that job. Since then he's had a few strokes of luck. One of the clients took a bit of a shine to him, left him that car he drives around and a bit of money when she passed away.' Samuel collected the glass ready to take it to be washed.

'Really? Who was the client?' Matt asked. This was all news to him. He had assumed Adam had earned the money for his car.

'An elderly woman, a Mrs Tromans, a widow. Terrible really, she fell down the stone steps outside the back of her house and broke her neck. They reckoned she probably slipped on the moss. It was damp weather, and she was wearing house slippers.'

'That's tragic,' Matt agreed, standing up from his seat. He was keen to return home to share this new information with Kitty.

He wasn't sure if any of it would help them to find the murderer, but it did at least provide them with more information.

CHAPTER TWENTY-ONE

Kitty listened attentively to Matt over dinner as he recounted his conversation with the club steward.

'Saul saved Adam's life from drowning? That was terribly brave and very quick thinking from such a young boy,' she said as they sat at the dining table eating the shepherd's pie their housekeeper had left for their supper.

'Samuel said the two younger boys had always been close. I suppose because they are nearer in age, even though it was only by a matter of months. It sounds as if Micah was always more the outsider of the three of them,' Matt agreed.

'They do still seem quite close now. What do you make of this tale about this poor woman who died and left Adam her car and some money? I suppose her death was an accident?' Kitty was troubled by this new revelation. Could Adam have been involved with the woman's death?

'I assume the coroner must have been satisfied and no one apart from Samuel has mentioned it before, so clearly it roused no suspicions at the time,' Matt said.

'I suppose it may be worth asking Chief Inspector Greville if he remembers anything about the case?' Kitty asked. She knew the chief inspector had a good memory for local cases.

Matt finished eating and placed his cutlery down on his empty plate. 'It may not have been his area, but he could always make enquiries if he did not know much about it himself.'

'I expect it will be another dead end, but perhaps there is something there. I don't see how it would tie into his brother and his father's deaths though. Adam has been very clear that he has no interest in farming.' Kitty finished her own dinner and sat back in her seat.

'I'll telephone the chief inspector tomorrow and ask. I think we should have something of a day off tomorrow, unless anything else comes to light. You have your evening out planned with Alice and I have agreed to meet Robert Potter and his father at the Ship Inn in Dartmouth for a game of billiards,' Matt said as Kitty collected their empty plates ready to take them away.

'I agree. I think perhaps a few hours away from the case might give us some perspective.' Kitty carried the dirty plates to the scullery and returned bearing two dishes of apple pie and a jug of cream. She knew a short break from thinking about their work usually helped to provide her with the solution.

Kitty set the desserts down on the table and Matt helped himself to cream. She refrained from asking him when he had arranged his billiards date. He regularly met up with Robert and his father in Dartmouth for a drink and a game.

She also knew he knew something more about Alice and Robert's parting of the ways. Since it seemed, however, that he had been sworn to secrecy she had never broached the subject with him, despite being tempted on many occasions.

After dinner they sat in the drawing room and listened to a play on the radio. Kitty's mind kept going over the case. It seemed to her unlikely that Abigail or Norma could have killed Micah alone. Together they would have had more motive, and it was clear the women had bonded over Norma's secret. They would have had the opportunity and they stood to benefit from both men's deaths.

Hedley too could have killed his brother. Feelings had been running high over the land and the water rights. Then he could have murdered Micah to ensure he could combine the farms and clear the way for Saul and Abigail to run Wassail Farm together.

Or he may have finally stumbled upon Norma's secret and taken his revenge on his brother. Micah may have discovered what Hedley had done, forcing the older man to kill his nephew.

Saul may have resented his father for his ill-treatment of Abigail and then murdered his brother so that he could marry her, and they could live at Wassail Farm. She supposed Adam might have helped him. He could have found out the conditions of the trust and Titus's will to try and help his brother.

Even Mr and Mrs Pickering were still in the frame. They too had opportunity and the constant arguments with Titus and his attempts to ruin their business would give them a motive. Then they might have killed Micah if he had inadvertently stumbled on something that could lead to their arrests, or if he kept trespassing on their land.

The play finished and Matt switched off the radio. 'You seemed very preoccupied during that?' he remarked.

'I keep thinking about this wretched case.' Kitty looked at her husband. 'There is just no evidence to put anyone at the scene. They all seem to have opportunity and motive, and I can't help feeling that whatever we are searching for to solve this is just out of our reach.'

'All the more reason to step back from it for a little while. I'll see if there is anything in that business with Adam that Samuel told me about. Apart from that, we've agreed to take tomorrow off and then perhaps on Thursday we shall have a better idea of where we need to follow up,' Matt said soothingly.

Kitty was forced to agree and followed her husband reluctantly upstairs, convinced that she wouldn't sleep a wink all night.

Much to her surprise she woke late the next morning. Mrs Smith had already arrived and she heard the low rumble of Matt's voice in the hall downstairs as he took Bertie outside.

She washed and dressed hastily, shivering as she did so. Despite the sunshine outside her bedroom window the scent of autumn was very much in the air as she hurried downstairs. After greeting the housekeeper and petting her cat, she took herself into the dining room to warm up in front of the fire.

'Boiled eggs suit you, Mrs Bryant?' Mrs Smith asked as she carried in the teapot and placed Matt's morning paper beside his breakfast place.

'That would be lovely, thank you,' Kitty agreed and sat herself at the table to await her husband's return from walking the dog on the common.

The telephone in the hall rang before she had a chance to pour herself a cup of tea. She rose to answer it, calling to Mrs Smith to ignore it.

To her surprise it was Mrs Pickering who was on the other end of the line. 'Mrs Bryant, I wonder if you and your husband might come to see us today. As soon as possible if you could.'

'Certainly, Mrs Pickering, is something wrong?' Kitty could hear the distress in the woman's voice.

'I'd rather not say on the telephone. If we could expect you shortly?' the woman asked, her voice wobbling as she spoke.

'Of course. Matt is out with our dog, but we'll come over as soon as we can,' Kitty promised.

She replaced the receiver and wandered back into the

dining room. Matt re-entered the house a moment later with Bertie bustling into the dining room ahead of him, sniffing hopefully at the table.

'Mrs Pickering has just telephoned. She wants us to call on her as soon as possible. She wouldn't say why but she sounded distressed,' Kitty said.

Mrs Smith carried their eggs and a rack of toast into the room and placed it on the table.

'We had better have a hasty breakfast then,' Matt said.

They ate quickly and set off for the Pickerings' stables, leaving Bertie with Mrs Smith. The gate to the stable yard was standing open but there was no one in sight as Kitty swung her car to a stop in front of the farmhouse.

The horses were in the stables and two of them popped their heads over the tops of the half-open doors as Kitty turned off the car engine. Mrs Pickering opened the door to the farmhouse before Kitty could raise her hand to the horseshoe-shaped brass door knocker.

'Mrs Bryant, Captain Bryant, thank you for coming so quickly. We just didn't know what we should do.' Mrs Pickering led them into the kitchen, where Mr Pickering was at the table.

Kitty was immediately struck by the expression of hopelessness on Mr Pickering's disfigured face. His wife went immediately to his side as he rose to greet them, shaking their hands before retaking his seat.

Lying on the table in front of them was a small pile of post. A circular, a couple of what appeared to be bills and in the centre of the table a cheap white envelope. Kitty could see it had been opened and the paperknife lay nearby.

'We received something dreadful in this morning's post.' Mrs Pickering's hand trembled as she indicated the opened letter.

'Who has handled it?' Matt asked as he pulled a clean, white-cotton handkerchief from his pocket.

'Just the two of us,' Mrs Pickering said, glancing at her husband.

Matt used his handkerchief to extract the contents of the envelope, taking care not to touch it.

'I don't expect there will be any useful fingerprints. I think every criminal these days has read of how this may be used by the police in their investigations,' Matt said as he opened the thin sheet of paper.

Kitty peeped over his shoulder to read the contents. It was as she had anticipated, an anonymous letter, compiled of words cut from presumably a newspaper and pasted onto the paper.

I know what you did. Pay me £100 and I can make this go away. Leave the money tomorrow evening at 6 p.m. at the Quay in Stoke Gabriel in the red flowerpot by the stone wall. Do not involve the police or it will be the worse for you.

Matt had read the letter aloud and Kitty saw Mrs Pickering's face blanch. Her husband placed a tender hand on his wife's arm. Matt placed the letter on the tabletop and, again, using his handkerchief, examined the envelope.

'It seems to be a local postmark. Posted in Churston yesterday evening,' Matt said.

Mrs Pickering threw up her hands to cover her face resting her elbows on the tabletop. Silent sobs seemed to wrack through her body. Mr Pickering patted his wife's back, his own puckered face bewildered and distressed.

'Do you have any idea what the writer of this note may be referring to?' Kitty asked in a gentle tone.

'No idea whatsoever. We can only assume that whoever sent this thinks we had something to do with the murders at Wassail Farm. Why else would they ask for such a large sum of money out of the blue in such a fashion?' Mr Pickering's moustache trembled with indignation. 'It's ridiculous.'

Mrs Pickering accepted her husband's offer of his handkerchief and blew her nose. 'We have no idea what this is about. We didn't do anything, we didn't see anything, anything we know we have told to you and to the police. Someone is out to drive us away from here. They want to ruin us and our business,' she gulped as she spoke.

'My wife, as you can see, is very distressed. This business is our everything. All our savings went into the purchase, and we work hard to make a living here. We are not wealthy people. We grow our own food and live simple lives.' Mr Pickering looked at his wife.

'Who hates us this much? When Reg was invalided out of the army, he couldn't get work. I did everything I could until we could get this place. This is supposed to be our sanctuary, and now this.' The woman burst into silent sobs once more that seemed to wrack her entire body.

'Needless to say, we have no fear of the police, but will they believe us? You know what people are like. If this got out, the gossip would ruin our business. Titus Blake had already cost us several of our boarders which has affected our income. The murders have put people off booking lessons or rides.' Mr Pickering sighed heavily. 'We didn't know what to do for the best.' He rose from his seat and paced about the kitchen as if searching for a way to relieve his feelings.

'I said to Reginald that you were a former military man, Captain Bryant, and you understand these things. You'd know how best to advise us.' Mrs Pickering turned a teary, hopeful gaze on Matt. 'My husband fought for this country. It's not right that we should be treated like this.'

Kitty could see the Pickerings' dilemma. Yes, if they were innocent as they claimed then they should simply give the note to Inspector Lewis or Chief Inspector Greville and have done with it.

On the other hand, she could see that they were fearful of

more damage being done to their business and the lasting implications that such rumours might have upon them. Mr Pickering was clearly a man who had suffered grave injuries during the Great War. She knew from Matt's experiences that having this kind of unpleasantness thrust upon such a man could cause untold mental anguish.

'I am flattered by your trust in me, Mrs Pickering. This will take some thought as to how it should be handled. I must double-check with both of you that you are absolutely certain that there is nothing at all that either of you can recall that the writer of this letter may be referring to?' Matt asked, looking at both of the Pickerings.

Mrs Pickering shook her head. 'Nothing.'

Mr Pickering's back was ramrod straight as he turned in his pacing to face Matt. 'No, Captain Bryant, we are quite certain. Our consciences are completely clear. We are both entirely baffled as to why this note was sent to us.'

Matt nodded. 'Very well. I think for now, do nothing. Kitty and I shall make some more enquiries first. It may be that our blackmailer has targeted others besides yourselves hoping to hit upon the right person.' He carefully picked up the note and envelope and passed it to Kitty, who dropped it inside her handbag.

Mr Pickering sucked in a breath. 'Then I think whoever did this is playing a foolish and dangerous game,' he said.

CHAPTER TWENTY-TWO

They left the Pickerings after promising to let them know what they managed to discover about any other letters.

'Do you believe them? That they have no idea about what the blackmailer is referring to?' Kitty asked as they pulled out of the Pickerings' livery yard.

'At this point in time, yes. Of all the people involved in this business they seem the least likely to resort to murder as a way of solving their problems with Titus and Micah Blake,' Matt said.

Kitty drove a few yards along the road and pulled to a stop in front of a farm gate. 'You are not being swayed by the military connection?' she asked. She phrased her question delicately, not wishing to distress Matt. It must have been hard for him to witness Mr Pickering's own discomfort at the farm.

'I don't believe so. Yet, I will admit I am very concerned for Reginald Pickering.' He glanced at Kitty, a thoughtful expression on his face.

'Oh? How so?' she asked.

'Pickering is struggling with all of this. I've seen it before in other men who have been in his position. He is a proud man living in reduced circumstances, forced to rely on his wife,' Matt said. He was clearly bothered about the interview they had just had at the stables.

'He clearly loves her dearly and she him,' Kitty said. She thought the affection between the couple was palpable. 'You don't think we should take this letter to Chief Inspector Greville?'

'No, not yet. There was a look about Reginald Pickering that worried me.' Matt was staring ahead of him now, as if his gaze was fixed on a spray of blackberries growing on a bramble in the hedgerow.

'What do you mean?' A shiver danced its way along Kitty's spine and it was as if a shadow had passed overhead temporarily blocking out the autumn sunshine.

'I've seen that look before. A man who thinks he has become a burden to the woman he loves and takes his own life thinking he is acting selflessly.' Matt's mouth was set in a grim line. 'I think Mr Pickering is close to that edge. This business of the letter could push him over. The police can wait for now.' He turned his head to look at Kitty. 'Let's call at Blossomdown and see if anyone there has received a letter today.'

Kitty could see her husband was deadly serious. 'Very well, Blossomdown it is.' She put her car in gear and continued along the road passing Wassail Farm. The gate there was closed and the farmhouse door shut.

She doubted that Abigail would have received such a letter. The girl had no money at all, something that was well known locally. A blackmailer would be wasting their time there. Of course, it could be that Abigail was the blackmailer, trying her luck to get some money for her future.

Kitty had just pulled her car to a halt in front of the farmhouse at Blossomdown when the farmhouse door was flung open, and Norma Blake came hurrying towards them.

'Captain Bryant, Kitty, I've been trying to get hold of you all morning. I called your office and your house...' She broke off breathlessly as Kitty opened her car door to get out.

'I presume you've received a letter?' Kitty said as Matt joined her at the side of the car.

'Yes, yes, I have. How did you know?' The woman stopped and looked at them in bewilderment as if they had performed some kind of conjuring trick.

'Perhaps we should go inside and discuss the matter?' Kitty suggested.

'Oh yes, yes, of course. It came this morning. Thank goodness I didn't open my post until Hedley and Saul had gone to the fields,' Norma babbled as they entered the farmhouse.

This time she took them into her kitchen and Kitty thought this was clearly a mark of Norma's distress. She was a lady that cared about appearances and liked her guests to preferably use her large and comfortable sitting room.

Once Kitty and Matt were seated at the scrubbed pine kitchen table Norma thrust a trembling hand into the front pocket of her pinafore and pulled out an envelope. It looked the same as the one the Pickerings had received and which was now nestled in the depths of Kitty's leather handbag.

Since Kitty was still wearing her driving gloves, she took the envelope and opened it to take out the contents. She placed it on the kitchen table so they could read it. It said virtually the same thing as the one the Pickerings had received, except it asked for five hundred pounds to be placed at the quayside at 6.15 p.m. the next day.

Again, it looked as if the words and letters had been cut from a newspaper and had been glued to cheap plain paper.

Matt let out a low whistle when he saw the amount. 'Our blackmailer is much greedier this time,' he said.

Mrs Blake stared at him. 'I don't understand. What do you mean?'

'You are not the only person to have received a note of this kind today. The other recipient was asked for one hundred pounds,' Kitty said.

Norma sank down on the vacant kitchen chair next to Kitty's. 'I thought I was the only one who would get this. I thought when it said we know what you did they were talking about...' Her voice tailed off and she swallowed as if suddenly realising what the letter writer was referring to.

'It's clear whoever wrote this means the murders at Wassail. Not the other private matter which you shared with us the other day,' Kitty said.

Colour started to return to the woman's pale cheeks. 'I never thought. I just immediately thought it had to be about the baby.'

Kitty could see why Norma had thought that. The phrasing '*I know what you did*,' would have immediately stirred the woman's conscience.

'Someone is hoping for a good payday tomorrow evening.' Matt looked thoughtful.

'Someone who is preparing to make a run for it?' Kitty suggested. 'And wants the money to get away?'

'Or who is hoping that if they try enough people, they might discover who killed Titus and Micah,' Matt said.

'I was on my own here when I opened it. I didn't know what to do. I thought it had to be about Sebastian, so I just panicked. I thought what if Hedley finds out? How can I get that sum of money?' Norma stared at the offending letter.

'The postmark is local, the same as the other one,' Matt said.

'Who else has had a letter?' Norma asked.

'We can't say for now, but we have it in our possession and are looking into the matter. May we take your letter too?' Matt asked.

'Will you give it to the police?' Norma asked, a shadow of something like fear flickering across her face.

'Not immediately,' Matt assured her. 'You are certain that

you have told us everything you know about Titus and Micah's murders?' His voice took on a slightly stern note.

'Yes, everything. I have nothing to tell as I don't know anything. I should hardly have asked you to investigate if I had anything to hide.' Norma sounded affronted by the suggestion that she had been holding something back.

'Of course, Mrs Blake,' Kitty soothed as she added Norma's letter to the other one inside her handbag.

'Please don't worry and don't think anything more about this note. Kitty and I will take care of things,' Matt assured the woman.

Norma seemed to relax once the letter was out of sight and safely stowed away. They said goodbye to Norma and went back out to Kitty's car.

'Right, now what?' Kitty asked as they both raised a hand in farewell to Norma and drove out of the yard.

'Let's go back to the house and get a closer look at these notes in case there is something we've missed,' Matt suggested.

'Very well. It's almost lunchtime anyway and I would rather Bertie didn't destroy any more of my soft furnishings because he thinks he is not getting his dinner,' Kitty replied with a smile.

Mrs Smith greeted them as soon as they entered the house, her usually easy-going expression replaced by one of annoyance. 'There is a Mrs Blake been after you. At least a half-dozen telephone messages she's left.'

'Thank you. I'm so sorry she troubled you. We've called to see her now, so she shouldn't call again,' Kitty said as she leafed through the pile of notes next to the hall telephone.

Mrs Smith raised an eyebrow as if doubting the veracity of this statement and returned to the scullery to finish mopping her floor.

Bertie danced around them, his tail wagging a welcome.

Rascal, as usual, had found a soft spot to lie where a pool of sunlight could warm his fur. Kitty took off her hat and gloves and fluffed up her blonde curls.

'Let's take those notes into the dining room where the light is better,' Matt suggested.

Kitty carried her bag into the dining room and opened it up. Matt used his handkerchief once more to extract the letters.

'The envelopes are both marked for Churston yesterday evening. The stationery is cheap and of the sort that can be found anywhere,' Kitty said, looking at the envelopes.

Matt placed the two letters side by side to compare the contents.

'I should say they were cut from the same source. It looks like a newspaper,' Matt said.

'Yes, and they have joined various parts of words together to form some of the words, presumably since they couldn't find what they wanted in the paper.' Kitty looked at the letters. 'It definitely looks like a fishing exercise to try and extract money without any real proof.'

'Whoever sent these has certainly distressed the Pickerings and frightened Norma Blake half to death. I wonder if anyone else has received a letter?' Matt mused.

'It's interesting the letter was addressed just to Norma and not to Hedley, don't you think?' Kitty said.

'You think he may have had a separate letter?' Matt looked at her. 'It's possible, but he didn't say anything to Norma, and she said he opened his post before he went out.'

Kitty gave a slight shrug. 'Unless he did receive one but there is something he did that the blackmailer has stumbled upon.'

Matt stroked his chin thoughtfully. 'Or our blackmailer has heard of Norma's inheritance. I wonder if Adam Blake has received one?'

'The blackmailer will have surely tried everyone who they

think may have money. Adam appears to be comfortable financially,' Kitty said.

'True. He is not at work though, and we don't have his address so we can't ask him,' Matt pointed out.

The telephone rang again, and Matt went to answer it before Mrs Smith could become annoyed at having her work disrupted yet again. He returned to the dining room after a few minutes.

'That was the chief inspector. He was answering the message I left for him about the woman who died in Totnes and left Adam Blake her car and some money. He remembers the case, although he was not working on it. The woman had a distant cousin who caused a bit of a fuss after the funeral when they found out about the bequests. However, since the cousin got the house and some other quite substantial assets, that didn't really go anywhere. The coroner was satisfied the death was accidental. The woman had a habit of putting out bread for the birds and they think she went out in her house slippers and slipped on the stone steps at the rear of the house,' Matt said.

'It seems there is nothing there then,' Kitty said. 'What do we do now, about these letters? We really should pass them on to Inspector Lewis.' She looked at Matt.

'Ordinarily I would agree with you. However, I think we have a golden opportunity to trap a blackmailer,' Matt said.

'You mean we should pretend to follow these instructions and lie in wait to see who picks up the goods?' Kitty said.

Matt grinned at her, the dimple showing in his cheek.

'You don't think that if the blackmailer has sent out other letters that we may not be aware of that there may be some danger involved in this?' Kitty said.

'If the murderer has received a letter you mean?' Matt asked.

'Well, yes.' Kitty could see someone who had killed twice would have no compunction about killing someone else who they thought might know their secret. If they lay in wait for the blackmailer, the murderer might do exactly the same thing.

She also couldn't help thinking that it might be wiser to give the letters to Chief Inspector Greville or Inspector Lewis and let the police set a trap for the blackmailer. She could see though that Matt was deeply concerned for Mr Pickering and what actions he might take if the police were involved.

At least they had until tomorrow evening to come up with a plan.

CHAPTER TWENTY-THREE

Kitty was still mulling things over when she set off to meet Alice at the picture house at Paignton that evening. Her afternoon had been spent catching up on the errands she had intended to run in the morning and discussing various ideas about what they should do the next day with Matt.

Matt had already left on his Sunbeam motorcycle to meet with the Potters at the Ship Inn at Dartmouth for his planned game of billiards. It was a pleasant evening but now the sun was much lower in the sky there was a distinct nip back in the air. Kitty snuggled down into her coat and adjusted the fur collar around her neck.

She decided to put the roof up on her car, anticipating that it would be cooler still when she and Alice emerged from the picture house later. She parked on the street near the seafront and hurried to meet her friend.

Alice was waiting for her as usual just outside the entrance. She looked very pretty, Kitty thought, in her pale-green summer coat and a soft-green hat trimmed with pink ribbon. Her auburn hair curling around her slim face.

'It should be a good one tonight,' Alice said after Kitty had greeted her.

'What are we seeing?' Kitty asked looking up at the posters. She always left the choice of film to her friend.

'*The Crimson Circle*. It's a crime one about blackmailers,' Alice remarked cheerfully. 'It should be right up your street.'

Kitty looked at the bright-yellow film poster and suppressed a sigh. It seemed she was unable to escape blackmail plots even on her night out.

'Lovely.' Kitty tucked her hand into the crook of her friend's arm, and they headed inside to purchase sweets and tickets.

When they emerged some two hours or so later, the street was dark, and the lamps had come on.

'You'm very quiet tonight,' Alice observed, looking at Kitty as they walked towards the fish and chip shop. 'Didn't you enjoy the film?'

'Oh, the film was good, and very appropriate at the moment. I've a lot on my mind with this case,' Kitty said.

There was a queue for fish and chips, so they stood in silence outside the steamed-up window until they were able to enter and get their portions of cod and chips. Once they were clutching their hot, newspaper-wrapped bundles and away from the small crowd, Alice asked, 'Want to tell me about it?'

They found a seat in one of the wooden shelters that over-looked the moonlit sea and dug into their supper. The hot chips and fish warmed their hands as they ate, and the delicious aroma of vinegar scented the air. Kitty told Alice of the latest developments in the murders.

'Mr and Mrs Pickering and Norma Blake have received black-mail letters implying they were involved in the murders. They have been asked to deliver quite sizeable ransoms by tomorrow evening.'

'Blackmail letters! That's like the film we just saw,' her friend exclaimed as she daintily nibbled on a piece of batter.

'Yes, except we don't have the benefit of Scotland Yard's assistance, instead we have Inspector Lewis,' Kitty remarked with a wry smile.

Alice giggled. 'Very true, and you say as Captain Bryant thinks as you ought to try and catch whoever wrote these letters yourself rather than go to the police?' Her brow crinkled into a frown. 'That's not like him. Normally it would be you wanting to do something hot-headed and him persuading you to do the right thing.'

Kitty sighed. 'I know, it is a bit of a switch. I think it's because of the Pickerings. Matt saw such dreadful things during the war. He is worried Mr Pickering may do something drastic. The poor man's nerves seem quite shot.'

'Do you think his sympathy is misplaced?' Alice asked.

'I don't know. I saw that Mr Pickering wasn't at all well. His wife looked very concerned.' Kitty stared gloomily at the waves lapping gently on the dark beach.

'He could still have done away with the Blakes,' Alice said.

Kitty grinned at her friend. 'Yes, I suppose he could. It would have to have been both of them I think, though. Mr Pickering's injuries are too severe for him to have acted alone.'

Alice was right. It was possible that the Pickerings were the killers. All afternoon Kitty had been trying to think who the blackmailer might be. Her most likely suspect was Abigail West, since the girl had no money and was familiar with all of the people involved in the case. Her other thought had been that Saul Blake also may have wanted money to start his married life with Abigail.

'Well, I can't say as I think it's a good idea for you and Captain Bryant to go trying to catch whoever sent them letters. Suppose the murderer turns up,' Alice said as she finished her supper and prepared to throw her chip papers in a nearby bin.

'I know. We at least have all of tomorrow to come up with a plan,' Kitty said as she too finished eating.

'Perhaps Captain Bryant might have a change of mind overnight and decide to go to the police after all. Surely Chief Inspector Greville would be tactful about Mr Pickering?' Alice said as she stood and took Kitty's papers to get rid of them along with her own.

'I think so. I'll see what Matt thinks when he has had time to reflect.' Kitty took out an old cotton handkerchief to clean her fingers.

'Where is Captain Bryant tonight?' Alice asked as she came back from disposing of their wrappers.

'He is in Dartmouth, at the Ship.' Kitty knew she didn't have to say anything more since Alice would guess who he was meeting.

Alice, as she had expected, refrained from commenting beyond giving a slightly derisive sniff. They walked the short distance to Kitty's car so that she could give Alice a lift back to her small flat over the top of her shop in Winner Street. The street was quiet again now since the cinemagoers had all dispersed and the fish and chip shop was preparing to close.

'I hope as Captain Bryant changes his mind and tells the police about those letters tomorrow,' Alice said, when Kitty pulled to a stop a moment later in front of Alice's shop. 'I don't like the idea of you both trying to catch a blackmailer.'

'Perhaps he will. In any case, we shall be very careful, I promise,' Kitty said as Alice opened the passenger door to leave the car.

'Well, mind you are, and telephone me later as I'm not spending all evening fretting,' Alice said.

'I will. Don't worry, it'll probably turn out to be nothing and no one will even turn up,' Kitty said.

Alice closed the car door and Kitty waited until her friend

was inside and a light switched on before driving off to go back home to Churston.

* * *

Matt had spent a pleasant evening at the Ship with Mr Potter senior and his son, Robert. They had played a couple of games of billiards and drunk a couple of pints of beer together. Mr Potter left shortly before closing time, leaving Matt and Robert to finish their drinks before Matt caught the last ferry of the night across the river.

'Kitty is meeting Alice at the picture house in Paignton this evening.' Matt glanced at his friend.

'Oh aye,' Robert said. 'Alice is fond of a film.' He gave a small, sad smile.

'Will she still not talk to you?' Matt asked. He could have asked Kitty about the situation from Alice's point of view, but he knew his wife would not think kindly of him asking questions.

Robert shook his head glumly. 'I tried to explain when I last saw her, but she wasn't in the mood to listen. Fiery lass is my Alice. Comes with her hair.'

'Perhaps she may come round in time,' Matt suggested.

'It's been months now and she's started her business and set herself up in that little flat over the top of the workshop. I think it's probably too late.' Robert stared morosely at the dregs in the bottom of his dimple-glassed pint pot.

'Never say never.' Matt clapped him on the shoulder.

'Anyway, how are you doing these days? You involved in those murders across the river?' Robert asked, after glancing around the pub to ensure that no one could overhear them.

Matt gave him a brief precis of all that they had discovered, leaving out a few of the details to spare Norma and Dora. He then went on to tell Robert about the blackmail letters.

'You going to give them to that Inspector Lewis?' Robert asked.

Matt knew Robert and most of Dartmouth were not enamoured of the inspector after the murder of a beauty queen contestant in the town several months earlier. His handling of the case had not gone well, and Matt and Kitty had almost been killed before the murderer had been caught.

'Kitty and I have been discussing it all afternoon. The problem is I am concerned for Mr Pickering. I met several men like him at the end of the war. The man's nerves are gone and any kind of pressure at this point might have a catastrophic, even fatal, effect on him,' Matt said.

Robert nodded gravely. 'Then go to Chief Inspector Greville. He has a bit more about him. You can tell him you'm worried about Mr Pickering.'

'True. Or we could try and trap this blackmailer ourselves,' Matt said.

'Why though? I mean from what you say whoever has wrote them letters clearly doesn't know who the murderer is, so catching them won't give you the killer.' Robert swallowed the last mouthful of his beer as the landlord rang the brass ship's bell for time.

'I suppose we hoped that the blackmailer might lure the murderer into the open.' Matt too finished his beer and placed his empty glass down on the bar.

Robert chuckled. 'Like a bit of cheese in a mousetrap.'

'Something like that,' Matt agreed. 'Either way, I intend to be near the quay at Stoke Gabriel tomorrow evening to see who might turn up.'

* * *

Kitty rose just after dawn the next morning. The matter of the letters and what they should do about them had continued to lie heavily on her mind all night. Matt was downstairs not long after her and he entered the kitchen to find her making a pot of tea.

'You're up early,' he said, bending to pet Bertie who was delighted to see both of them around at such an early hour.

'I couldn't sleep. I kept thinking about those letters and what we should do.' Kitty looked at Matt.

'You would prefer that I give them to Chief Inspector Greville, or our friend Inspector Lewis,' Matt said, taking the laden tea tray from her and carrying it into the dining room.

'Yes. I understand why you are reluctant and if it were only Inspector Lewis involved with the case I would agree that we should say nothing until after we have apprehended the blackmailer,' Kitty said unhappily as she took a seat on one of the polished rosewood dining chairs.

Matt set the tray down on the table. 'Very well. I shall telephone Chief Inspector Greville after breakfast and see if we can go and see him.'

Kitty brightened immediately. 'I am sure we can trust him to act discreetly. He may well let us be involved in setting a trap for the blackmailer.'

True to his word, Matt telephoned the police station at Torquay as soon as breakfast was finished and ascertained that Chief Inspector Greville would be happy to see them. The morning air was cool and misty with a heavy dew still lying on the grass as Kitty drove them to Torquay.

She would feel much happier once the letters were out of her handbag and on the chief inspector's desk. The desk sergeant greeted them affably as they entered the station. He knew both of them well from previous visits. A grizzled man approaching retirement, he had always been sympathetic to their work.

'Morning, Captain Bryant, Mrs Bryant. Chief Inspector Greville is expecting you.' He swung up the hatch to allow them behind his counter, before opening the door leading to the offices.

'Thank you.' Kitty smiled at the man as he led them along the cream and pale-green painted walls, passing the chief inspector's former office, now given to Inspector Lewis, before halting in front of a door near the steps that led down to the cells.

The sergeant rapped on the door and Kitty heard the chief inspector call for them to enter. The office was in the shambolic chaos that Kitty had come to find was usual for the chief inspector. Teetering piles of paper and brown manilla folders were stacked untidily on his desk. An overflowing metal ashtray and an empty used green teacup and saucer stood amidst the paperwork.

The chief inspector removed one of the piles from a bentwood chair in front of his desk and invited them to sit down.

'Now then, what can I do for you both?' He looked at them as Kitty took her place next to Matt, after brushing what looked like cheese crumbs from her chair.

She opened her handbag and using her gloved hand took out the blackmail letters. 'These have come into our possession.' She carefully didn't say they had been given them yesterday.

'Oh yes.' Chief Inspector Greville's moustache twitched, and he waited for her to extract the letters from the envelopes so he could read them.

'One to Mrs Norma Blake and one to Mr and Mrs Pickering,' the chief inspector said. 'Postmarked Tuesday evening.'

'Neither the Pickerings nor Mrs Blake have any further information about what it is the blackmailer is alleging they have done,' Kitty said, glancing at Matt.

'And they are both supposed to place large sums of money inside a plant pot on the quay at Stoke Gabriel this evening for whoever wrote these letters to collect.' Chief Inspector

Greville's brows raised as he read the arrangements. 'Hmm, has anyone else received a letter, do you know?'

'No, sir. We thought Adam Blake may have had one, but we have no way of discovering if that's the case. His employer has given him some time off work to make arrangements for the funerals and to assist his family,' Kitty said.

'The solicitor Adam works for is visiting Blossomdown today to make Hedley Blake aware of the ramifications of the trust, now it's been untangled.' The chief inspector continued to look thoughtful.

'I wonder what the Blakes will do about Wassail Farm?' Kitty said.

'Yes, that will be interesting. It will solve the argument over the land and water rights I imagine.' Chief Inspector Greville looked at the letters. 'I don't imagine we will be able to extract any useful prints from the envelopes. I presume the Pickerings and Mrs Blake have handled the letters themselves?'

'Yes, that's correct,' Matt agreed. 'Mr Pickering seems to have taken the arrival of this letter very hard. He is a war veteran, as you know, sir, and was badly injured. I was very concerned about his welfare when he informed us about the blackmail threat. He is a man close to the edge.'

Matt phrased his words carefully and Kitty hoped the chief inspector would understand the implications of what her husband was suggesting.

'In other words, tread carefully, eh? Perhaps best not to allow Inspector Lewis to place his size ten boots all over things.' The chief inspector gave a brief smile and Kitty was relieved he had picked up on their unspoken concern.

'Perhaps it might be as well to take care,' Kitty agreed.

'Well, the existence of two virtually identical letters to two different parties suggests that whoever wrote these is a bit of a chancer. They clearly don't know who the murderer is, they are just trying people who they think might have the ability to pay up rather than risk exposure of some kind.' The chief inspector's thoughts seemed to mirror their own conclusions about the author of the letters.

'We were worried that if the writer had sent more than these two letters and one had gone to the murderer, a third death might follow,' Matt said.

Chief Inspector Greville frowned as he looked at the envelopes. 'I'm afraid you might be right. I think we need to apprehend whoever wrote these for their own safety, as much as anything else.'

'Who do you think could have written them?' Kitty asked.

'Now there lies the problem. It could be Miss West; we know she hasn't two brass farthings to rub together. Her bequest in the will wasn't large. Then her sweetheart, Saul Blake, he might need some money, but I can't see him blackmailing his aunt after she's been so good to him. Or, the most likely thing, is someone outside the immediate family who we don't know of,' the chief inspector said.

'Like Jim, the Blakes' cowman?' Kitty suggested with a flash of inspiration. He would know all the details of the case and the people involved.

'Possibly, although I believe the man is illiterate. He signed his statement with a cross. I think the best thing we can do is to follow the instructions in this letter and leave a package in that plant pot this evening to see who collects it,' the chief inspector said in a thoughtful tone. 'Now, my problem with that is, who can leave it? If the blackmailer is watching, he'll expect either Mrs Blake or Mrs Pickering to drop off the money.'

Kitty could see where this conversation was leading. 'Would you like me to do it, sir?'

CHAPTER TWENTY-FOUR

By the time the afternoon had worn on and the plans had been made, Kitty was starting to regret her impulse to volunteer her services. She had been as jumpy as a kitten all afternoon. Chief Inspector Greville had been very busy getting everything set up as discreetly as possible.

Matt had been permitted to telephone the Pickerings to tell them not to worry, the matter of the letter was being dealt with and he would hopefully have more information for them later.

Norma Blake had been sworn to secrecy and had loaned Kitty one of her coats and a headscarf so if the blackmailer were familiar with Norma, he would assume she was the person leaving the money.

The money was a bundle of cut up newspaper in a brown envelope, carefully sealed to delay any opening to check the contents. The mist from the morning had continued to thicken throughout the day and the light was already poor by five o'clock in the afternoon.

The chief inspector had positioned himself in one of the cottages near the quay where he could look out from an upstairs window. From his vantage point, hidden behind a curtain, he could see the red flowerpot the letters had referred to and who was approaching and leaving the dock.

The tea shop on the green that led to the quay had closed early. The poor weather, no doubt, meant there hadn't been many customers. Chief Inspector Greville had arranged for Kitty and Matt to be dropped off just outside the village so Kitty could walk in exactly as Norma would do. Matt had gone on ahead to conceal himself nearby.

Kitty wished she could have driven herself in her own car, but she was aware that her red automobile would attract the wrong kind of attention from anyone watching the area. She heard the striking of a clock somewhere nearby marking the hour. Six o'clock and time for her to pretend to be Norma.

After adjusting her borrowed silk headscarf to cover her curls she walked along the street into the village. Stoke Gabriel was an ancient place nestled down in a hollow with steep lanes marked by high grey stone walls. With the mist now thickening as it came in off the estuary it cast an eerie air over the virtually deserted streets.

Even the sound of her heels on the uneven paving stones sounded muffled and anyone passing her by in the street seemed to loom suddenly out of the mist as insubstantial as ghosts until they came close. A few of the cottages had lamps lit, throwing pools of yellow light into the gloom.

Kitty's heart thumped in her chest as she rounded the final corner and made her way towards the red flowerpot. She looked around furtively for any sign that the blackmailer could be nearby watching her movements. The pot was on its own at the end of a row at the edge of the quayside.

She knew Chief Inspector Greville was in the bedroom of a nearby cottage and that Matt too had set himself up somewhere not far away. Inspector Lewis too was hiding nearby and there were also constables, dressed in their own clothes so as not to attract unwanted attention, stationed around the village.

Kitty shivered and reached inside the wicker shopping basket she was carrying over her arm. The bundle of newspaper clippings was concealed inside under a loaf of bread. The idea being that it would look as if Mrs Norma Blake were merely out getting some last-minute provisions for the farm.

She grasped the envelope and started across the wooden planking of the quay. The sound of her heels changing now she was walking on boards rather than stone. Once she was satisfied that she could see no one, she made her way to the red flowerpot and slipped the envelope inside the top underneath the pink flowering geranium, now almost past its best, that was planted there.

The chief inspector had told her to ensure the white label on the outside of the envelope was on top so it would be more visible from his vantage point in the cottage. Once the bundle was in place, Kitty took one final quick glance around and started to walk away. Her part in the plan was now complete.

She breathed a small sigh of relief and made herself focus on walking at a normal pace off the quayside and back onto the path. She kept her head down so her face would not be easily visible. Although in the mist it was hard to distinguish anyone. She wanted to look back to see if anyone had gone to collect the envelope yet, but instead kept her eyes on the path ahead of her.

Chief Inspector Greville had told her to return along the same route she had taken into the village and to wait at a certain spot where she was concealed not far from the bus stop.

She followed her instructions listening out for any sound or commotion behind her that might indicate the trap had been sprung. Instead, it all remained silent. Kitty walked to the designated spot and, after checking once more that she had not been followed, hid herself as directed behind a yew hedge.

After a minute she heard the rumble of a vehicle approaching along the road. She risked a peep to see it was the local bus, its headlamps shining dimly through the thickening mist. The bus halted at the stop with a wheeze of brakes to permit someone to disembark and then rumbled away again to follow the curve of the road leading it out of the village.

Curiosity getting the better of her, Kitty risked another quick peek to see who had stepped off the bus. To her dismay she recognised a slight figure in a spring-green coat carrying a large bundle hurrying off into the mist.

'Alice,' Kitty barely breathed her friend's name. What was she doing here? She must have been asked to make a delivery to one of her customers in the village.

There was no time to decide. Her best friend could be walking unknowingly into danger if she let her continue on her route. If she went after her though she risked giving the whole game away. She should have warned her friend where the drop-off point was to be.

Kitty slipped out of her hiding place. Alice was already almost gone from sight, swallowed up by the swirling grey mist. Perhaps if she followed her for just a short distance to ensure her friend was not headed towards the houses near the quay.

Kitty crept along the pavement following the curve of one of the grey stone walls. The closer she drew to the quay the thicker the mist became. She could just about make out Alice's green coat as her friend paused to seemingly consult a piece of paper she had in her hand.

'Turn off, Alice,' Kitty muttered under her breath as her friend hesitated as if unsure of her way.

To her relief, Alice peered at the front door of a cottage as if checking the number and turned as if to head out of the village on the same route the bus had taken a few minutes earlier.

Kitty leaned against the wall for support for a second, before turning ready to return to her hiding space. With luck she should be able to make it back before anyone saw her. At least the sea fret would be of some assistance there.

As she took her first step, she heard a commotion behind her coming from the direction of the quay. The sound of running feet and men's voices shouting. A police whistle shrilled eerily in the fog.

Kitty turned around to see that Alice had also turned and had run back to where the road split. A dark, male figure came hurtling out of the mist towards them and before Kitty had time to squeak whoever it was had taken hold of Alice and was pushing her back in the direction of the quay.

Her friend's parcel lay on the floor where Alice had dropped it when the man had captured her. Kitty followed behind at a safe distance, hoping the man hadn't seen her in his haste to capture a hostage.

'Stay back!' The man was on the dock now, his back to Kitty.

It was hard to see in the mist, but she thought she could see Chief Inspector Greville with one hand pressed to his side as if he had a stitch and another man, who she assumed must be Inspector Lewis, near the flowerpot.

'Come any closer and it will be all the worse for Miss Miller, here. I have a gun.' The man produced something from the pocket of his overcoat. Kitty saw the dull metal gleam on the barrel as a stray beam of light from the open door of the cottage momentarily pierced the mist.

Kitty wished she could see more of his face so she could be certain of his identity. She had a good idea, but the fog and the sound of the water seemed to distort everything. The man began to move towards the far side of the dock and Kitty wondered where he was heading.

She crept a little closer crouching down against the wall in an effort not to be seen. Nearer to where the man was holding Alice, she saw another dark shadow move. Someone else was also trying to get closer.

'This is the police. Give yourself up and let the girl go!' Chief Inspector Greville's voice cut through the fog.

The man half-turned and Kitty caught a glimpse of Alice's assailant's face. Adam Blake was the blackmailer. It made no sense. Why on earth would Adam be attempting to extort money from his aunt and the Pickerings? He had a good job and seemed well set up.

'Stay back.' Adam turned the gun in the direction of the chief inspector.

Kitty could see that Adam had his other hand clamped firmly over Alice's mouth preventing her from screaming.

The kerfuffle had led to more lights coming on in the windows of some of the nearby cottages as people looked out to try and see what was happening on the dock. The yellow squares of light cast shadows on the swirling sea fret throwing some things into stark relief and hiding others.

Chief Inspector Greville raised both his hands in the air and stood still. Kitty realised there was a small boat moored at the end of the jetty. It looked as if Adam intended to jump into that and make off across the water and out to sea.

Adam moved swiftly, edging back to the side before shoving Alice into the small wooden boat. The mast rocked and she heard the water splashing as Alice landed in the vessel. Kitty scuttled forward, keeping low trying to get a better view of where Adam might be taking her friend.

Inspector Lewis took a few paces towards where Adam was unfastening the rope tying the boat to the quay. Adam raised his gun and fired. A loud bang sounded and Alice, her mouth temporarily free of Adam's grip, screamed.

'That was a warning shot! Stay back!' Adam shouted to Lewis, who had thrown himself down flat onto the quay at the sound of the shot.

'Alice!' another male voice called out and Kitty turned to see Robert Potter hurrying down the road towards the quay.

'Stay back!' There was another loud bang and Robert dived

to the side, rolling over to end up crouching like Kitty under the shelter of one of the walls.

'Robert, stay where you are,' Kitty called across to him. She had no idea why or how Robert had ended up at the quay, but she didn't want to see any of her friends injured.

Adam was in the boat now and pushing off from the quay. It was hard to see from her position so far back, but Kitty thought she could see her friend hunkered down in the prow of the small boat. She hoped Adam hadn't hurt her.

With Adam's attention temporarily fixed on getting his boat away, the police spied their chance to draw closer. Kitty too followed them with Robert hard on her heels. She looked for Matt to see if he was anywhere in sight. She knew he couldn't be far away.

'Stop!' Chief Inspector Greville called out once more in an attempt to get Adam to return to the quayside.

The boat was already out on the water, the waves lapping at the side of the white-painted wooden hull. Kitty could barely see what was happening with the mist covering everything in a thick grey fog.

'Alice!' Robert called out again, desperation in his voice.

Kitty ran forward onto the quay to join the chief inspector with Robert close behind her. She was desperate to see what was happening out on the water. More of the villagers had emerged from their cottages and had started to gather on the far side of the dock as a constable tried to persuade them to stay back.

Something was happening out in the river. The boat started rocking back and forth and Kitty realised there was a struggle going on. Alice had clearly decided she was not going quietly.

Kitty gasped as she saw the two dark figures standing in the boat and she could see that Alice was trying to force the gun from Adam's hand. There was a muffled splash as the gun was sent overboard.

Adam's dark, taller figure then launched himself with a roar at Alice's slender green-coated shape, barely visible through the sea fret. Alice moved and the boat rocked violently before Kitty realised that Adam Blake was in the water.

'Alice, stay there,' Robert shouted as he saw Kitty's friend clinging to the side of the boat as it started to drift in the current.

Adam was splashing around in the water as if attempting to grab hold of the boat, which was drawing further away from him on the tide. Robert removed his shoes, coat and jacket and jumped from the side of the quay to swim out to the boat. Another male figure joined him, and Kitty's heart leapt into her throat as she realised Matt was now swimming alongside Robert to reach both the boat and the man flailing in the water.

Inspector Lewis called his constables to get the life-saving ring from the post. One of the fishermen offered the use of his boat, hurrying to untie it before the inspector could say yes or no.

Kitty could only watch and pray silently as she tried to keep her gaze fixed on the rapidly disappearing small boat as the currents took it out further towards the sea.

'Where on earth is Blake?' Chief Inspector Greville peered at the spot where the man had last been seen trying to grab hold of the boat.

'He can't swim very well. Someone told Matt he nearly drowned as a child. Saul saved him.' Kitty could scarcely make out Matt and Robert's heads amongst the waves as they continued to swim out.

The fishermen had launched their boat and were rowing towards Matt and Robert. The crowd on the quayside had swollen as more of the village had come down to watch the action unfold.

Kitty hoped Matt's strength would hold out. She knew he was a good swimmer, but his shoulder had been badly injured during the war and he had terrible scarring where shrapnel had damaged the nerves and tendons. The currents in the estuary could be treacherous, especially when, like now, the tide was running fast.

The fishermen had reached Robert and one of them produced a pole from the floor of the boat, extending it down for him to use. Robert hauled himself on board with help from the men. They then continued to look about on the water and Kitty guessed they must be searching for Adam.

Matt had continued to swim on in the direction of Alice's boat. He was almost out of Kitty's sight now and she fought back a sob as he vanished from view.

'Hold steady, Mrs Bryant. The other boat is going after them.' Chief Inspector Greville placed his arm around her shoulders and gave her a reassuring squeeze.

The men took up their oars once more, pulling with long practised strokes in the direction of Alice's boat. The pale-grey mist swallowed them up and all that could be heard was the splashing of the wavelets against the dock and the subdued murmurs of the waiting crowd.

Kitty's legs were like jelly and nausea roiled around her stomach as she peered desperately at the fog, willing it to lift so she could see Matt returning safely with Alice. From somewhere out on the water there was the sound of splashing and muffled shouts.

'I think they have them, Mrs Bryant,' Chief Inspector Greville said.

'I hope so.' Kitty could barely speak. She just wanted to see two boats coming back towards the quayside with Matt and Alice safely inside the second vessel.

The murmuring of the crowd grew louder and some of the other fishermen from the village had gone to the edge of the quay holding ropes. Kitty could only assume that they knew one or both of the boats was returning.

'There, Mrs Bryant, they're coming in.' Chief Inspector Greville pointed to a faint white shape out on the water.

The first boat rowed by the fishermen came more clearly into view. Progress was slower now as they were rowing against the tide, and they were towing the other boat behind them.

Kitty heaved a huge sigh of relief when she realised Matt was safely on board the following boat alongside Alice. He had one oar and was taking turns to place a stroke, first one side of the boat and then the other to try and assist the men in the leading boat.

As they drew nearer, the men on the dock threw out lines for their friends in the first boat to grab so they could be hauled closer to the quay and tied up safely. Kitty rushed forward, burrowing her way through the crowd to get to her husband and her friends.

'Matt!' she called to him as he and Robert helped Alice up the steps and onto the quay.

Blankets and towels were seemingly produced from nowhere for the two soaking wet men. Kitty flung herself at her husband disregarding any potential consequences for Norma's coat. She was simply grateful to have him back safely on dry land.

Alice was in Robert's arms, tears streaming down her cheeks. The two fishermen were being clapped on the back by their fellow villagers amidst many sorrowful looks at the mist covered stretch of water that had taken Adam Blake's life.

The police began to disperse the crowd. Inspector Lewis and one of the constables accompanied the two fishermen in the direction of the public house. Kitty suspected he needed to take a statement before the men accepted too many pints in recognition of their bravery and quick thinking.

'Are you all right, Matt?' She peered anxiously at her husband's face in the gloom.

'Perfectly. Just rather wet and cold.' He smiled at her and

dropped a reassuring kiss on the top of her head. 'I suspect my shoulder will ache tomorrow.' He winced as he moved the arm that had been damaged years before in the war.

'Yes, we need to go somewhere so that you and Robert can get warm and dry.' She looked around for Robert and saw that he and Alice were still huddled closely together.

Chief Inspector Greville was busy talking to a small group of local men who were all looking out at the water. Kitty could only guess that they were debating when to resume the search for Adam Blake's body. She shivered at the thought. Poor Saul had now lost his father and both of his brothers.

Chief Inspector Greville left the men he was with and crossed over to them. 'It seems there is little more that can be done now until tomorrow morning. The light is too poor and the mist too dense to search the water. Since the tide is going out, he may be carried on the current further out into the bay.'

'I wish I knew why he'd done it,' Kitty said. 'The blackmail and then abducting Alice.' She looked at the chief inspector.

'I think I may know some of it,' Alice said, overhearing part of the conversation. 'But can we go somewhere so Robert and Captain Bryant can dry off first?'

CHAPTER TWENTY-FIVE

It was quickly agreed that they should return to Matt and Kitty's house where the chief inspector could take their statements and Robert and Matt could dry off and get warm. Luckily, Robert Potter's build was not too dissimilar to Matt's so he could borrow some clothes.

Alice's bundle was retrieved from where she had been forced to drop it when Adam Blake had seized her and one of the constables promised he would take it to her customer.

'I wondered what on earth you were doing there when I saw you get off the bus,' Kitty said to her friend as they sat in Kitty's drawing room. Bertie was settled happily at her feet and Rascal was regarding them all with disdain, having been ousted from his favourite perch.

A small fire blazed in the hearth and Kitty had supplied her friend and the chief inspector with sherry while they waited for Robert and Matt to rejoin them.

''Twas Mrs Larkin's fault. She's a very good customer and puts a lot of business my way, but she's very demanding. She dropped off a pile of things that needed urgent work and wanted them back this evening. I thought, well, where's the harm? And I didn't want to upset her or lose her business, so I finished the work and took the bus to the village. I didn't know your stake-out thing was at the quay.' Alice paused to sip her sherry. 'And, even if I had done, I mean, I couldn't have said to her, I can't come because my friend is trying to catch a black-mailer, now could I?'

Kitty was forced to agree.

'I should have told you where the drop-off point was. But then why was Robert Potter there?' Kitty asked.

The lounge door opened just as she posed her question and Matt and Robert entered the room.

'Ah, that is my doing,' Matt admitted sheepishly as he took a glass of sherry from the silver tray on the table and sat down next to Kitty.

Robert followed suit, his already rosy cheeks colouring a deeper red under Alice's sharp gaze.

'I think both you and Mr Potter should explain yourselves,' Chief Inspector Greville remarked drily as he took out his notebook.

'We were discussing the blackmail notes the other evening and I was unsure at that point about what to do in the matter.' Matt looked at Kitty. 'I had grave concerns for Mr Pickering's well-being. Kitty and I had thought we might set a trap ourselves. We hadn't given the police the notes then and Robert suggested that he should come down to the quay around the time the blackmailer was expected and just be around as a backup if needed.'

Alice's mouth dropped slightly open at this, and she stared at Robert.

'I didn't hear anything else, so I thought I'd best do as I'd promised. Then I saw Alice and, well, you know what happened next.' Robert's face was now completely scarlet, and he shuffled uncomfortably on the end of the sofa.

'I didn't think to let Robert know of the police plans for the evening. By the time I remembered we were already in Stoke Gabriel.' Matt too looked shamefaced.

Kitty thought he and Robert looked like two naughty schoolboys who had been caught on a prank.

Chief Inspector Greville said nothing for a moment, he simply scribbled notes in his book.

'You could have completely derailed the operation,' he finally said in a stern voice. 'However, given the courage of both of you in trying to save Adam Blake and rescue Miss Miller, I think it best to draw a line under this matter.' He fixed them both with a steely gaze.

'Thank you, sir,' Robert mumbled, and Matt muttered his thanks too.

'Miss Miller, you said while we were at the quayside that you thought you knew something about Mr Blake's motives for his actions.' Chief Inspector Greville turned his attention to Alice.

'When we were tussling together on the boat, I was trying to get the gun from him. I asked him to turn around before it was too late. I asked him if a few pounds was worth all of this.' Alice shivered and paused, closing her eyes as she seemed to try to remember exactly what had been said. 'I said he had everything going for him. Why was he doing this? He told me that he needed to get away. He'd done terrible things, and he had no intention of hanging for them.'

'He killed his father and Micah,' Kitty said slowly. 'And I think I may have inadvertently given him the idea about black-mail.' Colour filled her own cheeks as she recalled the conversation she'd had with Adam at the tea room near Alice's shop.

'What do you mean, Mrs Bryant?' the chief inspector asked.

Kitty explained that she had asked Adam about anyone receiving threatening letters. 'Did he have money troubles?' she asked.

'He lived a little above his means, but not severely so. We

looked into the financial circumstances of all of the family,' Chief Inspector Greville said.

Matt gave Kitty's hand a comforting pat. 'I don't think your question could have sparked the idea of blackmail,' he reassured her. 'I think it sounded as if the knowledge of what he had done was gnawing at his conscience and he was simply trying to get money ready to flee.'

'I wonder what tipped him over the edge? He had left home and was away from his father so why did he kill him? He wouldn't benefit from his father's death.' Kitty frowned. 'And then Micah's death too. I know he had argued with Micah about him wishing to follow up the ownership of the farm but why kill him?'

Chief Inspector Greville finished his drink and closed his notebook. 'We may never know for certain what was going on in his mind, Mrs Bryant. He was clearly very unstable at the end.'

Kitty was forced to be satisfied with this for now as the chief inspector made his farewells and took Alice and Robert with him to drop them off at their respective homes.

'At least Alice and Robert are talking to each other again,' Kitty remarked as she collected the empty sherry glasses to take to the kitchen.

'Then something good has come from this evening,' Matt said.

Kitty took the glasses out and returned to her husband. 'You were very brave tonight. I was so frightened watching you both swim out. The currents out there in an estuary are really dangerous.' She rested her hand tenderly on his shoulder.

'We shall have to go and see Norma tomorrow and the Pickerings. I believe Inspector Lewis was being dispatched to inform the Blakes of Adam's death.' Matt's face was weary in the lamplight.

'Come, let's get an early night. We can pick up the threads tomorrow,' Kitty suggested.

. . .

The following day the mist had cleared leaving behind a murky morning with no trace of sunshine. Matt's mood still seemed as sombre as the weather as they ate breakfast together. Kitty's mind had been busy all night, thinking of what may have led Adam to kill his father and his brother.

She had a feeling the answer lay with Saul, the remaining Blake brother, and she hoped he would be around when they called at Blossomdown. Matt telephoned Norma and she agreed to see them, despite her distress at Adam's death. Kitty had sponged Norma's coat and folded her headscarf to return them to her.

They set off along the lanes, after taking Bertie for a quick trot over the common and leaving him with their housekeeper. Kitty had said little to Matt about her new theory of why Adam may have murdered his family. She desperately wanted to talk to Saul first to see if she was correct.

Norma opened the door to the farmhouse as soon as she saw Kitty's car halt outside.

'Do come through. We are all here this morning. As you can imagine we are desperately upset,' Norma said as she accepted her coat and scarf back from Kitty. She led the way into the drawing room. Hedley was seated on one of the fireside chairs, while Saul was on the sofa beside Abigail.

'I've made some coffee,' Norma said and vanished to fetch the tray from the kitchen, while Matt and Kitty seated themselves on occasional chairs near the others.

'Inspector Lewis told us that you and another gentleman tried hard to save my nephew, Captain Bryant,' Hedley said as Norma arrived back bearing a laden tray of coffee things.

Abigail immediately started to assist her with placing cups.

'I'm sorry we were unable to find him in the mist,' Matt said.

'It was a terrible night, right enough. We appreciate that

you did all you could. I hope the other gentleman and Mrs Bryant's friend are both recovered?' Norma asked anxiously as she poured coffee into the cups from a tall chrome jug.

'Yes, I telephoned Alice this morning and Matt has spoken to Robert,' Kitty assured her as she accepted her drink from Abigail.

'I still can't believe it. Why would Adam do such a thing? If he wanted money, he had only to ask, and we would have helped him. He was doing so well for himself.' Norma frowned as she handed another cup to her husband.

'I've been thinking about this all night,' Kitty said. 'I believe the answer goes back a long way.' She looked at Saul who was spooning sugar into his cup.

'Oh, what's that then, Mrs Bryant?' Hedley asked.

'I think you all agree that Titus was a terrible man. He treated all of his family appallingly. He was cruel, spiteful and vindictive and grew much worse after the loss of his wife.' Kitty paused and looked at the Blakes who all gave small nods of acknowledgement.

She looked at Saul. 'Growing up, Micah was older than you and Adam. He spent more time with your father and so you and Adam were close. You even saved his life when you were ten and he was eight,' Kitty said.

Saul nodded. 'That's right. At the same creek as took his life last night. Father were furious with both of us. He beat us within an inch of our lives and forbid us from ever going down there to swim again.'

'I think Adam always felt he owed you a debt. Your father was getting worse, and Micah seemed to be set to follow in his path. He could see you were happy here and settled, but he also knew how you felt about Abigail.' Kitty looked at the girl who grew rosy under her gaze.

'Adam come to Wassail Farm yesterday morning. He come to see how I was,' Abigail said in a soft voice.

'I think that he knew that Hedley and Norma saw Saul almost as the son they never had and intended that he would inherit Blossomdown someday.' Kitty looked at Hedley and Norma.

'Aye, that's no secret,' Hedley agreed.

'I think Adam had discovered how the trust worked when he was doing the research for his employer into the ownership of the spring and the field. Titus, however, had always said that Micah would inherit the farm. I think Adam thought this must be what was in the will that Titus didn't want him to see. The trust deed is complicated, and it took some time to sort out. He may well have believed that Titus's will could somehow negate the terms of the trust in the same way his father had taken the farm from Hedley.' Kitty paused to take a sip of her coffee before continuing.

'Why would he murder Father?' Saul asked.

'I think perhaps your father pushed him too far, perhaps goaded him when Adam called in. He probably said that you would all have a shock about who would get the farm. I think Titus had convinced himself that he could do what he liked, and he knew the trust was still in place. He had disregarded Hedley's rights to the farm and may have believed that Hedley didn't know or care,' Kitty said.

'So, you think Titus's death was unpremeditated?' Matt asked. 'That would make sense. The manner in which he was found indicated a deep hatred for him which would fit with how Adam felt.'

'Once Titus was dead, and the will became known, Adam thought that he had opened a way for Saul to get his share of the farm early and, by combining it with Adam's own share, they could outvote Micah. Saul could marry Abigail and take charge at Wassail, sidelining Micah who he thought would ruin the farm by running it like his father had done.' Kitty looked at

Saul. 'He could even combine his portion of Wassail with Blossomdown, leaving Micah with a smallholding.'

'Then Micah started to insist on seeing the solicitor and examining the trust deeds. He said that perhaps it wasn't as clear cut. That, in fact, Hedley might own Wassail.' Matt frowned.

'With Micah out of the way, and Adam stepping aside, Saul could take everything. He could marry Abigail and live at Wassail until such time as he took over Blossomdown as well. I think what really pushed him on to kill Micah was when you, Saul, couldn't find your mother's engagement ring. A ring you wanted to give to Abigail when you asked her to marry you.' Kitty gave the girl a small smile.

'When Adam was at the farm yesterday, there were a knock at the door. Mrs Bird, from the farm over yonder, were there. She had the ring on a chain about her neck. She'd come to give it back. Said it was a family thing and with Micah gone it should stay with the family.' Abigail looked troubled.

'And that was the first any of you knew about Micah and Dora being engaged and planning to marry at Christmas,' Kitty said.

This statement caused a murmur amongst the Blakes.

'Adam looked really shocked. I think he'd thought Micah or Titus had sold the jewellery.' Abigail cradled her coffee cup, her eyes brimming with unshed tears. 'Tell the truth, so did I. Mrs Bird were so upset when she give Adam the ring back. She said as they'd had such plans for a new life together and how good Micah had been with her boy, Freddie.'

'I think this was when Adam began to realise exactly what he'd done. In his attempts to make things right with Saul for saving his life all those years earlier, he had become the thing he dreaded. He had become like his father, playing with people's lives. He'd already sent the blackmail letters, but I think this was originally more to throw the police, and us, off the scent.

He was trying to direct and divert attention.' Kitty was certain she had the right idea now about why Adam had acted as he had.

'Then as the guilt set in and he realised the enormity of his crimes, he thought the money from his extortion attempt would help him to flee the country. He had that little boat all set up to make his escape, knowing the police would look for his car.'

Matt looked admiringly at Kitty. 'Yes, I think you're right.'

'I think he planned to go down to the quay that night, he knew how the tide was running. He'd grab whatever had been left in the flowerpot and then disappear in the boat he had readied earlier,' Kitty explained.

'I think he had hoped originally that Micah's death would be seen as an accident, that's why there was the business with the snares and the trap. When that didn't work, he needed to throw suspicion elsewhere. Titus's feud with the Pickerings made them an obvious choice.' Matt nodded approvingly at Kitty and she could see he was on the same thought process that she had followed.

'The appearance of the police last night and the confusion in the mist led to him taking Alice hostage. It all went wrong from then on.' Kitty gave a small shiver as she thought about the events of the previous night.

'Adam never owed me anything. It was all in his head. I'd give it all up to have him back. Micah too, for all his faults,' Saul said.

Abigail took his hand tenderly in hers. 'At least now it's over with. Terrible though it is,' she said.

They stayed a while longer with the Blakes and finished their coffees, before driving off to the Pickerings' stables.

Mrs Pickering was in the field behind the stable giving a riding lesson to a young woman when they entered the yard. Mr Pickering came out of the farmhouse to meet them. He extended his hand, first to Matt and then to Kitty.

'We heard what went on last night in the village. Tragic news about young Adam Blake. They found him this morning apparently.' Mr Pickering's expression was sombre.

'Yes, it seems he was responsible for the murder of his father and his brother,' Matt said.

'It's a terrible thing sometimes what goes on in families,' Mr Pickering said.

'We thought we should come and see that you and Mrs Pickering were all right. I hope now this is over things pick up for you both.' Kitty followed Mr Pickering's gaze where he was watching his wife instructing the young rider.

'Thank you, Mrs Bryant. I hope so. Thank you both for all your kindness to us.' The older man straightened almost as if coming to attention as he shook hands once more with Matt and then again with herself.

'Perhaps we might meet up sometime for a beer,' Matt suggested. 'It's good to meet with former comrades-in-arms.'

Mr Pickering nodded. 'Thank you, Captain Bryant, I should like that very much.'

'I hope they will be all right now,' Kitty said to Matt as they drove out of the livery for the last time.

'I think they will be, old thing, I think so.' Matt smiled at her, and she pointed the nose of her little red car towards Churston and home.

'Perhaps next time we fancy a bottle of cider for supper, or a trip out in the countryside, we should choose a different direction,' Kitty said as she changed gear.

'To be honest, I think a nice cup of tea when we get home will be perfect,' Matt said with a smile.

A LETTER FROM HELENA DIXON

Dear reader,

I want to say a huge thank you for choosing to read *Murder in the Countryside*. If you enjoyed it and would like to keep up to date with all my latest releases, just sign up at the following link. Your email address will never be shared, and you can unsubscribe at any time. There is also a free story – *The Mysterious Guest*, starring Kitty's friend, Alice.

www.bookouture.com/helena-dixon

The village of Stoke Gabriel is still a popular spot for people looking for crab fishing or a cream tea. The area is well known for cider production, and you can call in at a local farm, Hunts Cider, and take a tour and taste some of their drinks. Hopefully, there are no bodies! I do hope you loved *Murder in the Countryside* and, if you did, I would be very grateful if you could write a review. I'd love to hear what you think, and it makes such a difference helping new readers to discover one of my books for the first time. You can get in touch on social media or through my website.

Thanks,

Helena

KEEP IN TOUCH WITH HELENA

www.nelldixon.com

 facebook.com/nelldixonauthor
x.com/NellDixon

ACKNOWLEDGEMENTS

My thanks as always go to my Tuesday zoomers for their support and encouragement. Also to the Coffee crew, although we can't meet as often in person these days they provide me with friendship, laughter and support. Thank you to all the local people who continue to give me lots of information and assistance to ensure the books are factually accurate. Huge love to all of Team Kitty at Bookouture who work so hard to deliver the books. Special thanks to Maisie, my very patient editor, and Kate, my equally patient and brilliant agent.

PUBLISHING TEAM

Turning a manuscript into a book requires the efforts of many people. The publishing team at Bookouture would like to acknowledge everyone who contributed to this publication.

Audio
Alba Proko
Sinead O'Connor
Melissa Tran

Commercial
Lauren Morrissette
Hannah Richmond
Imogen Allport

Cover design
Debbie Clement

Data and analysis
Mark Alder
Mohamed Bussuri

Editorial
Maisie Lawrence
Sinead O'Connor

Copyeditor
Jane Eastgate

Proofreader
Shirley Khan

Marketing
Alex Crow
Melanie Price
Occy Carr
Cíara Rosney
Martyna Młynarska

Operations and distribution
Marina Valles
Stephanie Straub

Production
Hannah Snetsinger
Mandy Kullar
Jen Shannon
Ria Clare

Publicity
Kim Nash
Noelle Holten
Jess Readett
Sarah Hardy

Rights and contracts
Peta Nightingale
Richard King
Saidah Graham